Six men. With nothing to lose. Who dared to go…

THE FULL MONTY

FOX SEARCHLIGHT PICTURES ... MARK ADDY
MUSIC BY ANNE DUDLEY ... ORMAN B.S.C.

R RESTRICTED

For Dad

Wendy Holden is a journalist and author
of six books to date. She lives in Suffolk
with her husband and two dogs.

THE FULL MONTY

WENDY HOLDEN

Based on the screenplay by
SIMON BEAUFOY

HarperCollins*Publishers*

HarperCollins books may be purchased for educational, business, or sales promotional use. For information please write: Special Markets Department, HarperCollins Publishers, Inc., 10 East 53rd Street, New York, NY 10022.

FIRST EDITION

ISBN 0-06-095294-6

98 99 00 01 02   10 9 8 7 6 5 4 3 2 1

The Full Monty: *To go all the way, to have the lot. Various sources suggested, from a French proverb relating to Montgomery, a medieval chief who kept the spoils of war instead of sharing them among his men, to the full English breakfast enjoyed by Field Marshal 'Monty' Montgomery before going into battle. Other possible definitions relate to the 'full monte' or pile of cards given to the winner of a Spanish card game and the three-piece suit issued by outfitters Montague Burton to soldiers after the Second World War.*

CHAPTER ONE

The twelve-year-old boy stuffed his hands into the pockets of his baggy jeans and gaped in awe at the menacing hulks of machinery that littered the quarter-mile-long rolling mill. Dinosaurs from the days of heavy industry, they resembled giant metal monsters frozen mid-step and reminded him of a *Star Wars* set long abandoned by the special effects film crew.

The vast open floor space between the crumbling machines was pockmarked with pools of oily water and rusting piles of metal shards, adding to the atmosphere of mournful decay. Shafts of spring sunshine beamed through the high broken windows and onto a huge edifice at one end, the steelworks cauldron, now cold, but once the focus of the bustling factory, into which the sweat of a thousand men had mingled with the liquid steel.

This wasn't Nathan's first time in the redundant Harrison's steelworks and he suspected it wouldn't be the last, but there was something about the light and the atmosphere today that made it feel more ghostly than he had ever known it before.

Dragging his eyes away from the mesmerising scene, Nathan turned to watch his two older companions grunting as they selected an eight-foot-long length of steel and manhandled it onto the shoulder of the larger of the two men, setting off precariously towards him through the deserted building, their footsteps echoing eerily. As soon as he was sure the girder was safely balanced on his friend's shoulder, Nathan's father, Gary, slipped out from under the front of it, leaving his friend to do all the work. Walking three paces ahead of him he ignored his complaints that it was too heavy for one man to carry alone.

Red in the face, a barrel-chested Goliath of a man in his late thirties with short brown hair and rounded features, Dave Horsfall staggered under the weight and wondered once again how he had been roped into this caper in the first place. 'Gaz, who's gonna want to buy a rusty girder?' he enquired sullenly, wishing he'd stayed at home to do the housework, which is all that was planned for his day before 'Gary the Lad' had pitched up at his house with yet another one of his hair-brained schemes to supplement their meagre dole money.

'Come on,' urged Gaz, his hand on his son's shoulder as he strolled ahead. A wiry, angular figure – thirty-eight, unemployed and divorced – Gaz was wearing his trademark jeans, T-shirt and tatty black leather jacket, his collar-length streaked blond hair matted to his head, a single gold earring in his left earlobe. He was well accustomed to Dave's grumpiness and generally disregarded it. Dave was perfect for this job, all beef and no brains – Gaz had always prided himself on being the bright one of the pair – and he'd carry their valuable prize down to the scrap metal merchants in no time. It would only take a minute, he had told Dave pleadingly as he and Nathan stood on his front doorstep half an hour earlier and, as usual, the big-hearted bear had caved in.

Nathan, an angelic-faced boy whose looks largely matched his character, was much more concerned about the morality of the situation. 'Dad, it's stealing,' he complained. It was a hopeless plea, he knew, but something deep inside him told him to point out to his father that what they were doing was wrong. He never knew, it might act as mitigation later. Gaz smiled benignly at his son, that familiarly mischievous twinkle in his steel blue eyes. 'No, it's liberating, love, liberating,' he informed the boy, wondering again where he got his sense of right and wrong from. Not from his side of the family, that was for sure.

'Gaz, hang on,' puffed Dave, trying desperately to re-adjust the weight onto his broad shoulder as his knees began to buckle. But Gaz was already lost to them both, miles away in his thoughts as he wandered through the factory where he and Dave had started work as young men. Stepping into the centre of the huge rolling mill, his hand still resting fondly on his son's shoulder, he looked around glassy-eyed, remembering days long past.

He could almost smell the molten ore being poured into the pig-iron moulds, feel the heat on his face from the furnace, see the red-hot sparks flying, hear the unbearable din that used to pound in his ears long after his shift had ended. The ghosts of a thousand men – including his father and grandfather, brothers, uncles and cousins – appeared before him in caps and baggy overalls, wiping their blackened faces with the backs of their hands, toiling night and day to keep production going in Steel City, the soles of their hobnail boots melting as they walked the upper gantries.

'Ten years we worked in here. Now look,' Gaz told his son. He could hardly believe the changes he had seen during his lifetime. When he was Nathan's age, Sheffield was still the beating heart of Britain's industrial north, home to the world's greatest steel industry and the jewel in Yorkshire's crown. More than 100,000 men were employed in the city's rolling mills, forges and workshops, making everything from high-tensile girders to stainless steel cutlery, in a virtually non-stop metalworking production process that had begun 500 years earlier.

The massive manufacturing heartland of the Lower Don valley between the Yorkshire moors was layered with mile upon mile of working steel mills, nearly 200 furnace chimneys belching into the atmosphere. Jobs were virtually guaranteed and it had seemed that nothing could dent their optimism.

But within the space of a comparatively short time everything changed. The industry that had grown too big for the market was almost wiped out with the advent of cheaper steel imports from the Far East. One by one, the great steel factories began closing until there were just seven furnaces left. When the industries finally re-emerged from the painful metamorphosis, they were leaner, meaner and less labour-intensive. For those who couldn't find the only work they knew, real hardship set in, and with it came shame – a loss of honour at being out of work, out of cash and out of luck. All around them regeneration and re-growth meant new jobs for the next generation, but they were largely passed by.

It was the women who suddenly had to find jobs, and earn the money to spend. Not jobs that brought in enough for a steel man's family to live as well on, but just enough to scrape by, and which shifted the emphasis onto the women as the heads of the household.

Men like Gaz and Dave who had previously worked day, night and weekend shifts, with only two weeks off a year for holidays, were now terminally unemployed. They collected their fortnightly Giros and sat around at home, doing the housework, walking the dog, rolling their cigarettes and ducking and diving to make a few extra quid. On the Wander, they called it. The slow tread of those who had nowhere to go and a lot of time in which to get there.

Nathan watched his father mentally strolling down Memory Lane and recognised the symptoms. He had seen and heard it all before and learnt long ago to ignore his father when he got that faraway look in his eyes and started on about the good old days when men were men and women knew their place. His father's condition was not hereditary, his mother had often told him. Nathan had a bright future ahead of him, she insisted, and not one that involved slaving over a bubbling steel cauldron for the rest of his days.

It was that sort of talk, he reckoned, that made his mum leave his dad in the first place. Well, that and his father's spells inside for car theft, not to mention the disastrous fling with the barmaid of the Thomas Boulsover. Thinking of his mother now, Nathan chewed on his bottom lip and wondered what she would do if she found out that he and his dad had crept into the works to go thieving on one of the two days a week he was allowed to see him.

'But what if we get caught?' His tremulous voice of reason dragged Gaz back to the present day, his big blue eyes like saucers as he peered up into his father's gaunt face. The two of them had reached the huge open doorway they had come in by, in which an ancient maroon Austin Princess was parked – dumped, they presumed, from the state it was in.

Gaz looked down at him with a smile that said he had it all figured out. 'You don't get a criminal record until you're sixteen,' he explained, his Yorkshire accent distorting his vowels. As an afterthought, and with an image of Nathan's disapproving mother in his mind, he added the warning: 'Just don't tell your mum.' He ruffled his son's mousy brown hair while the boy flinched.

Dave, by now purple of face, blundered up behind them under the girder, relieved to reach the sliding metal doorway and fresh air. He didn't like being in the rolling mills any more than Gaz or Nathan. It held too many sad memories for him; memories of happy days when he worked alongside Gaz as a welder until they were laid off three years before; days when he sweated off his permanent diet of chips and steak which his wife Jeanie gladly cooked for him every night. Now he ate just as much but with no hard labour to burn it off, the fat stayed on.

If Jean ever found out he was there, nicking stuff with Gaz, it would be all the worse for him. His body twitching involuntarily with the strain of the girder on his back, he took a few deep breaths to stop the pounding in his ears before he realised that there was something other than his heart beating a drum in his head.

'Hey, listen,' he said, stopping suddenly, as Nathan and Gaz turned to face him. Faintly, they could hear an insistent, rhythmic thumping, which was getting ever louder and more menacing outside. The doleful beat of a big bass drum could now be clearly heard, accompanied by trumpeting and some sort of fanfare. 'Music,' said Dave, his expression puzzled.

'Yeah,' Nathan nodded. He could hear it too, sounding entirely out of place in the middle of a derelict steelworks.

He and Gaz stepped ahead into the daylight, past the parked car, and poked their heads around the doorway, their mouths falling open at the sight that greeted them. Marching towards them, in anoraks and jeans, was a phalanx of men and women, the full complement of a twenty-member brass band complete with baton waver, unfurled banner and band leader. The thumping strains of their marching song resounded around the empty factory walls.

'Bloody hell!' was all Gaz could manage before he stumbled backwards, grabbing Nathan by the scruff of his red checked jacket and colliding directly with the over-laden Dave. The steel girder toppled from the big man's shoulder and into his flailing arms before crashing to the ground with an almighty clang, narrowly missing his foot. The three of them scattered in terror and hunched guiltily together behind the door pillar.

Relieved that the tremendous clatter hadn't been heard above the noise of the band, they peered round the doorway in unison, one head above the other, Gaz and Nathan perched on a wooden box. 'What they doin'?' whispered Dave, as they watched the musicians approaching to the rousing strains of Elgar.

'It's the factory band,' Nathan explained, recognising them from the various functions they attended at his school. Unable to afford their own full set of instruments, the school and the works band shared the cornets, trumpets and tubas between them, and often joined forces for end of term assemblies and community events. It was a way of keeping the spirit of the steelworks alive, or that's what their head-master and erstwhile tuba player had told them proudly as he remembered the highly polished trophies the band used to collect in the good old days of brass band championships. 'They're still going, you know,' the boy added thoughtfully, while he, Gaz and Dave watched agog as the band members, heads held high, marched proudly past, their music sheets neatly clipped to their instruments, their feet stepping perfectly in time to the music.

''bout the only thing around here that is,' Dave commented morosely, as they waited for them to disappear. The band had almost reached the corner and vanished from view when a tall, skinny red-haired cornet player they recognised as Lomper – one of the works' few remaining employees – broke discreetly from the last row of the formation and ran towards the doorway where the three of them were crouching. 'Eh up, security guard's back,' Dave warned as the three of them shuffled as one into the shadows and listened intently, their backs pressed against the wall.

Seeing as he marched past that he must have inadvertently left a door open when he parked his car there earlier, Lomper hoped the band leader wouldn't notice if he slipped behind and shut it for safety. Sliding the heavy steel door closed with a crash, he secured the massive padlock and ran back to catch up with the band as they rounded the far corner of the concrete roadway once used by the works' fleet of massive articulated lorries.

The three of them collectively held their breath as they heard the doors bang shut and the padlock engage. Realising what it meant, Nathan dropped his head into his hands while Dave raised his big brown eyes to the heavens before glowering at Gaz. Jean had long referred to his oldest friend as 'a magnet for trouble' and this was yet another time when he wished he'd heeded her advice and told him to get lost when he came round on the make.

Nathan, entirely accustomed to his father's madcap schemes going wrong, shook his head woefully and peered up at Dave with a look that belied his years. Only last week the three of them had been nicked shoplifting and were lucky to get off with a caution after Gaz blamed it all on the boy who, he claimed, was on day release from a special needs home. Dave spoke for them both when he turned to Gaz in exasperation. '"Won't take a minute," he says … "Won't take a minute." … Well, now what?'

'Shut up, I'm thinking,' Gaz said, blinking hard, hand to his chin. Then, to his companions' dismay, a cheeky grin lit up his face, indicating that the boy inside the man had had another brain wave.

Fifteen minutes later, Nathan found himself perched precariously on top of the bonnet of an abandoned Mark III Ford Cortina partially submerged in the dirty waters of the Tinsley Canal that ran along the edge of the abandoned steel mill. His father and Dave were standing equally dangerously behind him on the car's roof; Gaz at the front, bent double, Dave behind him, his left arm outstretched and resting on Gaz's back for balance. The steel girder lying beside them on the roof of the rusting vehicle had just been used as a makeshift bridge from the smashed factory window they had climbed out. By shunting a second girder across to the towpath, Gaz had devised his ingenious escape plan.

This had been his great brain wave, a question of using his initiative, he had told them confidently, a way of breaking out of the locked mill and still retrieving not one, but two girders for their scrap value. He was very pleased with himself for coming up with the ruse, but as the rotten hulk they stood on rocked unsteadily backwards and forwards with their combined weight, even he was beginning to have second thoughts.

'Can't we do normal things sometimes?' Nathan asked, not for the first time. Setting off, as instructed, one foot carefully placed in front of the other, his arms horizontal, he edged his way gingerly across the four-inch-wide girder to the bank. He thought about all his school friends, sitting at home playing computer games, or down the terraces at Bramall Lane with their fathers, cheering Sheffield United on.

Gaz, watching every cautious step with fatherly pride as he leaned forward, hands on his knees and charted the boy's progress, smiled. 'What's up with you?' he asked his son. 'This *is* normal.' Getting no response from the unhappy Nathan, who was too busy biting his lip and concentrating on his footing to answer, Gaz sought moral support from his friend. 'Innit Dave?' he asked, shrugging his shoulders to prompt his reply.

Dave, his moon face still red and blotchy from the morning's exertions, nodded his head and tried not to look too deeply into the oily black water. 'Oh aye, everyday stuff, this,' he replied sarcastically. As Nathan's weight shifted to the far end of the girder, so the Cortina sank deeper into the mud. Dave pointed to the water and added, miserably: 'You know, I think this bugger's sinking.' It had been bad enough creeping across the girder like some Russian gymnast on the bar, he was now facing the prospect of a triathlon – balancing, swimming and a brisk walk home.

There was an audible sigh of relief from the towpath as Nathan reached the safety of dry land and turned to face his father. The boy hadn't fancied going back to Gaz's freezing cold flat with soaking wet clothes. He'd never have got them dry in time for school the next morning.

'Right, now pick it up and try and slide it across the other side,' Gaz encouraged, imitating the movement of shunting the girder towards his son.

Nathan looked doubtful, but did as he was told. At four feet eight inches and weighing less than six stone, he struggled valiantly as he bent his knees and lifted his end of the heavy steel girder in both hands, before trying to drag it towards him.

'That's it,' his father urged, nodding his head vigorously. But as the end resting on the bonnet of the Cortina slid off the radiator grill, its sheer weight sent it plummeting straight to the canal bottom, and Nathan's end slipped from his hands and quickly followed suit. The girder was lost. Gaz's face crumpled into a frown and he threw his hands in the air in an expression of bitter frustration. 'Oh, fucking hell, Nathe,' he castigated, as his son looked up at him in disbelief. 'They're twenty quid each, them!' Nathan, wounded and upset, turned to walk away, his shoulders hunched, his hands stuffed deep in his pockets. 'That were your bloody maintenance, were that!' Gaz called after him, his eyes

15

blazing. Realising his mistake at mentioning the crippling monthly payments he had to make to Nathan's mother, he muttered under his breath: 'Oh, shit!' as Nathan trudged off miserably.

Dave shook his head at his friend, never ceasing to be amazed by Gaz's stupidity when it came to his son. 'Oh, nice one,' he said. Dave and Jean didn't have kids, it wasn't medically possible for her, but Dave had always thought that if he did have a son, he'd want him to be like Nathan – kind, considerate, a gentle lad with his mother's good looks and little of his father's innate immorality. Only Gary 'Shifty' Schofield didn't realise how lucky he was – or how close he was to alienating Nathan for ever sometimes by opening his big mouth.

Seeing the accusatory look in Dave's eyes, Gaz knew he'd cocked up again. Turning back to his son, now several hundred yards away, he called out: 'Nathe! ... Nathan!' But the boy continued to stalk broodily up the towpath, pretending not to hear his father's plaintive cries.

Completely forgetting where he was, Gaz stepped down onto the bonnet of the car to get a little closer and call his son's name again but, as he did so, the car lurched dramatically forwards, almost throwing the two men into the water. The girder on the roof – their last chance of a dry escape – slipped sideways into the canal with a loud splash.

'Fuckin' hell!' Gaz cussed as he teetered dangerously on the bonnet. Dave scrambled forward and grabbed his arm to pull him back onto the roof as the car swung violently the other way.

'Shit! Come here, come here ... come here,' Dave yelled as he helped Gaz back up onto the roof of the Cortina, which then see-sawed gently back into a horizontal position.

'Stay still, stay still,' Gaz ordered as he checked the car's motion beneath him. 'All right.' The two men half-stood, half-crouched, their legs wide apart, their arms outstretched ready to save themselves, as they tried to find their balance on the floating wreck. Once it stabilised, they froze like panic-stricken statues and glared helplessly at each other.

'What's your bloody "initiative" got to say about this then, bog-eyes?' Dave cursed, his face purple, releasing his grip on Gaz's sleeve in disgust.

Gaz swallowed hard and looked around him feebly. Nathan was oblivious to their plight way up the towpath and from the same direction, a man and a dog were strolling towards them. 'Ey up, someone's coming,' he hissed.

The middle-aged man sauntered on, his ageing black Labrador sniffing audibly and trotting along on a lead beside him in search of new smells. Looking up, but without a trace of surprise on his face, the bearded passer-by called out a cheery greeting to the two men: 'All right?' He recognised them from the steelworks and, like them, was now left at home to do the household chores and go on the wander, with the dog.

'Aye, not so bad,' Gaz responded breezily with a jaunty flick of his head, hands on his hips. Without breaking stride, the man and his dog strolled past without another word, before disappearing around the corner.

Dave, his mouth open, stared at his friend in wonder. 'Not so bad?' he repeated, his voice incredulous. 'Not so bad? That's not much of a chuffin' SOS, is it?' This was absolutely the last time he was going to have anything to do with Gaz and his ill-fated schemes. He never learned and they always ended in tears. Waiting for a response, he watched Gaz peer down into the murky water at the two girders lost in the silt, and then across at the towpath.

'All right, all right,' Gaz soothed, flapping his hands at Dave to calm down. 'Don't get a benny on,' he added, looking around him for inspiration. As Dave waited, hands on hips, for Gaz to come up with something brilliant, he had a sinking feeling in the pit of his stomach, and it wasn't just the movement of the car.

For once, he was right. Having carefully considered all the options open to them, assessed the situation from all angles and taken everything into full account, Gaz rubbed his hands through his hair helplessly and looked up at his friend. 'Oh shit!' he cursed and Dave knew that all was lost.

The squelch from Dave's trainers as he walked down the steep steps two blocks from the steel mill was matched only by the swishing sound his wet jeans made as his thighs rubbed uncomfortably together. He was sodden from the waist down and a trail of oily black water dripped onto the pavement with each footstep. It was April, but unseasonably cold with a stiff easterly wind and as the late afternoon drew to a close, the temperature plummeted.

Gaz, completely dry and seemingly unaffected by anything as mundane as the weather, had just pulled his T-shirt down over his head and put his jacket back on. Doing up the last button on his jeans, he was still chuckling to himself at the memory of Dave belly-flopping into the canal from the car with an almighty splash, the filthy water shooting up his nostrils and into his mouth as he did so.

Nathan wandered along in front of the hapless pair, shaking his head and wondering if either of the others had ever noticed that he seemed to be the only one with any sense.

'Me jeans are bloody soakin'!' Dave complained, his face now white with cold. His jeans, jacket and T-shirt were wet through and his Y-fronts were chafing his groin.

Gaz grinned. 'Should've taken your kit off then, shouldn't you?' he said, repeating his earlier advice, after wading naked across the canal himself, his clothes held high and dry above his head. In a high-pitched voice, he mocked: 'What's up, are you shy?' He knew the answer only too well.

Dave pulled a limp packet of cheese crackers from his bomber jacket pocket – the only between meals snack he allowed himself on his latest diet – and grimaced as diesel-contaminated water poured from the packet. Tossing it angrily into the hedge, he scowled at Gaz, an image of him stripped off, his lithe body exposed to all and sundry on the towpath still in his mind's eye. There hadn't been an inch of fat on Gaz, not one inch, let alone any vast dimpled expanses of cellulite.

'Don't,' Dave warned Gaz through gritted teeth. The last thing he needed right now was someone starting in on him about his weight. 'Just shut it. All right?' He hated himself enough, without anyone else adding to his misery. He was sixteen-and-a-half stone the last time he weighed himself properly. He stared down at the impressive spread of his stomach, his wet T-shirt clinging unflatteringly to it, and felt disgusted with himself for the hundredth time that week.

He'd been overweight for as long as he could remember. The kids at school used to take the mickey, and the blokes used to rib him about it when they were all working together in the steel mill. But, somehow, it hadn't mattered so much back then – when he was still the man of the house, bringing the money in and able to keep Jean happy. Since he'd been laid off and his self-esteem had gradually been chipped away as he piled on the pounds, it began to matter more and more. Jean got a job as a sales assistant at the smart new Asda supermarket in the Meadowhall Shopping Centre, that vast cathedral to commerce, showcase for the new Sheffield. She was the one with the money now. He was left at home, watching daytime telly, secretly bingeing and picking at the food while he made dinner, ready for when Jean came home from work.

It seemed to Dave that his whole world had been tipped upside down. It had all gone to cock. Women like his wife, for so long taking second place, were suddenly no longer tied by their apron strings to the kitchen sink. They had money in their pockets, a new found independence and greater demands. Now it was the men who were expected to shape up, keep fit and get sexy in order to keep hold of their meal tickets. It wasn't all right to be a fat bastard anymore. But fat bastard he was and fat bastard, he knew, he would remain.

Lost in his thoughts, he hardly noticed a pretty young woman in a miniskirt approaching them as they walked slowly down the steps towards their short cut home. But Gaz did. 'Eh up, Dave,' Gaz winked at his sullen-faced mate. Turning to the young woman with his most winning smile, Gaz leered openly. 'All right, babe?'

Nathan and Dave were equally unimpressed by Gaz's behaviour. 'Dad,' Nathan chided, embarrassed as ever by his father's seemingly insatiable libido. It sometimes seemed to the boy that his father tried to overcompensate for his absence from his life the rest of the week by being overtly macho on the days he did see him. He was always asking Nathan if he had a girlfriend yet and openly discussing masturbation, sex and other similar matters in a way which tried to put the boy at ease, but which only made him shudder inwardly.

Gaz ignored his son's remark and accompanying glare, and stared back up at the young woman as she passed. Her blonde hair piled up in a scrunch on top of her hair, she was wearing a denim jacket, electric blue miniskirt and carrying a handbag over her shoulder with a black and white cow-skin pattern. She turned and winked at Gaz, knowing exactly who he was and what his reputation was like.

'What d'you reckon, Dave? ... Eight? ... Maybe even a Nine,' Gaz asked, giving her one last ogle as he considered the issue. He and Dave had been awarding marks out of ten since they first made eyes at girls in the playground at the Brinsworth Secondary Modern School thirty years ago. Coming to his final verdict, he awarded her eight-and-a-half, while privately bemoaning the fact that the unusually cold weather meant that the objects of his desire were wearing several more layers of clothing than normal for this time of year. 'You never can tell till you see their tits, can you?' he added thoughtfully.

Nathan clamped his hands to his ears in open indignation and screamed silently at his father, but Gaz only grinned even more. Dave squirmed on the boy's behalf and wished once again that Gaz would engage his brain before opening his mouth.

Rounding the corner and crossing the street at the bottom

of the steps as dusk began to fall, the two men and the boy almost stopped in their tracks at the unusual sight before them. Forming a noisy but orderly queue outside the now shabby Millthorpe Working Men's Club were three dozen giggling women, all done up to the nines and shrouded in a mist of hair spray and perfume. A smile tugged at the corner of Gaz's mouth at the sight of so many potential high scorers together. There were at least three Nines that he could see already. This was going to be too tempting to resist.

'What's all this then?' he asked aloud, not really expecting a response as the three of them ambled towards the queue.

Nathan – always the most clued up – supplied the answer anyway. 'It's them Chippendale efforts,' he said nonchalantly, remembering hearing his mother chatting excitedly about it on the telephone with a friend the previous evening.

'You what?' Gaz asked, staring down at his son as if he were seeing him for the first time. Nearing the club now, he could hear the music thumping out, and see the posters advertising the event. He realised with a shock that his son was telling the truth.

Nathan shrugged his shoulders. 'Them dancers – Mum were going on about it,' he explained apologetically. Gaz was appalled at his son's reaction. He was surprised that the boy even knew who the Chippendales were. Gaz only knew because he'd read a recent newspaper article about them and how they were taking Britain by storm. But the boy acted as if it were the most normal thing in the world for a troupe of pumped-up American male strippers to do a turn on the stage at the Millthorpe Working Men's Club – the very place where Gaz and Dave had spent many a testosterone-filled, beer-swilling night, watching Sheffield's finest tarts peeling off to their skimpy G-strings to the strains of a Barry White hit.

'Ah, you're joking,' Gaz replied, finding it equally hard to imagine his ex-wife getting excited about a bunch of over-oiled, muscle-bound poofs in bow ties. 'She must be getting desperate,' he added with an impish grin. Thinking of the wimpy Barry she was now shacked up with he wondered if Mandy was getting enough in bed. Computer-nerd Barry might have money, a job and prospects, but he'd bet his last quid that the freckle-faced little pillock was hopeless between the sheets.

Fired up by the thought, Gaz swaggered over to the line of overdressed women – several of whom he knew in the biblical sense – and decided to try his luck. Dave, embarrassed enough and still soaked to the skin, tried to call him off, while wringing canal water from his jacket. 'Away, Gaz,' he cautioned, as he and Nathan walked quickly past the queue, but Gaz – as ever – ignored them and headed directly for the hornet's nest.

'You all waiting for me then?' he called cockily to the first few women, who were standing on the steps chewing gum and smoking cigarettes, their clothing making no allowances for the unseasonably cold temperatures. Gaz did a quick nipple count.

'Yeah ...' replied one woman he knew only as Leanne, who could drink six pints of bitter a night and still hold her own at the bar. The queen of sarcasm, she added: '... to go home.' The women around her cackled in unison, relishing the sight of the 'Leery Lad' being put in his place for a change.

His blood up, Gaz rounded on them with a boastful strut, his arms outstretched as if welcoming them all into his bed. 'Well, you know where to find me when you're tired of looking at them poofs,' he proffered, his tongue firmly in his cheek. He cackled back at them while they shook their heads in awe at his inflated opinion of himself.

Nathan, mortified at the humiliating scene as the women ridiculed Gaz still further, called his father's name. 'Dad, come on,' he urged, hurrying past the club. It was bad enough that he'd had to watch his father make an idiot of himself all day, without him adding to the score at night.

Dave picked up the call. 'Come on, Gaz, I'm freezing,' he whined, keeping pace with the boy. It was starting to get dark and he wanted nothing more than to get home and get out of his wet clothes and into some dry ones. Sod the diet, he'd promised himself a comforting bag of chips on the way home, before he started on Jean's supper.

Gaz finally turned away from the baying women and headed away from the club as if he was going to let the matter rest there. But there was a look on his face that bothered his companions, and they feared that the night was not yet over. Grinding to a halt when he caught sight of the full-colour Chippendales poster stuck to the club wall, Gaz paced a small circle on the pavement – a sure sign that he was enraged. Afraid of what he might get up to without their guiding influence, Dave and Nathan faltered and waited for him in resignation.

True to form, Gaz strode up to the poster and studied it closely, his face black. The words 'For One Night, Women Only' and 'The Men Are Here' were plastered in red lettering over the front of a huge photograph of five half-naked and immaculately groomed men, one with long blond hair all the way down to his pert nipples. Dave wrung the other corner of his jacket out and let the water cascade to the ground as Gaz's face darkened further with anger at the headlines which he seemed to regard as a direct challenge to his manhood.

'Women only?' he said with great indignation. 'Cheeky buggers! It's a bloody working men's club!' Pointing dismissively at the smiling blond Adonis in the front of the all-male group, he scoffed: 'I mean, look at the state of that!'

Dave, well accustomed to Gaz's rantings, reached into his other pocket wearily for his cigarettes as he stood impassively with Nathan. Fishing out the sodden packet to see if any of its contents were salvageable, he extracted one soaked example, studied it carefully and then discarded it and the packet in dismay. Now it seemed he couldn't even have a smoke to warm him up while he was waiting. This was fast turning into a very bad day.

Gaz continued talking to the poster. 'I dunno what you've got to smile about,' he said to the muscle-bound man second from the left in the poster. Turning to Dave, he argued: 'I mean, he's got no willy for starters, has he?' Tapping accusingly at the unimpressive bulge in the man's half-unzipped trousers, he moved his face inches from the target of his criticism and shouted: 'There's nowt in a gym'll help you there, mate.'

Judging by the hyperactive way Gaz was carrying on, Dave and Nathan could tell that he was still in full flow. There was nothing to do but wait until he'd got it all out of his system. They might just as well have provided him with a soapbox to stand on and taken a seat themselves. There'd be no shifting him until he'd said his piece.

After railing on for a few minutes, Gaz finally turned away from the poster with a shake of his head. 'Nah,' he declared. 'No decent woman would be seen dead in there.' His verdict had been delivered. The Chippendales had been consigned to exile, and all those who had paid money to see them had been duly sentenced. Pleased with himself, he turned to his companions with a decisive nod, but his triumphant expression fell from his face when he saw the doleful look on Dave's.

'Jeanie would,' Dave answered miserably after an uncomfortable pause.

Gaz winced as if in pain. 'Ah, Dave? What's going on?' he said, his voice rising in pitch as he wondered for the umpteenth time why Dave let Jean walk all over him. This would never have happened in the old days, when Dave was still working. Something had gone fundamentally wrong with that marriage and Gaz was buggered if he knew what.

Dave shrugged his shoulders and tilted his head. 'It's her money, isn't it?' he mumbled, looking away down the street. They were exactly the words Jean had used to him when she told him she was going with a couple of mates. Try as he might to reason with her, she was right and who was he to blame her?

Gaz's hands shot from their pockets and onto his hips, his stance one of macho defiance. 'Fuckin' hell!' he exclaimed, his hackles raised. 'Are you gonna just stand there while some poof's waving his tackle at your missus?' Dave looked away and wished that he'd never mentioned it. But Gaz still wasn't finished. 'Where's your pride, man?' he asked, before moving in for the kill.

A recent image flashed up on the screen in his head of big Dave, a floral pinafore tied tightly around his belly, doing the housework. Gaz had spotted him at it through the living room window the previous week and had turned and walked away, deciding that it was best to say nothing at the time. But faced with this latest blow to all that he held dear, he felt it necessary to bring it up now. Rounding on Dave and imitating the vacuuming motion, he sneered: 'She's already got you hoovering ... I saw it and I let it go.'

Nathan stood awkwardly at Dave's side and peered up into his guilty face. The big man looked for all the world as if he had been caught playing with himself. Gaz didn't seem to notice, and carried on. 'But this? ...' he pointed at the club with his thumb. 'No, no, no.' His manner chilled Dave's heart. Standing head to head with Dave, Gaz challenged his friend and pointed to the club again. 'You wanna get her out of there and tell her what for.'

The colour drained from Dave's face at the very thought of dragging Jean from a club full of her screaming girlfriends. Unable to speak, he couldn't think of a reasonable response and was grateful when Nathan chipped in. 'He can't. It's women only,' Nathan reasoned, seeing where this was heading and dreading the thought.

Dave nodded a little too eagerly at the helpful comment, but Gaz's patronising expression and mischievous grin told them both that his initiative was about to come into play again. As Nathan and Dave eyed each other helplessly, swallowing hard, they felt instinctively that something disastrous was about to happen.

CHAPTER TWO

With an ungainly thud, Nathan dropped from the narrow window high up in the wall of the gents' lavatory and onto the tiled floor. He looked back up at his father struggling through after him, trying to get his footing on the narrow edge of the porcelain urinal.

Rubbing his hands together to clean off the dirt from the outside wall they had just clambered up, the boy paced the stinking room with his nose wrinkled, as the thumping beat of a Gary Glitter hit pounded the walls of the club just outside the door. Seeing his father still struggling he stepped closer to allow him to rest his foot on his shoulder if necessary as he prepared himself to drop the six feet to the floor. Nathan couldn't help but wonder what they were doing in such an unsavoury place on a Sunday night when he was thirsty, hungry and just about ready for bed. His father appeared to have completely forgotten that it was a school day tomorrow.

All that could be seen of Dave outside the toilet window were his two hands and the top half of his head as he stood on tiptoe and tried to peer in at them. 'Just hurry up will you?' he hissed. 'My feet have gone numb.'

Gaz raised his eyebrows to the heavens and addressed his comments to the hairline peeping over the ledge at him. 'Well, that's gratitude for you,' he complained. 'We're riding into the Alley of Death for you, you fat git.' As usual, Gaz had turned the entire episode around, so that he was apparently doing Dave a favour by breaking into the club and dragging Jean outside for a ticking off. Some favour.

Dave's fingers curled tighter around the ledge and his

26

voice took on its familiar apologetic whine. 'It's not my fault I can't fit through, is it?' he said, before dropping back to the ground outside with a thump. It had been humiliating enough getting stuck half in and half out of the window like Winnie the Pooh down the rabbit hole and having to be prised from his wedged position, but now Gaz was making him feel even worse.

Ignoring Dave's self-pitying tone, Gaz turned to his son and the mission they had come to accomplish. 'Right then,' he said, which Nathan knew indicated it was time for him to do his father's dirty work. 'I'll be waiting here, keeping guard.' He put his hands on Nathan's shoulders and pushed him towards the door. 'You find Auntie Jean and tell her David wants a word outside, all right?' As simple as that. Never mind what Auntie Jean – who Nathan was more than a bit afraid of – might have to say about it when she saw the twelve-year-old boy in such a place.

Nathan scowled and looked up at his father with a pleading look. 'Dad, do I have to?' he asked, knowing full well what the answer was. There was no way, having got this far, that Gaz was going to back down now. It was a matter of principle. Auntie Jean would have to be found and a reluctant Dave would be forced to make his point to her in front of them, although all three of them knew very well what her reaction would be, and what stick Dave would get for being persuaded into it.

Gaz patted Nathan on the back to remind him that he had no choice. 'Good kid. On you go,' he said, opening the heavy wooden door to push him out into the smoke-filled function room.

The noise and heat hit them in the face like the blast from an open furnace. Stopping mid-step, they stood and stared, open-mouthed and blinking, at the astonishing spectacle before them.

Illuminated by the flashing red strobe lights from the stage out of Gaz and Nathan's sight to their right, the legions of women they had seen queuing politely at the door less than an hour earlier in the twilight were crowded in around the stage, crammed side by side together at tables with standing-room only at the back. Some scrambled over each other in their eagerness to get nearer to the men who were on stage getting their kit off.

In the hot, smoky atmosphere of the club, the women were wearing even less than they had been outside – pink rubber boob tubes with midriffs showing, leather miniskirts, see-through blouses, satin dresses – and they were baying for blood. 'Off! Off! Off! Off!' they chanted in between cheering, clapping and screaming hysterically. These were housewives and mothers, young girls and old grannies, shop assistants and bank clerks, all fully made-up and out for a good time. All eyes were on the stage, all lipsticked mouths were open in screeches of appreciation. The sexual tension in the air was palpable. Gaz had never seen anything like it in his life and Nathan, a novice to all this, was quite speechless, blinking hard again and again to remind himself that he was not imagining it.

Coming to his senses, Gaz prodded Nathan in the back and pushed him forward as he stood watching half in and half out of the doorway. The boy stumbled reluctantly into the dimly-lit extremities of the club, the Glitter chant 'Come on! Come on!' deafening him. Staggering towards a row of plastic tables lined up against a segmented wooden partition that formed the only barrier between him and the baying pack, the boy's eyes gradually became accustomed to the gloom and, as he scanned the scene immediately in front of him, they sparkled suddenly with his father's mischievous twinkle.

On each table lay the flotsam of the evening's pre-show build-up – ashtrays overflowing with dog-ends; pint glasses with a few dregs of Stone's bitter left in the bottom; paper handkerchiefs smeared with scarlet lipstick; a few half-empty glasses of Pernod and black. Deciding that his mission could wait and transfixed by the astonishing scene that he could now see on the stage through the gaps in the screen,

Nathan moved from table to table, picking up each half-empty glass and draining it in one. His wide eyes lit up by the bright lights of the stage, he stared, mesmerised, at the male strippers going through their outrageously provocative routines.

Gaz watched his son disapprovingly, hissing his name to try and stop him drinking from a tumbler that could only contain whisky, but he found his own gaze drawn back again and again to the images before him. Womenfolk, his father would have called them, hundreds of Sheffield women-folk, more fired up and sexually aroused than he could ever have imagined, even in his dreams. It was an exhilarating moment, intoxicating in its throbbing sexuality, and yet he was strangely intimidated by the sight.

He felt as if he had stumbled across some ancient tribal ritual deep in the jungle that no outsider was ever meant to see. Afraid to stay in case he was caught and torn limb from limb by the bloodthirsty creatures whose sacrificial ceremonial he was unwittingly witnessing, and yet unable to free himself from the spell of the drama unfolding before him, Gaz was trapped in the glow of the stage, rendered insensible by the music, the overwhelming noise and the heady scents that filled the air.

Catching sight of one woman in the crowd, standing up, head and shoulders above her mates, howling for more, Gaz was shaken back to his senses when he realised it was Jean, Dave's wife, her face pink and shiny with perspiration, her short blonde hair plastered to her head. Dressed in a tight miniskirt and a skimpy top which left little to the imagi-nation, her normally hard features were flushed with lecherous womanhood. She looked like a bitch on heat.

Watching from the safety of his doorway, he realised to his horror that she had turned her attention from the stage and was heading towards him, slipping from the crowd as the first act drew to a close. Beckoning two of her mates, Sharon and Bee, Jean put her hand on her crutch to indicate her need to go to the toilet and led them straight towards the gents lavatory – that last male bastion, the one place Gaz had believed he would be safe from the relentless march of female liberation.

Cursing under his breath and horrified by the thought of being discovered, he flew backwards through the doorway, slamming the door behind him. Reversing at speed into one of the three cubicles, he pushed the door firmly shut with his hands. Bending over, he peered apprehensively through a small hole in the door left by the torn-off lock. Panic stricken, he waited, his breath held, as he heard the main door fall open and the three drunken women staggered in, giggling.

'Oooh, I'm not waiting in that bloody queue,' said Jean, referring to the ladies' lavatory, her voice already slurred by too many gin and tonics. Hoicking up her dress and pulling down her knickers as she passed Gaz's peep-hole, she crashed into the cubicle next to his and he listened as her urine tinkled into the pan.

Sharon, dressed in a turquoise satin blouse and black miniskirt and even more under the influence, stumbled around the room, a strange expression on her heavily made-up face, before settling in front of the mirror, directly in Gaz's line of vision. 'Oooh, I've always wanted a nosy in the men's toilets,' she giggled, trying to focus on some of the more legible graffiti.

Gaz flinched as Bee, an attractive Asian girl, who now resembled a poodle with her long dark hair bunched up on top of her head above a lime green satin blouse, rebounded drunkenly off the wall of the cubicle the other side of his and went to the toilet with the door still open, shouting out to her girlfriends: 'Phwoar, them bloody muscles!'

Jean, emerging with her dress up round her waist and her tights half way up her buttocks, confided in her knowingly: 'No, no. It's not their bodies, Bee. It's what they do with them that counts.' Gaz gallantly averted his gaze until his best friend's wife had readjusted her clothing and was decent once again.

Bee giggled her agreement, but told Jean: 'I don't know what you're worrying about, with you-know-who on your tail.' She came out of her cubicle, pulling down her short skirt and joined Sharon, still standing at the mirror, plastering even more make-up on her face as she hiccuped. Gaz could see them all quite clearly now through his spy-hole. The two women nodded knowingly at each other, despite Jean's obvious embarrassment. Before Bee could stop her, Sharon had launched into the 60s hit: 'Frankeee, do you want my body...' but the expression on Jean's face made her trail off.

'Hey, hey, hey,' Dave's wife scolded, her finger wagging angrily at them. 'Frank don't fancy me and I don't fancy Frank, all right? So bloody well give over!' It was obviously a line she repeated quite often. Her two companions looked genuinely contrite. They knew they had been pushing this thing about the attractive young man at work a bit too far lately and now it seemed Jean had really had enough of their teasing.

Bee, flanking the other side of Jean, adjusted the ponytail high on the top of her head and she and Sharon eyed each other warily in the reflection as they reapplied their lipstick. Bee started rummaging in her handbag for her blue eye shadow, trying not to make eye contact with Jean.

Seeing the looks on their two faces and wishing she hadn't snapped at them so, the inebriated Jean broke the silence with a sudden impish grin and a wink. 'Eh, do you think he might though?' she asked as the three of them cackled like the Three Witches. Gaz, his leg getting cramp from his crouched position behind the door, swallowed hard and hoped to God that Dave had got fed up waiting and wasn't outside listening to all this.

As she leant over the sink and peered at her thirty-something reflection in the mirror, Dave watched Jean's expression dull with a maudlin thought. 'No, I couldn't do that to Dave,' she said softly. 'Not even if I wanted to.' Her eyes moist, she looked up at her two friends standing behind her, the women to whom she had so often poured out her heart. 'But, you know, it's like ... it's like he's given up. Work ... me ... everything.'

Bee nodded supportively and patted her shoulder. 'Ah, love,' she said, well aware that Jean was having a lot of trouble at home. It was all the poor woman talked about. She and Dave were drifting towards the rocks, that was for sure. Despite all her efforts to keep him upbeat, he had succumbed to the hopelessness that enveloped many of the unemployed and his worsening depression was beginning to drag Jean down with him.

Sharon turned away, unable to deal with someone else's failed marriage when hers had long been foundering for much the same reasons. Her husband Mick had taken to the bottle as his way of coping with redundancy, and his drunken rages had her running for cover most nights.

Winking at a forlorn-looking Jean and patting her arm, Sharon promised: 'Here, love, this'll cheer you up.' She swaggered over to the urinals on the wall, hiccuping and smirking back at her two friends. Gaz pressed his eye socket as close as he could to the hole in the door, following Sharon's progress across the room and wondering what she was going to do. Hitching up her skirt and pulling down her knickers, she thrust her hips forward dramatically, moved her hands to her groin and started to urinate, her little silver handbag dangling by her left buttock as she did so.

Gaz squashed his face against his peephole in appalled disbelief as he watched a stream of yellow urine hit the wall directly in front of Sharon and trickle to the drain below. The sight made him draw back for a second, not sure he could believe his own eyes. He peered out again to be sure. It was true. She was pissing standing up, just like a bloke! He couldn't believe it. Neither could Jean and Bee, who both collapsed into uncontrollable fits of laughter, roaring their approval.

'I weren't in t' Girl Scouts for nothing!' Sharon yelled at them over her shoulder. Her astonishing performance completed, she pulled her tights up over her bare ass, readjusted her clothing and turned to face her delighted audience, thoroughly pleased with herself. The three women crashed back through the door and into the club, still laughing at the best party trick they'd seen in years.

Speechless, Gaz cautiously opened the cubicle door and stepped out, still staring in amazement at the urinal wall. The colour had drained from his face and he felt quite wobbly at the knees, what with the fear of being discovered and the shock of what he had just witnessed. He was beginning to think this whole escapade had been a very bad idea.

Behind him, Dave's two hands suddenly appeared at the window. A forlorn voice called: 'Gaz, Gaz. That were our Jean, weren't it?' Dave had heard some but not all of the conversation, but thought he had caught snippets of Jean's voice, joking about some bloke at work fancying her. He hoped he was wrong.

Pulling himself together, Gaz shook himself. 'No, no, er, just a couple of old tarts,' he responded brusquely and headed for the lavatory door. 'I'm going back in for Nathe,' he announced, having suddenly lost his taste for adventure.

Pushing forcefully through the door as the Donna Summer hit *Hot Love* pounded its beat throughout the club, he no longer cared who saw him. Hands over his eyes to accustom them to the glaring spotlights, he spotted Nathan sitting rather haphazardly at the farthest of the tables, pouring assorted drinks into a dirty pint glass. The boy took a brief quizzical look at his toxic cocktail, before downing it in one, spilling most of the contents down his chin and onto his jacket.

Realising that the women were far too busy having fun to notice him, Gaz stalked over to where the boy sat and snatched the glass from his hand, thumping it down on the table. Hoisting him up, he hissed: 'You're in big trouble,' and yanked him to his feet, arm clamped around his shoulder to keep him upright.

The crowd had started a slow hand clap as the heavily tanned Chippendales came back on stage and started their final pelvis-grinding routine to the music belting out over the massive loudspeakers. Wearing little more than bow-ties around their necks, the men were at the front of the stage, beckoning women to come up and slip £5 notes into their G-strings. The women were queuing up in their droves.

'What about Auntie Jean?' Nathan asked, his eyes glazed, his breath stinking of booze. Gaz spotted Jean hard at it once again, on her feet and dancing this time, twirling her arms around and singing along in perfect time. Pummelling her arms in the air like a boxer, she roared lasciviously as she watched Sharon make it to the stage and stuff a crisp fiver straight down the front of one dancer's skimpy pants.

'Auntie Jean's busy,' Gaz remarked sadly and dragged Nathan back towards the gents' lavatory and their escape route as the crowd around them erupted into the chorus.

Nathan hardly said a word to his father the following morning. The pair of them fell straight out of their beds into their crumpled clothes and sat down in Gaz's debris-filled kitchen for breakfast. Sniffing the curdled half pint of milk left out of the refrigerator overnight, Nathan had vomited. He couldn't even face the piece of buttered toast his father offered him. The pair walked in silence to school, Gaz nodding a hello to all the other unemployed fathers similarly delivering their children.

As they rounded the corner near their destination, Nathan finally turned to his father and admitted weakly: 'I don't feel well.' Pale and unwashed, his teeth unbrushed, he looked as if he had been up all night.

Gaz punched his son lightly on the shoulder with a smirk. 'Of course you don't,' he chided, trying not to laugh. 'You've got a hangover.' Softening, he added: 'Take a day off, hang about at home.' It was a suggestion he often made to the boy, anxious to spend as much time with him as possible and seemingly unfazed by the warnings Mandy had given him about Nathan's schoolwork suffering as a result. What did it matter if the boy missed the odd day here and there, he would argue. He was only a kid and, anyway, school hadn't done Gaz much good.

Nathan was, however, unimpressed with the latest offer to play truant. 'Your house is messy. It's cold an' all,' he complained, rubbing his empty stomach, the taste of vomit still in the back of his throat. He was actually looking forward to a hot school meal and the chance of a nap in the uninterrupted boredom of his geography lesson. Anything was better than his father's dismal council flat in one of the city's most notorious tower blocks. The housing estates might have been state of the art in their day, but many were now occupied by single mothers, drug addicts and the unemployed. Gaz couldn't afford his heating bills and so he didn't bother turning it on. He advised Nathan to wear more clothes instead.

Gaz had another suggestion. 'All right then, come down the Job Club. That'll be a laugh.' His eyes told Nathan he was lying. Warm it might be, but fun it wasn't. Sitting with a load of grim-faced men on the dole, watching them play cards, inhaling their cigarette smoke, listening to them complaining about the way of the world wasn't his idea of a fun day out.

Nathan squinted up at his father with a frown. 'Mum's house is always warm,' he said quietly, thinking of the deep shag pile carpets throughout, the numerous radiators belting out heat, and his cosy bedroom with its goose down duvet. He wished he could be snuggled under it now, and that the throbbing pain in his head would stop.

Gaz hated this line of conversation. It had been coming up more and more lately and he knew he couldn't possibly compete with the comforts Mandy's well-financed home life had to offer. Climbing the hill with Nathan to the school gates, he shook his head and held out his hand pleadingly. 'I can't always have the red carpet out for you, can I?' he reasoned. A muscle in his jaw started to twitch. 'Anyway, it's not your mum's house, it's what's-his-name ...' He gestured back over his shoulder with his thumb while he tried to bring himself to say the name. Finally, and with great effort, he blurted: 'Barry's.'

Nathan wondered why his father always pretended he

couldn't remember Barry's name. It had been more than two years since Barry and Mandy had moved in together; he'd have thought his dad would have got used to the idea by now. The boy did his best not to mention Barry's name in Gaz's company, he knew it upset him, but it was ridiculous to pretend he didn't exist. And anyway, Nathan liked Barry. He was all right. He bought him presents and took him on outings. Next holidays he was taking him to EuroDisney.

Gaz dismissed the odious Barry from his mind and entertained a more amenable thought. 'Tell you what, next weekend I'll have a big tidy around … I promise.' Nathan's eyes were fixed firmly on his feet. He'd heard that one before. It usually meant that he got roped in as well and spent his entire weekend cleaning his dad's flat while he lay on the sofa with a cigarette, supervising. Seeing that he was unimpressed, Gaz offered a sweetener: 'Even go and see a footie game,' he said.

The boy's head shot up and he appeared interested for the first time that morning. 'Yeah?' Football was his passion; he and the boys at school collected football cards and watched all the big matches on the telly. Barry had even bought him the new Sheffield United strip for his birthday.

Gaz nodded enthusiastically, pleased to see Nathan animated at last. 'Sunday League going on down at the park. It's got some right good players.' He tried to make the most of the only football game he could afford to take his son to, a free knock-around in the local playing fields. Well, it was still football, and he knew his son adored the game.

Nathan's face fell. 'United playing Man U, aren't they?' he asked tentatively, looking across at his father with hope. Barry wouldn't have just taken him down the park, he felt like adding but didn't.

Gaz took a deep breath and stopped walking. It was his turn to look despondent. 'Oh, Nathe, you know I can't stretch to that,' he complained. The cost of two tickets to a professional game would eat up most of his week's dole money, not to mention his bills and the maintenance he was meant to be paying Mandy and was already well behind on.

The Child Support Agency had been hounding him for the arrears for months and he knew that unless he did something about it soon, they would stop just threatening to take legal action and start instigating some. It was a thought which filled him with such dread that he hadn't even bothered opening his latest post, in case it had already begun.

Nathan, who understood very little of the financial pressures his father was under, was still sulking. He resented the fact that his father seemed to have a lot less money than those of his mates. Scowling at Gaz as they reached the school gates, he told him: 'You're always making me do stupid stuff, like last night.'

It wasn't just breaking into the factory or sneaking into a nightclub through a window he was talking about, it was all the other madcap escapades his father had dragged him into over the years – collecting empty beer cans; checking discarded lottery tickets for winning numbers; entering newspaper competitions, shoplifting. Schemes which became more and more desperate as his father's need for cash increased. Still pouting, Nathan added hurtfully: 'Other dads don't do that.'

'Don't they?' Gaz responded crossly, wondering for the first time in his life what other single fathers did with their children on the weekends they were allowed to see them. Nodding at his son, he conceded: 'Aye,' but he was still smarting from the accusation. He thought the kid enjoyed tagging along on their little capers together. He thought it had been a bit of fun. Something to do.

Nathan couldn't bear to see the pain in his father's eyes, so he mumbled a goodbye and, with nothing more to say, turned on his heel to walk in through the school gates, striding across the playground without another word.

Not wanting to part on such bad terms if they weren't going to see each other for another week, Gaz kept pace with him outside the wrought-iron railings, calling through them to his son. ''Ere, Nathe!' he shouted. 'We could try and sneak into Man U ... Terry were telling us about this gap in the fence.' His face was animated, the mischievous sparkle back in his eyes.

Nathan spun round with a frown. 'No!' he scolded, looking uncannily like his mother for a second. The boy was furious. His father obviously hadn't listened to a word he said. He didn't want to do stupid stuff any more. That was what he was trying to tell him. He stalked off unhappily.

His hands gripping the railings, Gaz tried one more time. 'All right, I'll, I'll, I'll get tickets – I will.' Nathan's expression was one of open disbelief. He hitched his rucksack higher onto his shoulder and continued walking with a sigh.

Clambering up the railings to get a better view of his son now halfway across the playground, Gaz clung to them and broke into his son's favourite football chant, a tirade against the former Manchester United player Eric Cantona. 'Ooh, ah, Cantona, has to wear a girly bra!' Several of the children in the playground turned and watched him with a smile, highly amused by the grown-up's unusual behaviour. But Nathan kept his back firmly to his father and headed purposefully for the classroom door, eager to get inside and escape the embarrassing scene.

As the boy finally disappeared from view, Gaz yelled: 'We'll stuff 'em, Nathe.' But the boy was long gone. Gaz slammed his forehead against the railings and swore out loud, frustrated with himself and the unfairness of the world.

The dismal surroundings of the ironically-named Job Club – the politically-correct new title for what used to be called the Labour Exchange – did not constitute a fun day out for a twelve-year-old boy, Gaz had to admit, as he leaned back on his red plastic bucket seat and studied the grimy glass-panelled walls around him.

Plastered with encouraging red and white stickers informing people how to apply for jobs, and with the few meagre job vacancy notices stuck on a board in the corner, this cheerless zone of the human soul did little to inspire the hardened long-term unemployed who slouched around within it day after day. Dave and Gaz, along with twenty or so other old mates from the steelworks, pitched up here three or four times a week – mainly for the free cup of coffee and a chance to warm their feet. Today was no exception, and the motley crew gathered together rarely changed.

Luke Marcus, the Job Club manager, a stocky but dapper man in his late thirties with his sights firmly set on a senior Civil Service job, was addressing them in his usual patronising manner. 'I want your application letters finished by the time I get back, right?' he said, sounding like a primary school master. He was part of the latest Government initiative to get the jobless back to work by talking to them like children and making them do their homework – pretending they were applying for a job which didn't exist. Nice one.

Luke knew it was a complete waste of time with most of this lot. They sat behind rows of grey plastic tables staring at him blankly, waiting for him to bugger off and leave them be. Unemployment had sapped their will and crushed their self-esteem. They wanted everything handed to them on a plate and they no longer even pretended to care.

But despite their unresponsiveness, he still went through the motions and duly filled in all his reports, writing glowingly of his sterling attempts to help these unfortunates get back on their feet. There were one or two of the older men who appreciated his help, who didn't mind his ubiquitous red pen criss-crossing its way through their day's work, and it was to them now that he directed his final comments. 'Any problems, I'm outside,' he concluded, shutting the door behind him as he retreated to the sanctuary of his own smoked-glass office, a room – the lads knew – in which the bottom drawer of his desk hid several pornographic magazines.

As soon as the door clicked shut behind him, the casually-dressed incumbents set to work. Out came the ashtrays and thermos flasks hidden under the tables, the packs of cards, hand-rolling tobacco and newspapers. The plain pieces of paper on which they were meant to write their application forms were fashioned into paper planes or crumpled into balls and bounced off the walls. The four men on Gaz's table sorted out their recently dealt hands of cards in their morning's poker game while Gaz resumed his story.

'I tell you,' he repeated with a sigh, 'when women start pissing like us, that's it.' Several of those in the room nodded Aye and drew on their cigarettes, fuelling the smog that already formed a haze above their heads. Gerald Cooper, a greying middle-aged man in a suit, sitting at a computer terminal to one side, listened in to the conversation, his expression wholly disapproving. Oblivious to his hostility, Gaz smirked at Dave, sitting pensively at his side and said: 'We're finished, Dave. Extincto.'

Dave frowned and turned to Gaz, trying to find the right words to express his confused thoughts. 'Yeah, but I mean ... how, you know?' His hand flapped uselessly in mid-air, trying to get to grips with the problem, his mind boggling at how a woman could possibly urinate standing up. He didn't have that much experience with women – well, truth be known, he'd only ever had sex with one girl before Jean – but in both instances their pissing tackle seemed to him to be in completely the wrong place for such a feat. 'How?' he asked again, utterly perplexed, his finger pointing at his groin, his eyes cast downwards.

Gaz shuffled the pack and shrugged his shoulders. He'd seen it with his own eyes and yet he still didn't really know how Sharon had done it. He wasn't even sure he wanted to know.

Terry, a thick-set moustachioed former colleague from the works, who was slumped in the chair opposite them studying his cards, piped up: 'Genetic mutations, isn't it? They're turning into us.' A few of the men sitting around and listening in nodded sagely, but none of them really knew what he was on about.

A cigarette wedged high up between his fingers as he dealt

40

the cards, Gaz thought about a wildlife programme he'd seen on female toads evolving to mate with themselves. 'A few years and men won't exist,' he said ominously. 'Except in a zoo or summat.' Sitting up, he shuffled his cards and brooded. 'I mean, we're not needed no more, are we?' Shaking his head, he added forcefully: 'Obsolete.' Allowing a few seconds for that thought to sink in, he said: 'Dinosaurs.' He paused for effect. 'Yesterday's news,' he concluded.

Dave, who was still finding it very hard to take it all in, brightened at the last phrase. He recalled reading a newspaper article by that name about fads and fashions that made the headlines one day and were forgotten the next. 'Like skateboards?' he offered helpfully, as Gaz looked askance and wondered again at the mysterious workings of his friend's mind.

The banal comment was the last straw for Gerald Cooper, the only man among them making any attempt to fill in his application form. Swivelling round in his seat in front of the computer terminal, the man who was nearly twenty years their senior scowled at them. 'Button it, you lot! Some of us are trying to get a job,' he spat. The deep lines around his eyes hinted at the considerable stress he was already under, without having to listen to this lot prattle on all day, interrupting his concentration with all their talk of genetic mutation and men not being needed any more.

Seeing that he had grabbed their attention, he pointed angrily at the sign on the wall above their heads and added, for good measure: 'Hey! And it says "No Smoking" in here.' He glared up at the sign and for the first time in six months realised that it was heavily pockmarked with holes where darts had been thrown at it.

Gaz snorted through his nose at Gerald's outburst and rocked back in his seat, cigarette in hand. 'Aye, and it says "Job Club" up there, and when were the last time you saw one of them fuckin' walk in?' He dropped his cards onto the table as the men sitting with him laughed out loud.

Gerald turned back to his screen and tapped angrily at the keys. But Gaz had an audience now and he couldn't let it go. 'You forget, Gerald,' he reminded the older man, 'you're not our foreman any more.' A few of the lads nodded. Cooper had never been particularly popular among the men; he had engaged in too much brown-nosing with the management for their liking, although to be fair he had supported their industrial action at the end. Forgetting that, Gaz went on: 'You're just like the rest of us ... scrap.'

Gerald turned to Gaz, his eyes on fire. 'Shut it. Right?' he warned. Gaz was surprised at the intensity of the warning and decided not to push it for a change. Pulling a childish face at Gerald instead, he drew on his cigarette and returned to the issue of the inevitable decline of the male gender.

Dave's mind was clearly still two conversations back. 'Hang on, though,' he said, as if he had just thought of something meaningful. 'Why were all them women in working men's club in first place, eh?' He looked around him with a nod and a finger held up for added impetus. Not waiting for an answer as his fellow players carried on examining their cards, he provided it for them. 'Now then,' he added, '... 'cos of us ... Men.' His expression was triumphant.

Gaz turned his nose up at the suggestion and sneered with indignation. 'You call them Chippendales men?' The man who had spent much of the morning staring at the topless model adorning Page Three of *The Sun* newspaper added: 'Degrading, that's what it were.' He spoke with the weight of one who had witnessed something remarkable first hand, who knew what he was talking about. A few of the lads nodded, trusting his assessment.

But Dave wasn't going to let Gaz spoil his moment of glory quite so easily. 'How many lasses were there, though?' he asked, half-smiling, his eyebrows halfway up his forehead with excitement.

'Thousands – baying for blood,' Gaz answered glumly, shaking his head at the memory. 'Ten quid an' all, to watch some fuckin' poof get his kit off. Ten quid!' He took a deep draught of his cigarette and continued shaking his head as his audience mulled that sobering thought over.

Dave smiled smugly and pointed across at Terry. 'Right. Times ten quid by a thousand, right ...' He looked down at his sausage-like fingers and started to count out ten thousand, his lips moving silently as he counted, '... and you've got ...' Giving up the attempt almost as soon as he had begun it, he added hastily: 'Yeah well, a lot ... a very lot.'

Gaz shook his head disparagingly. 'Nah,' he said.

Terry sat opposite them, hunched into his tan leather jacket, his eyelids flickering as his brain clicked into gear. 'Ten thousand quid,' he suddenly offered, his eyes widening as he spoke. Even Gerald looked round. The whole room fell silent.

'How much?' Gaz asked quietly, stubbing out his cigarette with a frown and staring up at Terry in astonishment.

'Ten thousand quid,' Terry responded confidently. It had been his job to count the coils of steel at the works and everyone knew he was good at adding up. The figure must be right.

Dave turned smugly to Gaz with a look that said 'Told you so'. But the pound signs spinning in Gaz's eyes were not what he had expected to see and his own face fell slightly at the sight.

'Hey now, Dave. I mean, er ...' Gaz started, sitting up in his seat, his mouth twisting into a smile. Turning to him and repeatedly stubbing out his dead dog-end, he added encouragingly: 'It's worth a thought though, isn't it?' wiggling his eyebrows expressively. Dave, inwardly recoiling in horror at what his friend was suggesting, waggled his eyebrows back at him nevertheless in an attempt to show a bit willing.

It was too much for Gerald Cooper to resist. Swivelling round to face them, his expression gleeful for the first time in months, he guffawed loudly. 'Oh, aye,' he tittered, hardly able to speak for his mirth. 'Could just see Little and Large

prancin' round Sheffield with their widgers hanging out ...
Now that would be worth ten quid!' The men in the room
couldn't help but snigger along with him at the thought.

Gaz straightened his neck and looked decidedly annoyed.
'Don't be so bloody daft,' he said, retracting hastily and
fiddling nervously with his cards. 'We were just saying, you
know.' Dave had flushed crimson next to him.

But Gerald had the floor now and he was loving every
minute of it. 'Widgers on parade. Bring your own micro-
scope,' he cajoled, swaying his head from side to side and
wiggling his two little fingers in unison to the sounds of
stifled laughter across the room.

Dave took instant exception to the suggestion that his
personal attributes were less than impressive. 'I don't see
why the chuff not, Gerald,' he challenged, before Gaz could
stop him.

Gerald rose quickly to the bait. 'Because you're fat,' he
pointed an accusing finger at Dave, '... and he's thin,' he
pointed at Gaz, his voice rising to a hysterical cackle as the
laughter turned into a roar. 'And you're both fucking ugly!'

Gaz could take no more. Tossing his cards to the floor, he
jumped to his feet and, with one fluid motion, was up on the
table, eyeing Gerald blackly. 'You bastard!' he shouted,
before leaping down in front of him, meeting him in the
middle of the room with an attempted head butt. The two
men pushed and shoved each other in the chest angrily as
Terry, Dave and a few others tried to separate them.

This showdown had been a long time coming. Both men
had been winding each other up for weeks, and as they fell
flailing to the floor in a flurry of fists, each giving as good as
he got, the rest of the crowd began to cheer.

Later that evening, Gaz found himself staring up at a redbrick detached house on a smart new estate in one of the
better suburbs of Sheffield, thinking of what might have
been. This was Barry's house, Barry and Mandy's and
Nathan's house, with its fancy brickwork, festoon blinds

and perfectly manicured lawn trimmed with flowers. Parked in the drive was a brand new Rover. He felt sick to his stomach as he marched up the York stone path and banged his fist on the door.

Checking his bruised knuckles for damage from his earlier brawl, Gaz took a deep breath and paced a small circle on the pathway, trying to decide whether he should do to Barry what he had done to Gerald. He was taken aback when the door was opened by Mandy, her arms folded defensively across her chest, her head tilted to one side, a hostile expression on her face when she saw who her uninvited caller was.

Slim, pretty and pixie-like, her dark hair pulled back in a ponytail behind her head, she was still very attractive even though she was now well into her thirties. Mandy had been all Gaz ever wanted at school and afterwards. They'd married young, struggled to get a home and have a family for years and then, just when Nathan came along, things started to go badly wrong.

First and foremost, he'd got caught nicking cars on his first return to his old ways of petty crime, in an attempt to raise a bit of extra cash for her and Nathan's Christmas presents. He ended up doing eighteen months in Wakefield Prison. By the time he came out, Nathan was a toddler and Mandy had hardened to him. He could no longer fool her with his wild dreams and by then, she had a job of her own and an attitude to match. He got his old job back at the steelworks, but as the recession pinched and people started to be laid off, he became one of the first casualties, and the dream lifestyle Mandy had set her heart on was lost to them for ever.

Miserable at his financial castration, and unable to cope with being a househusband, he started drinking too much and not long afterwards he began fooling around. When Mandy came home unexpectedly and caught him in their marital bed with the barmaid from the local pub, she walked out. No verbal warning, no yellow card, no second chances.

Gone. Goodbye to Nathan too, and the divorce papers in the post.

It wasn't long after that Barry appeared on the scene. A computer wizard at the clothing factory where she was in charge of the machine-room, with his flashy cars and his fat pay cheques, he could give her and Nathan all she ever wanted – this house, financial security, a cast-iron guarantee that he would come home every night, sober. He was boring as hell, but he wasn't going to break her and Nathan's heart and that was all she could expect as a single mum. She glared at Gaz now, her jaw clenched in anticipation of what he had come for and he doubted if he could ever win her back.

Waving a sheaf of documents in her face angrily, he demanded: 'What's all this about sole custody?' A rope of veins in his neck throbbed.

'You know what it is, Gary,' Mandy said, as if to a child, her Yorkshire accent far more shrill than his. It was not as if this could have come as a surprise to her ex-husband; he'd been served all the papers and she'd warned him time and again what might happen if he didn't get his act together. 'If you want joint custody then you have to pay your share ... seven hundred quid,' she reminded him, her arm held protectively across the doorway, barring his entrance in case he tried anything stupid.

Gaz seethed. That was Barry talking, not Mandy. 'I'm on't dole, in case you hadn't noticed,' he shouted, his hackles raised.

Mandy had heard it all before and she was tired of the same old song. There might not be work in the steel mills any more but there was work, other work, if Gaz could only bring himself to swallow his stupid male pride and do it. 'Then get a job ... I'll give you a job,' she offered.

Gaz laughed derisively. He could just see himself sitting at a machine, sewing ladies' underwear in her sweatshop, alongside a hundred women. 'Two pound fifty an hour in black hole of fuckin' Calcutta? No thank you,' he snorted, his head jerking forward on his neck.

Mandy bristled. 'Fine. Whatever.' She clamped her arms tightly across her chest. 'If you want to go off and play your games, Gary, then you do that. But from now on, Nathan's gonna have two parents.' She felt ashamed even saying it. She knew Gaz loved his son, and that the feeling was largely mutual, but she was afraid that he might lead the boy astray, tempt him to do things that he knew he shouldn't do; she knew he already encouraged him to play truant. At least with Barry's guiding influence, the boy might have a future on the right side of the law.

Gaz sneered openly at the thought of Barry taking his place as Nathan's father. 'Oh yeah, and your bloody live-in lover's gonna do that, is he?' His voice had that same edge it always did when Barry's name was mentioned. She wished it were different but it wasn't, and she was fed up with trying to make Gaz understand that this was how things were now. As Gaz spoke, Barry, tall and gangly with freckles and pale ginger curls, appeared behind Mandy, his arms swinging loosely at his side. 'Oh, abracadabra, here he is,' Gaz said acidly. 'Evening, Barry.'

Barry stood close behind Mandy and smiled sarcastically at his ex-love rival. He knew better than to try and engage this no-good lunatic in any meaningful conversation, especially when it came to money or Nathan. He'd listened to the doorstep conversation from the lounge and when he heard Gaz raise his voice, he'd decided it was time to come and give Mandy some moral support. The woman they both loved, always deeply uncomfortable at such confrontations between them, stiffened. 'That'll be for the court to decide,' she told Gaz defiantly. She wished he would just go and leave well alone.

Gaz stared daggers at her. 'No it won't,' he said through thin lips. Stepping closer to her, he spoke urgently, a catch in his voice. 'Nathan's yours and he's mine,' he reminded her, waving the legal documents angrily in her face. Jabbing his finger in Barry's direction, he shouted: '... and he's fuck all to do with him!' There were tears in his eyes.

Mandy hung her head as Barry interjected for the first time. 'As if you've ever given a toss,' he said, hands on his hips now, shaking his head at the audacity of this man who had treated his wife and child so badly. Gaz mulled over the options of punching him or not. He had once, a long time ago when the freckle-faced git had first started sniffing round Mandy but, despite bloodying his nose, it hadn't got him very far.

Mandy tilted her head again and tried to reason with him. 'Face it, Gary,' she said gently. 'He don't even like staying at yours.'

Gaz was deeply wounded at the suggestion and tossed his head back. 'Course he bloody does!' he yelled. 'Ask him.' There was silence. 'Ask him!' Taking two steps back and looking up at the window he knew to be Nathan's bedroom, he called out his name. 'Oi, Nathe!' he shouted. 'We have a laugh, don't we?' Barry shifted uncomfortably from foot to foot and looked around anxiously, hoping that none of the neighbours were listening.

Mandy, keen to protect her son from this emotional blackmail, stepped forward, her arm outstretched to touch her ex-husband's arm. 'Gary, don't,' she urged.

But Gaz was all fired up. 'Is he in?' he shouted. Mandy looked away, her face pained. 'Nathe!' Gaz yelled, his bottom lip trembling. He looked up at the window again, but there was no response, not even a flickering of the muslin curtains. Looking back down at the couple in the doorway and stepping towards them, he blinked back the tears and said breathlessly: 'Well, he can't hear through your triple bloody glazing.'

Mandy, her eyes glassy, spoke softly. 'He can hear all right,' she told him.

Gaz, still blinking hard, his feet twitching, waved the papers at her again, his head shaking angrily. 'This is ... this is all wrong, this is,' he said, his voice breaking. 'It's all to fucking cock.' Seeing the self-satisfied look on Barry's face, he hissed at the man now sleeping with his wife: 'I'm his dad

48

and you … you're nobody.' Mandy looked as if she might burst into tears.

Barry decided enough was enough. Putting his hands on his girlfriend's shoulders, he pulled her in from the doorway. Leaning forwards slightly towards Gaz, he smiled and said: 'Goodnight, Gary,' before slamming the white-painted mock Georgian door in his face.

Standing desolate in the twilight, his face lit by an ornate carriage lamp by the front door, Gaz stared again at the legal documents in his hand and fought to control the emotions raging within him. The worst part of breaking up with Mandy had been losing his daily contact with Nathan; missing the boy's grumpy face first thing in the morning; hearing all about school when he came in at teatime; being a major part of his life. Now it seemed that even the two days a week he was allowed to see him might be snatched from him, and the very thought left him fighting for breath.

Walking back along the neat garden path, he turned and looked up at his son's bedroom window once more, willing him to come to it and give him a wave, to reassure him that everything would be all right. 'Night, Nathe,' he called, his left hip swung out to one side as he stared and stared at the window. Running his hand roughly through his hair, he sniffed and added dolefully: 'See you, kid.'

CHAPTER THREE

High on the moors and ancient slag heaps overlooking Sheffield's vast Don Valley, Gaz and Dave, dressed in sweatshirts, tracksuit pants and running shoes, were silhouetted against the cloudy sky as they jogged along a deserted single-track road. Dave, fighting for breath as he climbed the steep hill, was beetroot-faced and wheezing badly. Gaz, hardly out of breath at all in his red, black and white-striped Sheffield United T-shirt, was five paces ahead of him.

'No,' Dave gasped between great lungfuls of air as he made an ineffectual attempt to keep up. 'Not doin' it.' He shook his head as vehemently as he could manage in the dire circumstances. His heart felt like it was about to burst through his chest and he was in real trouble. 'I'm not stripping.'

Gaz's face was pained. 'Dave,' he whined. 'They're taking him away. All I need is seven hundred quid and they've got nowt on me.' He had been on at Dave all week, but was getting nowhere fast with this line of persuasion. He didn't know how else to seduce his partner in crime into joining him on his latest and most daring escapade.

'Gaz, no.' Dave could now only manage words of one syllable and felt as if he might pass out. A strange rattling noise was coming from somewhere under his rib cage.

'Dave, he's me kid,' Gaz pleaded, half-turning to his puffing running companion. He hoped that by appealing to the generous heart he knew Dave had when it came to children, his friend would be moved.

'No,' Dave said for the fortieth time that morning as they reached the final ascent.

Sulking now, Gaz jogged silently alongside Dave for a

while, his head bowed. After a pause, he said, half under his breath: 'Suppose there's nicking cars.' It was his trump card and, as he saw the look of horror on Dave's sweat-stained face, he knew his suggestion had hit the mark.

'No!' Dave said, as firmly as he could muster. The last time Gaz went nicking cars, he had got caught red-handed and ended up inside. Dave only escaped sharing a cell with him in Wakefield Prison because Gaz persuaded the Old Bill that he hadn't known the car was stolen and was an innocent passenger. Jean had gone ballistic.

'Well, then?' Gaz whimpered, making the clear inference that he had no other options open to him and that if his oldest and dearest mate didn't back him up on this one, then he would be forced back into a life of petty crime. He looked back at Dave with begging bowl eyes.

Dave slowed his pace slightly with the increased gradient but continued panting furiously, great clouds of steam coming off him like a locomotive. 'Look, I'll help, all right?' he said, his voice no more than a rasp. 'I'm running, aren't I?' He opened his arms expressively and waited for some sign of acknowledgement from Gaz, who had turned his head away impatiently. 'But I'm taking nowt off ... Final!' His hand made a quick slicing movement through the air to emphasise his point.

Gaz remained in silent thought as they made their way slowly up the hill and past the gas works, the city spread out before them like a huge grey quilt. He had to think of something, anything to get hold of the money Mandy wanted. This was serious.

Failing fast, Dave dropped back more and more, his heart and lungs bursting, his vision blurred. Gaz sped ahead of his friend, running effortlessly. 'Come on Dave, don't stop now,' he urged over his shoulder, an insistent tone in his voice, but Dave was slowing rapidly. When encouragement didn't work, Gaz resorted to hurling abuse. 'Keep up, you fat bastard,' he yelled from further up the hill, speeding up on the steepest gradient to demonstrate how easy it was.

Dave, almost ground to a halt, called after his mate: 'Gazza, you tosser,' but he was long gone and couldn't hear him. Hands on his knees, Dave gasped for air, every muscle in his body twitching involuntarily as they struggled against the blood and oxygen pumping through their veins. Looking up at last but with his eyes still pressed shut against the pain in his head, he heard a familiar whirring noise in his ears, and opened his eyes to identify the cause.

Parked just a bit further up the hill from where he had stopped in a state of semi-collapse was a shabby maroon-coloured Austin Princess, its bonnet up, its starter motor whirring ineffectually as the driver attempted to get it going. Dave half-recognised the vehicle. This was just the excuse he needed to take a breather. He sauntered towards the car with the intention of offering his services and giving himself a much needed break into the bargain.

'D'you need a hand?' he called to the driver, hidden from his view by the open bonnet lid. Without waiting for an answer, he wandered over to the engine and peered down at the ageing machinery, looking for the problem. Leaning heavily on the front of the car, tilting it down with his weight, he reached in and fiddled about with something hot.

Forced to sell his own Morris Marina two years ago, Dave's front garden was still littered with the rusting remnants of a dozen of Longbridge's finest models, all ready to be done up the day he got some money again. Initially he had collected the bits and pieces as a way of making a bit of extra cash; acting as an unofficial breaker's yard to friends and neighbours who might need the odd spare part. Jean had never approved; she was always on at him to get rid of the mess, but he never did and nowadays he didn't even bother fiddling around inside them, like he used to. The irony was that Jean would be delighted now if he did show some interest in the old bangers – anything to get him out of his favourite armchair.

Well at home under the bonnet of this British Leyland classic, Dave delved expertly into the engine, coughing up a lungful all the while, and deftly extracted a spark plug lead. Giving it a quick blow with his mouth and polishing it on his T-shirt, he called out: 'Yeah, it's your HT leads, I reckon,' once he had re-emerged. Disappearing behind the bonnet once more, he replaced the plug and shouted: 'Give it a go at that,' from deep under the bonnet.

The driver turned the key in the ignition and the engine sparked into life, sending a filthy cloud of exhaust fumes along the plastic hose that he had carefully attached with tape to the tail pipe and in through the passenger window to where he was sitting, quietly attempting to kill himself.

Well pleased with his success, Dave chuckled, dropped the bonnet shut and wiped his oily hands on his now grease-stained T-shirt. Leaning towards the driver's window, Dave was completely oblivious to the smell of fumes and the hose pipe on the other side of the car. He looked at the driver for the first time, recognising him as Lomper, the steelworks security guard and cornet player in the works band. That was where he had seen the car – the previous day at the rolling mill.

Lomper's distinctive hair was like a shaggy red mop on top of his head, his freckled complexion pale. The young man said nothing in reply but rolled down the window slightly, a strange expression on his face. He wanted nothing more than to be left alone to complete his morning's task.

Watched by the perplexed driver but completely unde-terred, Dave rested his huge bulk against the roof pillar and peered into the car. 'Didn't you used to work up at Harrison's afore it shut down?' he asked, wiping his palms on his sweatpants. There were so many men working there at the peak, but Lomper had stuck in his memory because of his hair – and the fact that he had seen him the previous day, playing in the brass band.

Lomper, mortified by the exchange at such a crucially personal moment, glanced up briefly but then stared straight ahead of him and nodded dumbly as the cabin of the car gradually began to fill with fumes. His hand was in position on the window winder, ready to seal himself in. He wished to God the bloke would just piss off.

'Yeah, I thought I clocked you,' Dave added, chattily, staring into the distance dreamily. 'I were on't floor with Gaz.' Getting no response whatsoever, he pointed to his running partner, who was now waiting for him leaning against a burned-out Mini at the top of the hill. 'Him up road,' he added helpfully.

Lomper lowered his head and studied the plastic insignia on the steering wheel intently, willing his Good Samaritan to disappear and go and help some other poor sod. It was embarrassing enough being unable to restart the engine once he'd launched himself on his fatal plan, then to have been discovered in such a pitiful position. But now this. It really was too much to bear.

Never one to give up in the face of a hostile response, Dave carried on chatting, smiling cheerily. 'How's it goin' then?' he asked as Lomper's cheek twitched incredulously at the question. 'You got any work?' Dave asked. He knew the security guard job could only be part-time and unlikely to last beyond the massive refurbishment planned for the industrial estate later that year.

Unable to speak for the choking sensation in his throat and the shame in his heart, Lomper looked blankly at the floor, the whites of his eyes reddened by the acrid smoke, his lips becoming drier and drier by the second.

Getting the impression that somehow Lomper wasn't in the mood for a chat, Dave nodded sagely. 'No, there's not a lot about is there?' he mused. Still eliciting no response, he tried one last time and, referring to the faulty HT leads, he added: 'Yeah, well, like I say, get some new 'uns when you get the chance. All right?'

Lomper glanced up at him with a glazed look on his face, nodding slightly, his lips blue, the air around him filling with smoke.

Dave shrugged his big shoulders and looked up the hill with a frown. 'No, no, my chuffin' pleasure,' he said to himself, shaking his head in disbelief, before pushing off from the car to follow Gaz up the hill.

Lomper, frowning heavily, watched the smoke belching from the hosepipe and quickly rolled up the window to speed his despatch. Leaning back on the headrest, he stared ahead of him and inhaled deeply, trying to think positive thoughts about the better place he was going to.

Gaz was still resting on the burned-out Mini, smoking a cigarette and looking down over the valley, watching the M1 motorway cutting a swath through the city at the bottom of the hill. All those busy people in their gleaming cars rushing to and fro, people with jobs, couples with kids and cash to spare. There had been a time in his life when he could have had all that. But that was lost to him now. He was deadly serious about this Chippendales lark, though; it was the best way he knew right now of getting hold of seven hundred quid and he was prepared to do anything to keep seeing Nathan.

Despite what Mandy, Dave and others might think of him – and he knew he had hardly led the life of a saint – his son meant everything to him. The prospect of seeing him at weekends was what had kept him going through all those terrible dark days after Mandy left, when there had been times when he had even considered ending his life, but he had always been dragged back from the brink by the thought of Nathan. He wasn't going to give him up now, he couldn't, and he'd just have to find a way, some way, of getting the money and keeping Mandy and Barry sweet.

Turning to see an unusually thoughtful Dave jogging slowly up the hill towards him, panting heavily, he reached into his pocket for a packet of cigarettes, pulled one out and lit it from his own, ready for his mate. He'd have to go easier on him, he decided, appeal to his sense of fairness. He'd soon win him round.

Dave had almost reached Gaz, but the lines on his forehead were heavily furrowed as he tried to figure out what was bothering him. He couldn't put his finger on it, but there was definitely something wrong. Gaz held out the lit cigarette for him like a baton, a prize for getting to the top of the hill. Just as Dave reached him, his head jerked up, his mouth opened into a silent scream and he did a little dance with his feet before turning in his tracks and sprinting back down the road as if possessed.

'Dave?' Gaz called, holding the cigarette out to him and wondering what on earth was going on. He hadn't seen Dave move as fast as that since the police had pulled them over on suspicion of taking and driving away.

Gathering momentum as he raced back down the hill, Dave reached the Austin with a thump and grabbed the door handle, yanking it open as fast as he could. A great cloud of fumes billowed from inside the car. Grasping Lomper by the collar of his quilted anorak, he dragged him from his seat and hurled him onto his back on the ground, where the dazed young man lay choking and coughing his lungs up.

In equal pain, Dave stood bent double beside him, clutching his stomach and head, bellowing in pain from his record-breaking sprint, starved of oxygen. Finally able to speak, he leaned against the car and croaked: 'Are you all right, kid?'

Lomper, who had fallen into blissful unconsciousness just moments earlier only to be rudely awoken by the same fat git who had earlier taken it upon himself to fix his car and remove the final obstacle to his oblivion, looked up in utter dismay. 'You bastard!' he cried, distraught. It had taken weeks to build up his courage enough to finally go through with it, to end his miserable, misunderstood life and now here he was, still alive, thanks to the very man who had inadvertently helped him along in the first place.

Indignant at the ingratitude, Dave's mouth fell open, unable to believe his ears. Reaching forward without a word, he picked up Lomper forcibly by the lapels, hurled him back into the fume-filled car and slammed the door shut behind him. Leaning heavily against it and pointedly ignoring Lomper's frantic knocking on the window, Dave drank in the air wheezily and wondered at the thanklessness of modern youth.

An hour later, Dave, Gaz and Lomper sat silently side by side in the long grass at the top of the hill, gazing up at the sky. Dave was flat on his back, staring at the clouds and deep in thought; Gaz was semi-prone and puffing furiously on a cigarette; Lomper, the newcomer to the gang, sat uncomfortably in the middle, his hands locked self-consciously around his knees, rocking backwards and forwards.

'You could shoot yourself,' Dave offered, trying to be helpful. They had spent the previous half hour discussing Lomper's determination to end his life and his lack of nerve when it came to the method. The young man had given no explanation as to why he wanted to do it, he had simply presented them with a *fait accompli* and asked their advice on how best to go about it.

Gaz tutted aloud at the impracticality of the suggestion. 'Where's he gonna find a gun from round 'ere?' he asked. Even Gaz didn't know any criminals bad enough to use shooters.

Lomper, looking from side to side at each of the men, nodded in silent agreement. He was never very good at operating machinery anyway.

Gaz was considering other possibilities. 'You want to find yourself a big bridge, you do,' he said, looking across at Lomper thoughtfully.

Dave concurred with a smile: 'Yeah, like one of them bungee jumps.' As the other two eyed him quizzically, he added hastily: 'Only without the bungee bit.'

Lomper rocked back on his bottom and blinked hard. 'I can't stand heights, me,' he said through tight lips, his red hair ablaze in the sunlight.

Dave puffed on his cigarette and exhaled the smoke into the cool evening air. 'Drowning. Now there's a way to go,' he said to no one in particular.

There was silence as they all considered the suggestion. Lomper's eyes darted from side to side before he finally decided it wasn't the best way for him. 'I can't swim,' he said flatly, staring into the middle distance.

Gaz made a loud snorting noise through his nose and tore a blade of grass in two. 'You don't have to fuckin' swim, you divvy,' he said, his words clipped. 'That's the whole point.' As the lad raised his eyebrows apologetically and looked contrite, Gaz added: 'God, you're not very keen, are you?' shaking his head in exasperation.

Lomper eyed Gaz warily, still unsure what to make of the man he knew had a bit of a Jack the Lad reputation around town. 'Sorry,' he said softly, his sixteenth apology that hour. He hung his head in shame.

'I know,' Dave interjected, his expression suddenly animated. 'You could stand in the middle of road and get a mate to drive smack into you right fast.' He smiled at the thought of all the people he would like to do that to. Both he and Gaz glanced at the potential suicide, awaiting his response.

Almost ashamed to admit it, Lomper stuck out his bottom lip and whimpered: 'I haven't got any mates.' These two weren't to know, but that was the whole crux of the problem, really. Truth was, he'd never really had any friends, not even at school. He'd been the outsider, the loner, the Mummy's boy with poor personal hygiene that nobody wanted to pick for their team at sports because he was so useless. Conjuring up such miserable childhood memories, Lomper looked as if he might burst into tears.

Gaz, ever uncomfortable in the face of other people's emotions, bristled. 'Listen you,' he told the redhead crossly. 'We just saved your fuckin' life, so don't tell us we're not your mates, all right?' He thumped the arm of the young man least likely to have counted himself among Gaz's circle of friends before now.

Lomper's pale grey eyes misted over, this time with happiness. 'Yeah?' he asked brightly, his head turned hopefully towards Gaz, the beginnings of a smile tugging the corner of his mouth.

'Yeah, me an' all,' Dave piped up supportively, as Lomper swung his head happily to face his other new friend. In an effort to show how much of a mate he was, Dave added: 'I'd run you down soon as look at you.'

Lomper grinned from ear to ear and nodded enthusiastically. 'Oh, cheers,' he said, happier than he had been in months. 'Ta.' Turning to Gaz, now chuckling to himself at the thought, he added: 'Thanks a lot.'

After the rest of the day spent happily with his new friends, Lomper returned to his Victorian redbrick terraced house feeling like a new man. Turning his key in the lock, a shy smile still on his face at the prospect of seeing his mates later on, he opened the door to see his mother's empty wheelchair at the foot of the stairs, and her frail, half-paralysed body clinging precariously to the banisters halfway up. His buoyancy was instantly deflated.

Tossing his keys onto the hall table, he raced up the stairs, two at a time, to her side. 'What are you doing, Mum?' he asked gently, enfolding her in his arms. She knew she wasn't meant to attempt the stairs without him. She had her commode in her ground floor bedroom and he'd left everything else she could possibly need downstairs for her, knowing that the kind woman from Meals on Wheels would arrive in the morning and find his suicide note on his bedside table.

'Where have you been?' she asked weakly, her face ashen from the effort of the last twenty minutes of trying to haul herself painfully up to her son's bedroom to see if there was any clue to his sudden disappearance. Her pale grey eyes were fearful. She'd been so worried about him recently and she knew that he was finding her failing health a terrible strain.

Lomper couldn't meet her steady gaze. 'Driving,' he answered softly, lifting her tiny frame effortlessly into his arms. Now she was almost upstairs, he might as well carry her up to the bathroom and give her her evening wash.

'Driving where?' she pressed, as he cradled her in his arms on the climb up the steep stairs. She buried her nose in the white flesh of his neck.

'Just driving,' Lomper replied, looking straight ahead of him and resolving to tear his suicide note into a hundred pieces just as soon as he'd got her into the bath.

The old woman half-smiled and stroked her only son's cheek fondly. He was a good lad, if a little too quiet sometimes. 'I thought you'd gone,' she said, her voice catching, and she leaned her head against his neck again with a sigh. Lomper said nothing as he steeled himself for the nightly bathing and undressing tasks that had been his duty since his widowed mother's stroke five years earlier.

It was Dave, Nathan and Gaz's second visit to the steel rolling mill that week, only this time – unusually – they had been invited. Sitting high up in the glass-fronted security office where Lomper worked, overlooking the deserted building, they blinked at the row of closed circuit television monitors on Lomper's desk, each showing a deserted and slightly spooky factory shrouded in darkness

Dave snooped in all the cupboards, flicking switches, while Nathan sat glued to the unexciting images on the television screens and Gaz sat in a battered leather swivel chair, his feet resting on a desk, an ever-present cigarette in his hand. Lomper had gone on an errand for them and wouldn't be back for a while, so they talked freely about him. Waving his hand indifferently at the bank of screens and shaking his head, Gaz commented: 'Security guard in 'ere, no wonder he wants to kill himself!'

Dave nodded and paced the room thoughtfully. 'Well, at least one bloke got a job out of this place being shut down.'

Referring to Gaz's decision to ask Lomper to come in on his stripping caper, Dave added: 'What d'you tell him for any road? … Kid's a nutter.' Even in Dave's worst moments, he'd never contemplated suicide – it just wasn't in his character – and, as far as he was concerned, anyone who did was headed for a straitjacket and a padded cell. Furthermore, the more people Gaz got involved in this crazy scheme, the closer it came to becoming possible. And Dave wasn't taking his kit off for nobody.

'He's a bugle player,' Gaz answered matter-of-factly, as if that explained everything. Seeing the look of incomprehension on Dave's face, he added: 'Could come in right handy. Might need a bit of music.' Dave picked up a Rubik's cube and started twisting it round and round in his hands, undoing weeks of painstaking work by Lomper, as Gaz carried on. 'He's got a car; somewhere to practise. Besides, it's good what's-its-name for the lad. Therapy.'

Dave stared down at the infuriating multicoloured puzzle and tried to force the movable cubes into position. 'Oh, aye,' he scoffed. 'Jiggling about in the buff. Therapy.' Turning to Gaz with a meaningful bob of his head, he added: 'I tell you, he won't be the only one trying to kill himself if you carry on with this caper.'

Nathan, bored rigid with the whole subject, and wishing he was home watching some football on the telly, swivelled round in his chair and looked pleadingly at his father. 'Dad, I'm hungry,' he whined, his chin sinking to his chest and staying there.

Gaz, twiddling his cigarette end in his hand, spotted some movement on one of the television screens behind Nathan and watched as Lomper's car pulled up at the factory's electronically operated gates. Hearing a car horn honk twice, he commented: 'Eh up.' Dinner had arrived.

For the second time in as many days, Dave Horsfall delved around under the bonnet of Lomper's car. Only this time, he was helping himself from the assorted tinfoil cartons that Lomper had placed on the hot engine to keep them warm on the ten-minute drive from the Chinese takeaway. Pulling out a full tub of pork spare ribs that was almost too hot to

61

handle, Dave set them down on the edge of the engine in preparation to devour his meal with his fingers, returning to the car to see if there was anything he'd forgotten.

Up in the operations room above them, Lomper jabbed a crispy pork ball with a fork and watched the television screens like an automaton, glancing down occasionally at his new friends in the loading bay below, happy for the company. Gaz emerged from the engine with his single carton of chicken chow mein and Nathan retrieved a box of plain fried noodles. Dave poked his head up with a frown from the bonnet and yelled up to the redhead, 'Hey Lomper, where's me rice?'

'Try the cylinder head, tubby,' Lomper called into the microphone, his voice booming out over the ancient Tannoy system, as crackle and feedback echoed around the deserted factory. Dave cursed him under his breath and returned to his search.

Nathan had been miserable all evening and his mood wasn't improving. Turning to his father, his untouched carton of food outstretched in his hand, he said accusingly: 'I don't like Chinese.'

Gaz laughed. 'Course you do,' he sneered, but then seeing the serious expression on his son's face, he frowned. 'Don't ya?' he asked, amazed. He thought everyone liked Chinese. Nathan raised his eyes to the ceiling and shook his head, wondering how many times he'd told his father he hated foreign food and would much prefer a burger.

Wounded by Lomper's insult, Dave lost his appetite temporarily and, abandoning his food, began rummaging around on the back seat of Lomper's car. 'Let's see his records,' he called to Gaz, emerging with a pile of tattered old LPs. The two of them had asked him to bring a selection of music along with him that night, so that they could practise dancing.

'What we got then, Dave?' Gaz asked, licking his fingers of noodles and gravy so that he could light a between-bite cigarette.

Dave flicked disparagingly through the pile in his

hand. '"The Floral Dance",' he recited. '"Marching With Hepworth"?' His expression was pained. Brass band music wasn't exactly what they had in mind for a striptease routine. If this was Lomper's idea of sexy music then no wonder he tried to top himself.

'Jesus Christ!' Gaz exclaimed, staring up at Lomper with disdain. But he stopped himself from saying anything more when he saw Dave's face brighten.

'Ah, *Hot Chocolate*. Now we're talking,' said the big man before breaking into a tuneless rendition of 'I Believe In Miracles', swivelling his broad hips around ridiculously in a vain attempt at sultry dancing.

Nathan, aghast, watched as his dad joined in, thrusting his hips backwards and forwards and lifting his hands alternately in the air while taking up the lyrics of the chorus, before they both finished in unison. They looked like a pair of uncoordinated Thunderbird puppets. Nathan decided he would rather be doing his homework than watching this excruciatingly painful spectacle.

'Stick it on, Davereemo,' Gaz instructed. 'I'm there.' As Dave made his way up the steps to the operations room, pulling the record from its sleeve ready to place it on the turntable Lomper had rigged up, Gaz abandoned his noodles and skipped over to the car. Leaning in through the open driver's window, he turned the headlights on to full beam. Lomper reached up to a control switch and killed the lights in the factory, before descending the stairs to take his place on a bench next to Nathan in the full glare of the headlights, ready for the show.

Slicking his hair back with a greasy hand and pulling the collar of his black leather jacket up around his ears, Gaz positioned himself in front of the car with his back to them, silhouetted in the head lamps and striking a dramatic pose. Legs wide apart, head tilted down and sideways, his arms frozen in the air above his head, fingers outstretched, he looked for all the world like a character from the 70s film *Saturday Night Fever*.

Nathan, sitting uncomfortably next to Lomper, his mouth open, wanted the earth to swallow him up. 'Dad,' he pleaded. 'Dad, don't.' He'd rather go back to nicking stuff than have his father make such a complete fool of himself.

Gaz misinterpreted his son's tone. 'No, it's all right, Nathan,' he called, reassuringly. 'This is right, this is. Seen 'em do it.' His head half-hidden in the turned-up collar of his jacket, an expression on his face designed to tell his reluctant audience that here was a man bursting with sexual energy, Gaz was ready.

When Dave tapped the microphone a screech of feedback nearly deafened them all. Nathan clasped his ears and Gaz winced. In a high-pitched voice, Dave announced: 'Good evening shoppers, tonight's special offer ...'

'Dave!' Gaz remonstrated. The moment was ruined, his concentration lost. Lowering his arms, he stood up, hands on his hips and scowled at the fat controller.

'All right, all right,' Dave conceded, and placed the stylus carefully on the record. 'You Sexy Thing', he announced, as Gaz got back into character. 'One, two, one, two, three, four ...'

The opening chords of the 70s *Hot Chocolate* hit crackled through the speakers as Gaz, posing provocatively, began jerking his left knee slowly to the beat. Lomper, his supper forgotten in his lap, sat next to Nathan, transfixed.

Playing to the gallery, Gaz leered openly and, cigarette wedged firmly between his lips, thrust his hands deep into his jacket pockets, using the angle of his elbows to slide the garment suggestively down over his shoulders, which were shunting backwards and forwards in perfect time to the music. Pulling his jacket off one arm in a single slick movement, he lifted it into the air with the other arm, his wrist still inside the sleeve and whirled it round and round high above his head.

Assorted coins, keys, cigarettes and a lighter scattered at high velocity from the pockets, hitting Nathan and Lomper full in the face. They cowered under the bombardment,

Lomper shielding his supper from the shower, Nathan squinting into the headlights to try and see where the next missile was coming from. Struggling to free his wrist from the jacket sleeve, Gaz beat it again and again on the floor as if he was killing some sort of rabid animal and, having extricated himself finally, he left it there in a heap, carrying on with his routine as if nothing had happened.

Unbuttoning his shirt with rhythmic movements in time to the music, he smirked sexily at Nathan, who squirmed and eventually covered his face with his hands. Dave, his bottom jaw resting where it had fallen, shook his head in astonishment in the control room. Gaz gyrated and strutted on regardless, swaying his hips sexily from side to side while peeling off his checked shirt. Spinning it in a giant circle behind him and tossing it flamboyantly into the air, he swivelled a perfect pirouette, cigarette still between his lips, only for the shirt to fall back on the floor in front of him, temporarily veiling his face as it fell.

Unfazed and kicking it quickly to one side, he winked at Lomper, who had a four-inch long fried noodle dribbling from his lips. Strutting slowly back and forth in front of them, his toes pointed, his pelvis thrusting from side to side, Gaz crossed his muscular arms in front of him, pulling his T-shirt up over his head, his hips gyrating in a wide circle above his feet, which were simultaneously doing some sort of Fred Astaire fancy two-step.

Dave couldn't help but look wistfully at the well-defined biceps in Gaz's arms and the ladder rack of taut muscles that ribbed his slim stomach as the T-shirt exposed his body. Glancing down at his own bulging beer gut, now spattered with grease spots from various dropped particles of Chinese food, Dave tried breathing in but quickly gave up.

Centre-stage and still struggling to lift the T-shirt over his head, his arms locked across him, Gaz completely lost his rhythm and managed to get himself into dreadful contortions. His face hidden from view, he mumbled inaudibly and coughed chestily as his lit cigarette caught on the material and singed his hair. As he wrestled on with his T-shirt, Dave couldn't stand another second of it and stopped the music suddenly with a loud scratch, dragging the needle forcibly across the record. At that precise moment, Nathan jumped up and fled.

Gaz, coming up for air and spitting out the smouldering cigarette end, shrugged his shoulders as he dusted burning ash from his clothes. 'Need an audience,' he told Dave and Lomper sheepishly, strands of tobacco stuck to his bottom lip.

'You need a doctor,' Dave's voice boomed over the Tannoy, and all three of them sighed, individually grateful that it was over.

By the time they realised that Nathan was no longer with them, it was quite late. Piling into Lomper's car, they drove slowly up and down the adjacent streets and those heading into the city, looking anxiously for the boy.

Gaz, his face pinched with worry, sat in the front passenger seat, peering frantically left and right. Mandy would have him for breakfast if she ever found out that her son was out on his own in a less than salubrious area of Sheffield at eleven o'clock on a Saturday night. 'I tell ya, there's something up with that kid,' he told the other two, as they scoured the deserted city streets. 'Are you sure you checked the whole top end?' he asked Dave, sitting on the back seat, but so far forward that his head was between them both.

'Yeah,' Dave nodded, wondering where the boy could be.

'There's no point,' said Lomper, turning up the heater so that the windscreen wouldn't steam up. 'He went out.'

Gaz's head spun to face him. 'What?' he asked angrily. Lomper hadn't said anything before.

Lomper looked apologetic. 'I seen him go,' he added, wiping away the mist with his hand. He had identified immediately with Nathan, a young boy, an only child, misunderstood and confused. When he'd run off like that,

Lomper had thought he would come straight back, and decided to cover for him to give the kid some time to himself for a while. Now, seeing Gaz's fury, he realised he should have spoken sooner.

Suddenly there was a shout from the back. Dave's broad arm shot forward between them and pointed straight ahead. 'There's the beggar!' he yelled, triumphant at the sight of Nathan, walking briskly along the pavement, illuminated by the lights from a twenty-four-hour petrol station.

Gaz had the passenger door open before the car even drew to a halt. 'Oi, Nathe!' he called, but the boy ignored him and hurried ahead, his arms pumping at his side. 'Nathan!' Gaz tried again. 'Nathan.' The boy increased his pace as his father leapt from the car and caught up with him outside the garage forecourt. Placing a hand on his shoulder, he spun him round to face him. 'Hellfire. What are you doing out here, kid?' Gaz asked, his tone conciliatory, relief in his eyes.

Nathan didn't even look up. Head down, he turned to walk away, striding ahead of his father as he replied: 'Nowt. Walking home.' His cheeks were flushed red and he was obviously upset.

Gaz grabbed his arm and stopped him again. 'It's miles home. You know that.' Nathan, his hands dejectedly in his pockets, tilted his head at Gaz but said nothing.

Standing facing his son in the neon light, Gaz tried another tack. 'Why did you run off like that?' he asked, gently. There was no reply. Nathan hung his head once more. Standing back a pace, he challenged the boy. 'You're embarrassed, aren't you?' Gesturing to himself, he added: 'You think your own dad's a dickhead.'

Nathan couldn't think of an answer, so he said nothing and just stared his father out. Gaz had hit the nail on the head. Nathan thought exactly that and he didn't want any part of it.

Gaz looked away and tried to find the right words to say all that he wanted to say. His leg twitching, he said to the boy: 'We're not doing this for a laugh, you know. I'm trying to get some brass together so as you and me can keep seeing each other.' He used his hands expressively, pointing to himself and then to Nathan.

Deeply uncomfortable, Nathan wrested himself free from his father's stare and stalked off. He kept walking as his father followed and tried to explain as best he could. 'They're, they're trying to stop us, you see,' he said, hoping that Nathan would understand what he meant. He didn't want to have to go into all the whys and wherefores, because he knew he'd quickly come unstuck. Trying to explain to a twelve-year-old all the reasons why Mandy and Barry deemed him an unsuitable parental influence would only end in tears.

But the boy simply carried on up the road. Gaz stopped and set his jaw. 'Oh well, I may as well not bother,' he shouted after Nathan. '... 'cept I'm your dad.'

Nathan's step faltered and finally he stopped walking and turned to look at his father uneasily, wondering what to say.

Gaz moved hesitantly towards him. 'That counts for summat, don't it?' he said quietly, hopefully. Getting no response, he stood awkwardly in front of his son and looked around. 'I like you,' he said, falteringly. Leaning in towards Nathan, he added: 'I love you, you bugger.' Nathan half-smiled as his father asked: 'All right, kid?'

He punched Nathan's arm again in a friendly gesture. The boy, blinking hard to keep back his tears, punched his dad's shoulder back harder; Gaz cuffed him on the shoulder, Nathan returned the gesture, really letting him have it. They looked at each other and smiled. Gaz pulled his son towards him suddenly and gathered him into his arms in a hug. Kissing the top of his head, he looked down into his eyes with a smile. 'All right?' he asked softly.

Nathan grinned back and nodded. 'Yeah,' he said, as the two of them turned and sauntered back to the waiting car, arm in arm. Ruffling his hair, Gaz added, for good measure: 'Nutter!' The boy smiled up at his father warmly.

CHAPTER FOUR

Teetering dangerously on tiny wooden infants' chairs in a darkened first floor primary school classroom, Dave, Lomper, Gaz and Nathan peered through the high window plastered with brightly coloured plastic sunflowers, and down into the next room, a school hall where a dozen cardigan-wearing middle-aged couples were performing pompous, if technically perfect, tangos. This was *Come Dancing*, Yorkshire-style.

Nathan sighed at the sight and said defensively: 'Well, you said dancin'.' As soon as he'd seen the sign on the school notice board for Dance Lessons, he'd thought of his dad. After the previous night's disagreement, he wanted to do all he could to help, to show willing. He was sorry he'd ever doubted his father's intentions.

Gaz reached across and ruffled his son's hair affectionately. 'Oh, it were a great idea, kid. Just not the right sort of dancing.' The two of them studied each other companionably, contemplating where they might find the right sort of dance class, as the others remained glued to the window.

'Gaz, Gaz,' Dave suddenly hissed. 'Hey, look here.' He beckoned his friend to look back through the window and take a peep at what he had spotted. Quickstepping towards them, his chin tilted upwards, his elbows held out at right angles, was Gerald Cooper, their old foreman, deftly manoeuvring an over-manicured, uptight woman around the dance floor, his hand placed firmly in the small of her back.

Gaz's face broke into a wide grin. 'Oh, my God,' he said,

as they watched Gerald sashay expertly across the floor, twisting his partner this way and that, stomach held in, spine ramrod straight, toes pointed. 'Gerald my lad, you're gonna be famous down the Job Club.' The others giggled in anticipation of the merciless teasing Gaz would give him.

Dave stopped smiling as Gerald, in a sea-green cashmere sweater, casual slacks, shirt and tie, shimmied towards them and performed a particularly complicated double shuffle right under their noses. 'Hey, he's not bad for a bastard, though, is he?' he said admiringly, thinking of his own sorry ineptitude when it came to dancing. A drunken blancmange, his brother-in-law had once called him at a family Christmas party, and Dave had never got up to dance again.

But Gaz was still thinking of the mileage he could make from seeing Gerald here. 'He's dead. That's what he is,' he beamed, delighted to have new ammunition against the man who'd grazed his knuckles with his chin.

As they continued to ogle him through the window, Gerald, completely oblivious to their presence, swung his partner round and danced smoothly with her towards them. Glancing up at the window mid-step, Gerald was horrified to see the four faces squashed against the glass in assorted grimaces like gargoyles; Dave sticking two fingers up at him, Lomper grinning, Nathan's mouth like a Halloween pumpkin. With a cross-eyed smile, Gaz's hand gave a slow but evil wave.

Almost causing an unscheduled interruption in his fluid progress across the floor, the shock of seeing his associates from the Job Club at the window all but took Gerald's breath away. His expression was one of absolute horror. Glaring at them over his partner's shoulder-pads, he mouthed the words: 'Bugger off!' and – much too quickly for her liking – manoeuvred her across to the other side of the room. She frowned up at him, a crack appearing in the smile fixed to her face for the duration of the tango.

'Hey, you said you wanted a dance teacher,' Lomper remarked as they all admired Gerald's fancy footwork, which continued apace despite the look of extreme consternation on his face.

Dave's eyebrows shot up his forehead. 'Gerald?' he asked, sceptically. 'Go get chuffed,' he said. 'He'd tell every bugger. We'd be laughed out of Sheffield.' He could just imagine the reaction of the boys down the Job Club. Gaz's expression was more thoughtful.

The four of them watched as the dance teacher turned off the tape recorder and congratulated her pupils. As a short break began, Gerald leaned forward and whispered in his partner's ear, before marching past her across the floor towards their classroom. A man with a mission.

'Eh up, lads, bandits at six o'clock,' Gaz warned, as they all dropped to the floor of the classroom, sniggering. Taking their places on the tiny children's chairs, Gaz smoking, they watched the reinforced glass door as Gerald burst in, his eyes blazing, and switched on the light.

Sitting astride a child's chair and playing absent-mindedly with a large plastic doll-house, Gaz looked up with a grin. 'Ah, come in Torvill,' he smirked, referring to the female half of the Olympic ice-dance partnership. 'Park your sequins over here.' He patted the chair next to him.

But Gerald wasn't in the mood for sarcasm. His greying fringe flopped onto his forehead as the Brylcreem lost its hold. He rounded on them. 'All right, you've had your little laugh, now you can piss off!' Trying to regain some composure, he straightened his tie and tried to look as if he meant business. The last thing he wanted was this lot, here at his dance classes, in one of the few places where he felt safe from the miseries of the outside world. Whatever else had happened in his life, whatever other goals he now realised, at fifty-three, he was never going to achieve, he could still do a good turn on the parquet flooring with his wife Linda and their chums, and he didn't want that ruined by the lads from the Job Club.

'It's a free country,' Lomper began quietly, sitting to one side, but stopped himself when he saw the deadly look in

Gerald's eyes. Dave sat wedged into a chair in the corner, next to some children's plastic toys and absent-mindedly slipped a plastic throwing ring over his wrist. Nathan sat guiltily next to his father.

Only Gaz's eyes were sparkling. 'I thought you were rather good, actually,' he winked. 'Very nifty footwork,' he told the others glibly. Nathan, trying not to smile, nodded. It was true, the old man he'd only ever seen hunched over a computer terminal at the Job Club when he went there with his father, was surprisingly agile and stylish once he was on the dance floor. They were genuinely impressed.

Just as Gerald looked as if he was about to jump on Gaz and finish their earlier business, Gerald's heavily made-up dance partner appeared in the open doorway, calling his name. 'Oh, hello,' she said, surprised to find a room full of men. Dressed in a bright pink and white full-length diamond-pattern cardigan and black skirt, her tinted auburn hair piled up on top of her head, her gold jewellery jangling, Linda Cooper half-smiled. Turning to her husband, who had frozen to the spot, she said pointedly: 'Gerald, we're missing the rumba.'

His hands flapping, his body language one of obsequious-ness, Gerald tried to think of something to say. 'S-sorry, love,' he stammered, bending down towards her. This was the last thing he wanted, Linda meeting this lot. He had to get her out of here. With his mind racing and his heart pounding in his chest, he stuttered: 'I, I, I was just having a bit of a chat with some pals ...' he swallowed hard, '... from, from work.'

Gaz and Nathan shot each other a look of puzzlement, followed by one of sudden realisation. Gerald looked pleadingly across at them not to give the game away. Dave hadn't even registered what had been said and was far too worried about the throwing ring now wedged firmly on his wrist.

Mrs Gerald Cooper smiled hesitantly and looked around at the motley crew in amazement. She had never met any of her husband's work mates before; he'd never brought anyone home for dinner, despite her repeated requests. She'd some-how expected – well, a slightly better mix of people. 'Oh,' she said, taken aback. Wanting to make a good impression, she asked politely: 'Not thinking of joining our class?'

Gaz bobbed his head and nodded in all seriousness. 'Well, funny you should mention it ...' he began, but Gerald laughed nervously, almost hysterically, and turned quickly to his wife to usher her out of the door.

'I think we, er, we better be getting back now, eh?' he said, pushing her unceremoniously through the doorway, a firm hand once again in the small of her back, guiding her out.

Linda Cooper looked almost disappointed. 'Oh well, goodnight,' she said, giving them her most appealing smile, her eighteen-carat gold earrings quivering. All but Dave nodded a farewell. He was still tugging furiously on the plastic ring still jammed on his wrist, which was beginning to swell.

Gerald, his shoulders hunched over, shook his head and made as if to follow his wife out. His skin had gone the colour of parchment and he no longer bore the dignified carriage of a man proud of his ability to dance.

'You get back to your rumba,' Gaz told Gerald with sarcasm as he and Linda reached the door. 'We'll see you later, Gerald,' he called out to the dejected figure standing motionless in the doorway, waiting for the words he knew would come. Pausing for effect and arching an eyebrow, Gaz added meaningfully: 'At work.'

Gerald turned slowly and stared at Gaz, his chest heaving up and down as a panic attack stifled his breathing. If only he hadn't said anything, if only he'd kept quiet, he thought. God only knew what someone like Gaz would try and do with information like that – the dire consequences of blackmail raged in his head. He might even be forced to tell Linda the dreadful truth. The colour draining further from his face at the very idea, he swivelled on his patent leather heel and quietly closed the door behind him.

* * *

73

At precisely eight-thirty the following morning, immediately after dropping Nathan off at school, Gaz and Dave were in position at the end of the driveway outside Gerald's bungalow. Appropriately named *Quicksteps*, it was identified by the ornate wrought iron name plaque – which Linda had had made for him one birthday – next to a wooden five-bar gate.

Overlooking the city on a well-appointed Sheffield estate, the middle-class bungalow with its double-fronted loft extension was like every other house in the street. Identical homes with identical conifer hedges, mock stone walls, fake Georgian carriage lamps at the door. Gaz felt decidedly out of place, braced against the cold at the gate, puffing on a cigarette, waiting.

Dave, sitting on the end of the gate, rubbing his wrist from the chafing the plastic ring had given it before Gaz had finally melted it off him with a cigarette lighter, studied the neat house and its trim garden critically. 'He's got gnomes,' he said, his nose wrinkled in disgust at the thirty or so gaily-painted plaster gnomes in fishing and gardening poses carefully positioned under stone toadstools. A tiny pond, plastic heron and miniature wishing-well adorned the middle of the freshly mowed lawn.

'Aye, he bloody would have,' Gaz commented, not in the least bit surprised, as he stood staring intently at the ornate frosted glass front door, willing it to open.

A few feet the other side of the door, Gerald was standing in front of a full-length mirror in the hallway, humming happily to himself as he adjusted his checked wool tie and smoothed his hair in the reflection. Linda, dressed in a salmon-coloured all-in-one lounge suit, packing her husband's sandwiches into a pink plastic lunch box in the adjacent kitchen, listened to him humming softly and smiled. 'Things looking up?' she asked, pleased to see her husband more light-hearted than he had been of late.

Gerald grinned at his reflection. 'Do you know, love, I think they just might be,' he responded cheerily, slipping his grey quilted anorak on over his suit.

'Good,' Linda said, pressing down the lid of his lunch box and holding it out to him. 'You've been working too hard.' Watching him while he packed his sandwiches away into his leather briefcase, she added: 'About time you let one of your colleagues do the lion's share for a change. I wish you'd be firmer, Gerald.'

She didn't like the long hours he worked, or the fact that he hadn't had a pay rise in three years. They hadn't been on holiday together since the previous summer and she was worried he was letting his obsessive fears about being made redundant affect his standing at work. If only he'd bring some of his more senior colleagues home, let her prepare a nice dinner party for them, then she could use her charm to good effect on his behalf. Or at least see what they made of him. She hated the idea of him being a laughing stock at work.

Uncomfortable with the line of conversation, Gerald nodded at his wife and half-smiled. He knew she thought he was too soft and was letting others walk all over him. Well that had been true, when he had had a job, but now it was too late and it didn't matter any more. Closing his briefcase, he said breezily: 'Oh well, mustn't be late,' and turned towards the front door, eager to escape her piercing gaze.

Holding up a skiing brochure she'd been clutching most of the morning and waving it at him, Linda gave her husband her most persuasive look. 'Er, so, it's all right, if I, um ...' she said, tapping a false pink fingernail on the brochure and tilting her head.

Gerald's face fell. He threw his head back in despair. 'Oh, Linda, love, you know, I don't ...' he began, his eyes pressed shut against the horror of what she was suggesting. He already had a £10,000 overdraft at the bank, all his redundancy money was gone, he was well behind on his mortgage and hire purchase payments and, try as he might, he couldn't get her to cut down on her costly weekly shopping trips to the Meadowhall Centre with her friends.

Linda frowned moodily at the expression on her

husband's face and interrupted him. 'Oh, don't be so mean,' she sulked, reaching out and patting his arm. 'Things are looking up, you said so yourself.' She had no intention of letting Gerald scupper her plans to knock them dead in the French Alps. She'd virtually booked the holiday already with that lovely young man in the travel agent and she'd put a deposit on a delightful ski-suit in cyclamen that she knew would turn a few heads on the slopes. Fluttering her eyelashes at her husband in a way which always won him over, she added, with conviction: 'You'll love skiing.' She made it clear there was no room for manoeuvre.

There was an uneasy pause as Gerald held his breath and looked down at his wife with glassy eyes. 'Linda,' he said, his forehead knitted into a frown, wondering where on earth he would start, how he could begin to tell her that he'd been made redundant six months ago, one of the last to go before Harrison's finally closed, but had never had the courage to let her in on the secret.

Linda cocked her head quizzically at her husband's strange expression and thought she saw tears welling up in his eyes. His mouth opened and closed, but no sound came out. Finally, giving her a little shrug of his shoulder, he said softly: 'Oh … don't matter,' losing heart yet again and making for the door. 'Bye.' He leaned forward and kissed her on the cheek before releasing the lock and stepping out into the crisp morning air. The door had not even clicked shut behind him before his wife was on the telephone confirming the holiday booking with the travel agent.

His head bowed as he set off down the garden path, Gerald didn't notice Gaz and Dave until he was almost at the gate. When he did lift his head it was to see Dave holding one of his gnomes in his hand, imitating its sweet-faced expression and picking its nose, before laughing lewdly at the hole in its bottom. Ignoring them, he walked on, but Gaz blocked his way. 'Off to the office, are we, Torvill?' the younger man asked, his tone one of pure sarcasm.

Gerald bristled. 'As a matter of fact, yes, I bloody am,' he said. Turning to Dave, still cradling the gnome, he yelled: 'Put that back!' When Dave hesitated and looked to Gaz for further instructions, Gerald repeated firmly: 'Put it back!'

Dave duly placed the small creature gently in its rightful position on the lawn and followed Gerald down the drive sheepishly. Rounding on Gaz, Gerald reached into his anorak pocket and pulled out a letter, waving it in his face. 'See that?' he asked, his blood up after the confrontation with Linda. 'Interview. In the bloody bag. Mate. I know him from Harrison's.' If he could only clinch the job, then Linda could have her bloody holiday and never be the wiser.

Putting the letter back in his pocket, he set off briskly down the street, Gaz and Dave in hot pursuit. 'I can do the job standing on my head,' Gerald added confidently, getting into his stride. Waving a hand at the pair of them he added, with feeling: 'And I won't have to look at your ugly mugs ever again.'

Gaz skipped along beside the tall middle-aged man, trying to keep up. 'Come on, Gerald, we just need a bit of help,' he begged, hands stuffed in his pockets. He had hoped that Gerald would have been more compliant after they had found out about his little secret. He was rather disappointed to find him so ebullient.

Gerald shook his head vehemently. 'Well, I'm sorry, pal, there's nothing I can do to help the likes of you. Nothing.' His manner was brusque and he increased his pace, his legs far outstretching the others'.

Dave decided to have a go. Maybe the earlier problems between Gerald and Gaz were clouding the issue. 'We just wanna know about dancin', that's all,' he asked dolefully. Surely it wasn't too much to ask.

Still marching forcefully down the hill, Gerald remarked acidly: 'Dancers have co-ordination, skill, timing and grace.' Turning his head sideways at Dave wobbling along beside him, puffing to catch his breath, he added pointedly: 'Take a long, hard look in the mirror.'

Stopped mid-stride by the rebuke, Dave and Gaz fell back

as Gerald stomped on. 'Now, I'm busy,' the ex-foreman shouted back at them. 'Don't be late for the Job Club, lads,' he added by way of a farewell and quickly disappeared around a corner, en route to his big interview and the chance to finally put his life back on track.

Gaz faked a head butt at Gerald to show his disgust. 'Bastard!' he said, a muscle in his jaw twitching. The wounded expression on Dave's face only fuelled his anger. Slapping the back of his hand on Dave's chest with a vengeful look in his eyes, Gaz turned and walked quickly back up the hill.

Gerald tried not to appear overconfident but he knew the interview was going very well. He'd answered all the key questions correctly and with the appropriate level of enthusiasm and the three-man board of directors facing him behind a long table looked suitably impressed.

The chief executive, his former acquaintance from Harrison's, had all but told him the job was his. It was very different now, the steel industry, he had explained. All automation and clinically-clean environments. Gone were the days of hard labour and high unionisation. The remaining factories in Sheffield were producing more steel than ever before but at a fraction of the cost. It would be Gerald's new job as deputy foreman to supervise machines, not men, and he would have to answer to their world-wide investors as much as to the local directors.

Gerald, sitting bolt upright on a chair in the middle of the room opposite the panel, his briefcase on the floor beside him, nodded in response and listened as he was taken through the terms of the new job.

'Starting at sixteen thousand, plus the pension scheme,' the director was reminding him, leaning forward over the large desk. He was well aware that it was a lot less money than Gerald had been on previously, and that he might have had to pay more to someone else, but these days beggars couldn't be choosers and he knew Gerald would be suitably grateful.

Gerald smiled. It was in the bag. 'It will be a relief to get back to work,' he told his new employers, clasping and unclasping his hands on his lap. 'It's not been an easy six months, granted. But I'm up to date with the latest industry developments.' The men nodded their approval.

Gerald carried on. 'And I've kept myself ...' His voice tailed off inexplicably as an expression of horror flashed across his face. The three men facing him studied him closely and wondered if he was all right. Beetroot-faced and blinking, he seemed to recover and picked up the sentence where he left off: '... um, busy, you know,' he added, trying very hard not to look at the garden gnome being waved jauntily at him through the window behind the panel of directors.

Looking down at Gerald's CV, the chief executive coughed to attract his attention. 'Well, all the qualifications are there obviously, Gerald.' But the best candidate they'd yet interviewed for the job wasn't listening, he was staring intently above the executive's head, his face ashen. The director carried on. 'And we go back further than I care to remember.' He paused for effect.

'Sorry?' Gerald said hoarsely, a lump in his throat, trying desperately to recover himself while the gnome – controlled by an invisible hand – paced backwards and forwards along the outer window ledge. He tried to smile and concentrate on the questions he was being asked.

Puzzled, the director turned in his seat to look back up at the window behind him just as the gnome disappeared from view. Shaking his head at his fellow panel members, he turned back to Gerald with a worried frown.

'What we're asking, Gerald ...' he began, as two gnomes suddenly appeared at the window behind his head, pursuing each other '... is after such a long lay-off ...' Gerald began trembling visibly as the gnomes engaged in a silent argument the other side of the glass before one head-butted the other, breaking his plaster head clean off ' ... do you think you're up to the job?' the director concluded.

Completely lost, his eyes darting from the panel to the window and back again, Gerald looked at his interviewers with a glazed expression, his mouth open and yet unable to speak. Each of the board members glanced meaningfully at each other before turning to their notes.

Back at the Job Club later that afternoon, still chuckling about their morning's activities, Gaz and Dave were making an attempt at holding mock interviews with each other while the Job Club manager supervised. All around the room, other pairs of men were doing the same.

Suddenly, the glass panelled door crashed open with an almighty bang to reveal Gerald, shaking with rage, his face purple, his briefcase clenched in his hands across his chest. Scanning hastily around the room, his eyes locked onto Gaz and he snarled. 'You bastard!' he roared and launched his briefcase bodily at him across the room.

'Fuckin' hell,' Gaz gulped and jumped up from his seat, backing into a corner and holding his hands up in front of him like a shield. 'Now just a minute,' he told the raging ex-foreman. 'Calm down!' But Gerald was quickly upon him, casting chairs and tables aside as if they were made of polystyrene.

'Hey now, Gerry. Just calm down, Gerry,' Dave soothed, reaching out to grab his arm, but Gerald shrugged him off and chased Gaz round a table.

'Hey, Gerry, Gerry,' Gaz tried, his hands still held in front of him as he reversed at high speed. 'Mate,' he added hopefully. He knew he'd gone too far this time.

But there was no calming Gerald. 'Come here you, you bastard!' he bellowed as Dave tried to tackle him again, blocking his path. Gaz, heading as fast as he could for the door, asked Gerald lightly: 'You didn't get it then?' referring to the job. His insensitive question only fired Gerald up even more, and he lifted Dave clean off his feet and hurled him into a filing cabinet, sending him crashing to the ground before giving chase to the fleeing Gaz.

'Out of my way, come here!' he thundered. Gaz deftly side-stepped Gerald to skip out through the doorway and into the club's main reception, but the older man was hot on his heels, lunging for his jacket as he passed and holding onto it for dear life.

'Look, leave it!' Dave shouted, staggering to his feet and rushing after him to try and keep him from committing murder. But Gerald was too fast for him and he soon had Gaz by the lapels of his leather jacket, shaking him like a rag doll and smashing his head against the wall.

'Bastard!' he roared, his voice cracking with emotion. 'That were mine, that job,' he shouted, his eyes filling with tears, his breath hot on Gaz's face. Releasing his hold in disgust, he shoved Gaz forcibly to one side, back towards his mates who had formed a crowd in the doorway to watch them. His clothes and hair dishevelled, his face still flushed, Gerald raged at them all. 'You don't give a toss, you kids,' he said, looking as if he was about to have a heart attack. 'It's different for me.'

Gaz stood unsteadily, ready to fend off another assault, to hit back if necessary. But Gerald was past that. He pushed Gaz further away, his eyes moist. 'I've got a standard of living, responsibilities,' he tried to explain, crumpling physically. 'I were on me way up.' Standing erect again and jabbing himself in the chest with his hand, he shouted: 'I *am* on me way up.' Staggering back against the notice board, he covered his face with his hands and sobbed openly.

Lowering his hands to stare at Gaz again, to try to make some sense of it all, he wept: 'It were me first interview in months.' He held his left hand out plaintively. 'I could have got me first month's in advance.' Referring to his wife Linda, still blissfully unaware of his plight, he whispered: 'She'd never have known.'

Gaz stood gasping for air in the face of Gerald's outburst, deeply remorseful for what he had done, wishing he could undo the wrong. Dave stood a few steps beyond, wishing the same.

Gerald was a broken man. Thinking of his wife and what her reaction would be, his eyes widened further. 'Now what?' he asked nobody in particular. Looking up at Gaz and Dave, he added with bitterness: 'She's still got the credit cards, you know.' Waving his hand towards the window, his voice choked with emotion, he said: 'She's out there now ... let loose on't high street with a fuckin' Mastercard ... spending!' He spoke the last words through gritted teeth before slumping back heavily against the notice board on the wall, his fury all but spent.

There was an awkward silence as his fellow Job Club members stood watching him, seeing themselves in a few years time in his eyes, wondering what they would have done in the same situation, hoping that they would never be that desperate. Up until this moment, they had all dismissed Gerald as an outsider. He'd been their foreman, he was never one of the lads and when he, too, had arrived at the Job Club – redundant like the rest of them in the final great purge – many had seen it as a just and fitting end.

Now they realised that he was just the same as them, hurting like hell from an injustice that had badly affected them all. And when they saw the tears coursing down his cheeks in this very public display of weakness, they understood for the first time that in many ways it was even worse for him to come to terms with unemployment because, with his high moral standards and social standing, he had so much more to lose.

Gaz was the first to speak. 'Why can't you just tell her?' he asked softly, his Adam's apple like a boulder in his throat.

The tears spilled from Gerald's eyelashes as he answered. 'How can I tell her?' he asked, his mouth twisted in pain. 'After six months?' He paused and looked up. 'A woman who wants to go skiing for us holidays?' Half-laughing, half-crying at the thought, he clamped his hand to his forehead and could hardly believe it had come to this. 'Skiing, for fuck's sake!' he added.

Staggering falteringly towards Gaz, he clung to his lapel

and peered into his face. 'Why did you do it?' he asked despairingly. Clenching a fist in front of him and pounding an imaginary beat, he gasped: 'It was my job ... It had to be – my – job.'

Realising that Gaz simply couldn't give him an answer, he released his grip and hauled himself into a more upright position. Suddenly embarrassed, he pushed past Gaz and stumbled slowly towards the door, a defeated man. Gaz and Dave stood silently watching him go, shame etched on their faces.

Surrounded by pigeons hopeful of a snack, Gerald sat forlornly on the park bench and tried to regain his composure. Delving into his briefcase, he pulled out his lunch box and the job application letter. Staring at the latter for several seconds before tearing it into a dozen tiny pieces, he tossed it up into the air and watched the hungry pigeons pecking greedily at the scraps of paper as they fell. Reaching into his lunch box unenthusiastically for one of Linda's low-fat ham sandwiches, he no longer felt hungry and cast that to the birds as well.

Maybe if he went back to the steelworks, to see his old mate, to explain his strange behaviour, he might get a second chance, he thought. When the interview had come to a rather abrupt end in that way, he had all but fled from the building, hunting for Gaz, wanting revenge. He hadn't even tried to explain himself, to make up for his rambling responses. The panel of directors must surely have crossed him off their list before the door even closed behind him. It was no use.

Looking up wearily, he groaned inwardly as he saw a delegation comprising Gaz, Dave, Lomper and Nathan, fresh from school, heading cautiously towards him, their hands behind their backs. 'Can't you just leave me alone?' he asked dejectedly as they arrived in a group before him. He was not in the mood for any more teasing.

The four of them stood in a huddle and said nothing as Dave, on Gaz's nod, reached into a white plastic carrier bag he was holding and pulled out a gnome, handing it to Gerald as a peace offering. Gerald raised his head and looked at the yellow and red plaster character, recognising it as the one that he had earlier seen decapitated by its fellow outside the factory window.

'Stuck it with Super Glue,' Dave said self-consciously. 'You can't hardly see join, look.' His podgy fingers pointed it out with pride before he retreated back to the rest of the silent group.

Gerald looked up and searched their faces, wondering if this was some sort of malicious joke. Suspiciously, he took the gnome and examined Dave's handiwork closely. He saw that the former welder had, indeed, done a fine job. Unable to formulate the words he needed to respond, he lowered his head still further to hide his tears.

Nathan looked up at his father, standing at the front of the group, and nudged him with his elbow. 'Go on,' he encouraged, as Gaz nodded and removed his hands from behind his back, to reveal a small wooden cart.

'Oh, aye, I, um ... got this in a jumble, like,' Gaz stammered, shuffling forwards. 'To, er ... to say sorry.' His right hand shot out and dropped the little cart into Gerald's lap, as the other three nodded their agreement.

Gerald took it and turned it over in his hand, still unsure of what to say. He tilted it and examined it as closely as if he were buying a used car.

'Wheels go round and everything,' Lomper added helpfully from the back, his finger imitating the motion. They all nodded again.

Choked, Gerald spun the little wheels with his fingers as they all smiled with relief. When Gaz had tried that at the jumble sale he had dragged them into en route to the park, one of the wheels had come off in his hand. Gaz used it as an excuse to knock the price down to fifty pence. Dave, recent restorer of the headless garden gnome, had used his leftover glue to stick its axle.

'It, it, it's for your gnomes really, not you, but ...' Dave began to explain, but he stopped when he saw Gaz's impatient glare.

Gerald raised his head, his eyes moist. 'I, er ... I don't know, er ...' he started and then broke into a smile. 'It's marvellous this,' he said, examining the fully restored gnome and fighting back the tears.

Gaz, still at the front of the awkward delegation, tried to fill the uneasy silence. 'Er, we were thinking, er, you could maybe put it next to the wishing-well,' he suggested. 'Make a bit of, er ...' The word escaped him as he searched his memory banks, but Lomper quickly provided it from the back.

'Feature,' said the redhead.

'Yeah,' Gaz nodded enthusiastically. 'What do you reck?'

Gerald looked down at the little cart and nodded too. It was a good idea. He too could see it right next to the little wishing-well, by the pond.

Lowering his head once more and losing the battle to keep his emotions in check as he stroked the gnome's head, he mumbled: 'Ta, lads, eh ... Ta very much.' When he looked up again, his cheeks were wet.

Staring resolutely into the middle distance, himself close to tears, Gaz couldn't stand it any more. Shrugging a shoulder at Dave, he hissed: 'Cigarette me, for fuck's sake,' as Dave reached into his jacket pocket.

Gerald looked up at them and half-smiled, their childish prank forgiven. He knew they hadn't really meant any harm and, in his heart of hearts, he suspected that he wouldn't have got the job anyway. He was too old and far too out of touch with all the far-reaching changes in the steel industry. He must have been kidding himself if he thought he could get a job now, after all this time.

Strolling through the park half an hour later, the five of them said little as they watched some of Nathan's fellow pupils playing and studied a few young girls larking around on the slide. Admiring a group of teenagers spinning on the roundabout, Gaz asked: 'Think any of them could dance?'

Gerald turned to Gaz in surprise, his gnome wedged in his open briefcase, cradled lovingly in his arms. 'You're not still on about this Chippendale malarkey, are you?' he asked. He genuinely thought it had all just been a big joke; Gary the Lad mouthing off again.

But Gaz bobbed his head. 'A Yorkshire version,' he affirmed. 'Them buggers can, we bloody can.' He'd even considered a name – the Yorkshire-dales – although he wasn't sure that would work. Dave and Lomper exchanged glances nervously.

Gerald, the oldest among them by far and their former boss, thought it was time to talk some sense into these lads. He was probably the only one who could stop this before it got out of hand. 'You can't dance!' he exclaimed.

'We know, Gerald,' Gaz said, as if that was his whole point.

Dave let himself fall to the back of the group, wondering for the hundredth time what he thought he was playing at, going along with Gaz on this lark. He had always believed it would never actually come off, but Gaz had a way of making things happen, and now here he was, about to win Gerald round as well. Shuddering at the thought of having to take his clothes off with the light on, he hurried ahead, trying not to think about it.

A welcome distraction appeared in the shape of a highly attractive young woman walking towards them up the hill, her shapely legs on display for all to see below her tight leather miniskirt. 'Eh up, Gaz,' he said with a chuckle. 'Niner on its way.'

To his astonishment, Gaz – that hormonally imbalanced lecher who normally went for anything with a pulse – let the woman totter past him in her high heels as if she simply didn't exist. Nathan couldn't believe it either, as he and Dave eyed each other in surprise. Even the woman stared back at the group indignantly, wondering if she had lost her pulling power if even the likes of Gaz didn't notice her.

But Gaz had much more important things on his mind.

His charm offensive was being used to great effect on Gerald, and he decided it was time for some unashamed flattery. 'Why d'you think we're trailing you all over town?' he asked the older man.

Realising that Gaz was truly serious, Gerald slowed his pace and shook his head. 'Oh, I don't know,' he said slowly, mulling it over in his mind. 'It's not my kind of dancing, is it? It's all arse wiggling and that.'

Gaz flashed him a smile. 'Well, I've got a degree in arse wiggling, mate,' he said. 'You learn us dancing and I'll learn you the rest.' Turning to him and waving his hands expressively to reiterate his intentions, he added: 'Look, Gerald, for once I'm dead serious. I need your help.' He stared his former foreman out.

Gerald nodded his understanding but then frowned with a sudden terrible thought. 'What if someone spots me?' he asked, his eyes fearful. 'What if Linda finds out? I've got standing, me.' It would be bad enough Linda discovering that he was unemployed, let alone that he had started teaching a group of male strippers to dance. She'd kick him out and change the locks.

Gaz, undaunted by Gerald's panic-stricken expression, knew he had won him round and sauntered a few paces ahead confidently. 'Aye, you've got an overdraft an' all, mate,' he said wryly, leading his new dance teacher and his first three recruits back down the hill in triumph.

CHAPTER FIVE

Gaz wasn't stupid. Even with Dave, Lomper and Gerald on his side, he knew he needed to audition for some quality talent, to get some blokes in who would be worth seeing at ten quid a go, or they'd never earn enough for a packet of cigarettes between them.

He was happy with his own contribution, always had been. Wiry he might be, but his physique was pretty well up to scratch, give or take a bit of honing, and at least he had some basic sense of rhythm. Lomper, the keenest of all, was eager to go along with the plan – anything to keep in with his new-found friends – but he was so skinny and pale he could have won first prize in a Mr Puniverse contest. Gerald, good-looking as he was for his age, was well past his prime, even if he was a bit canny on his feet. And Dave, the most reluctant stripper in town, was hardly Arnold Schwarzenegger, what with his beer belly, terrible posture and inability to keep time when dancing – that was if he even went through with it.

No, the troupe needed something more. Someone with a little bit of magic. Something that would lift the rest of them and cover for the likes of Dave and Lomper. Gerald accepted that too. He hadn't entered the regional finals of the ballroom dancing championship three years running not to know that beauty counted for everything. If Linda had only let him pair up with the lovely Clare Hudson instead of her, he was sure he might have stood a chance in the national final.

Self-appointed talent-scouts, Gaz and Gerald discussed their plans for a major recruitment drive. Adopting the Government's welfare to work initiatives, they decided to start by tapping their best supply of potential employees and advertise at the Job Club. It would have to be done discreetly, covertly almost, but Gaz promised to take care of that. Other recruits would be found elsewhere, through scrupulous assessment of those they met on the street, in the local cafés and down at the dole office.

As their quest for new members began, Gaz and Gerald found themselves fully engrossed in the finer attributes of the male physique. They watched athletics and football on the television with a hitherto unknown zeal. They found themselves awarding points out of ten to men instead of women. Sitting in a café one lunch time, watching Dave demolish two king-size burgers and a plate of chips, they gave one fellow diner seven out of ten for his legs, another eight points for his buttocks and a third an iffy six if he cut his ponytail off. 'There's talent everywhere, Gerry mate, they'll be eating out of our knickers,' Gaz told his new dance partner with a grin as Dave watched them in disgust, worried what they were turning into.

Keen to recruit some of that new talent while they still had the momentum, Gaz and Nathan scribbled together a hasty advert for potential strippers and stuck it on the Job Club notice board, asking candidates to present themselves at the empty steelworks the following Saturday morning at eleven o'clock. No names were mentioned, no numbers given. Gaz figured out that anyone desperate enough to come wouldn't spill the beans on them if they guaranteed not to let the others at the Job Club know they had applied. It all seemed very logical.

For sounds, Nathan 'liberated' Barry's portable hi-fi system, and Gaz and Dave rifled through their old 60s and 70s classics on cassette. In preparation for their first major audition, they filled Thermos flasks, bought cans of cold drinks, crisps and sandwiches, and dragged five chairs and a trestle table to one end of a room they'd sectioned off at the steelworks. Sitting in a row behind the table facing an open space illuminated by several enormous mock-Georgian arched windows, their panes smashed by vandals years ago, they waited apprehensively like expectant parents.

Eleven o'clock passed. Midday came and went and nobody had turned up. The daily tabloid newspapers had been fully digested by all of them – even Nathan – Lomper had chewed his way through two pencils and his fingernails, Gaz had smoked twenty cigarettes and Dave was feeling decidedly peckish. Gerald was just plain annoyed, sitting miserably, his anorak still on, thinking of all the job applications he could be filling in instead of wasting his time here.

Just as they were about to give it all up as a bad idea and call it a day, there was a tentative knock on the door and a head popped round it sheepishly. It was Reg, a forty-five-year-old widowed father of six, a former furnace hand at the works, and the least likely stripper they could possibly imagine. 'Sorry lads, I'm – er – looking for …' he began shyly, afraid that he'd come to the wrong place.

Anxious not to let the others see how disappointed he was at Reg being their first proper candidate, Gaz put on a brave face and waved him in enthusiastically.

More than a little taken aback by the idea of four men and a young boy watching him strip, however, Reg went red in the face and stepped inside, reluctantly closing the door behind him. He didn't know what he'd had in mind but this certainly wasn't it.

Telling him roughly what they were after and writing his name with great aplomb on a blank sheet of paper, Gaz was secretly as uncomfortable as his fellow panel members as Reg put down his heavy bag of shopping and took up his position in front of them. Dave leaned back in his chair, his arms folded and wondered at the courage of the man. Lomper, perched on the edge of his seat, sitting on his hands, coughed timidly. Only Gerald, bolt upright in his chair, an expectant smile carved into his features, was hopeful. They never knew, they might have a budding Gene Kelly in front of them.

With an uncertain nod of his head, Gaz indicated for Nathan to turn on the music and the first few bars of that stripper's favourite *Je t'aime* blasted from the speakers incongruously. Reg, still blushing from the dimple in his bristly chin to the top of his receding ginger hairline, froze momentarily, wondering where to begin. 'Shall I start then?' he asked, as Gaz nodded. Moving his hips jerkily in time to the music, he tugged on the hem of his quilted Parka jacket and unzipped it awkwardly, constantly looking up at the men facing him for some sort of reassurance that this wasn't all some terrible joke.

Taking his jacket off to reveal a blue and green striped rugby shirt, navy jeans and trainers, he hurled it to the ground without any grace and looked less than enthusiastic about the next part. Squirming in their seats and hardly able to watch, each member of the panel wished he was somewhere else, anywhere but where he was, as the distinctly unerotic music increased its breathless intensity.

Losing heart rapidly, Reg moved his hands round to his back, untucking his striped top from his jeans while he sort of bounced up and down as if he was on a trampoline. Gaz held his hand over his mouth to suppress his embarrassment. Lomper poured himself a cup of tea and hardly dared watch.

Pulling his rugby shirt off over his head in a series of ungainly movements which tousled his hair, Reg, his arms still caught in the sleeves, got into a terrible twist and ended up yanking each sleeve off one by one. Apparently unable to perform one movement at the same time as another, he stopped swaying his pelvis as he did so, but then abruptly began again as he remembered. It was an excruciating spectacle.

Removing his top finally and dropping it onto the floor to reveal a distinctly middle-aged girth and a chest covered in a fine down of orange hair, parted down the middle by a large, ugly scar, Reg swallowed hard and frowned at the panel as he moved on to the next and most embarrassing stage. Bent double as he fumbled with his belt and top button, preparing to undo his jeans, he was hoping beyond hope that they would end his suffering before he had to.

Gaz came gallantly to the rescue. Jerking upright in his seat and shaking his head No, he tried to speak. This was more than flesh and blood could stand. Motioning urgently to Nathan to stop the tape, he looked apologetically at Reg, who now stood, half-naked and deeply mortified in front of them.

'I'm sorry,' Reg mumbled when the music stopped, his hand gesturing his apology. 'Sorry.' No one on the panel could think of anything to say in response. 'Thought I'd give it a go,' he explained, clutching his stomach. 'I got a bit desperate, like – you know how it is.' Gaz nodded, trying to think of something positive to say. A picture of dejection standing before them, Reg looked close to the edge. His eyes moist, his fists clenched, angry with himself, he added bitterly: 'But I can't even take me kit off properly, can I?' He bent down to pick up his clothes from the floor with a sigh.

The others looked to Gaz, willing him to say something, anything, to make Reg feel better. But all he could do was stand awkwardly behind the table and say: 'You're … you're all right, Reg.' Hoping to fill the awkward silence that followed, he added: 'Er, there's a cup of tea if you like,' pointing to Lomper's battered Thermos flask.

Retrieving the rest of his clothes from the floor and clumsily putting them on, Reg shook his head, desperate to escape the pitying looks on their faces. 'No thanks. I've got the kids outside,' he said with a nod of his head, pointing out to the loading bay where he had left his four youngest playing football with an old tin can while Daddy was inside 'seeing someone about a job'.

Gaz brightened. 'Well, bring 'em in,' he said, smiling. He loved kids and Reg's were nice boys who had lost their mother to cancer a few years before.

Reg, all his clothes gathered, his composure regained, looked Gaz straight in the eye. 'Nah,' he said with feeling, picking up his shopping. 'This is no place for kids.' He nodded meaningfully at Nathan, who looked up guiltily. Gaz shot him a glance and wondered for the first time at the wisdom of involving his son in such a cheerless escapade. Maybe Reg was right, maybe seeing grown men so desperate for money that they would do anything, even take their clothes off, wasn't the best education for the boy. He felt suddenly ashamed. Before he could say anything, though, Reg, still not fully dressed, had picked up his bags and gone, slamming the door shut behind him.

Breathing out for the first time in several minutes, Gerald, his hands clasped together on the table in front of him, twiddled his thumbs and looked to the heavens. 'This is crazy,' he said quietly. Reg was right. This wasn't a place for kids. It wasn't even a place for grown-ups. What did they think they were doing? He could hardly believe he was sitting here, a party to what he had just been forced to witness. From the expressions on the others' faces, it was clear he was voicing the feelings of them all. Gaz sat down heavily, scribbled a thick black line through Reg's name and threw his pen down on the table, bitterly disappointed.

They would have all got up and walked out there and then, only a minute later, their next candidate strode confidently into the room and stood in front of them, legs apart, his hands in his pocket, ready to give them his best. Gaz, his confidence restored, took a few details and began the interview. 'So, er, it's Mr Horse?' he asked their next hopeful, a middle-aged black man who stood coolly before them.

'Horse,' the Scouse grandfather of four corrected him, his chin covered in fine silver bristle. He was dressed in a steel grey single-breasted suit, comfortable brown leather moccasin-style shoes and a pale blue open necked shirt. Dave thought he looked more like a bus conductor than a stripper. None of them seemed much impressed.

'Yeah, well, er ...' Gaz started, not sure where to begin. Lomper, sitting to his left, tugged on his sleeve to indicate that he wanted to ask something. 'Just a minute, Mr Horse, um, my colleagues on the panel …' Gaz rocked back on his chair and in towards Lomper to hear what he wanted to say. Gerald and Dave leaned in the other side.

Staring at Horse wide-eyed, Lomper gripped Gaz's arm and whispered: 'Ask him why he's called The Horse.'

Gaz looked at the redhead crossly and pulled away from his grip. 'You bloody ask him,' he said, not bothering to whisper back. 'It's not 'cos he does the Grand National, is it?'

Gerald, on the other side of Gaz, leaned in and spoke out of the side of his mouth. 'Yeah, that's all very well, but what's the point of having a big wanger if you need a Zimmer frame to tout it in, eh?' He gave Gaz a disapproving sneer. 'I mean, he must be fifty if he's a day.'

Gaz sat up suddenly in his chair and leaned forward, ignoring the Doubting Thomases at his side. Gerald was one to talk, having reached that milestone himself some years before. Giving the waiting candidate an encouraging smile, Gaz enquired: 'So, Horse, what can you do?'

Horse raised his head and faltered. 'Don't know really, um …' he began as Gerald tutted aloud and the rest of the panel glanced sideways at each other. Gaz groaned inwardly but tried not to let his disappointment show. If this one was no good, he knew he'd probably have to call the whole thing off.

Coming to his senses, Horse pulled a hand from his jacket pocket to count items off on his fingers. 'Let's see, there's the, er … there's the Bump … the Stomp … the Bus Stop.' Three fingers were held out in front of him as Gerald's mouth fell open. 'My break dancin' days are probably over,' Horse added honestly, 'but there's always the Funky Chicken.' His rasping Liverpudlian accent cut the air like a knife.

Speechless and suitably impressed, the panel sat in open appreciation. Gaz sneered at Gerald who, apparently forgetting all the criticisms he had just made about the man in front of them, recognised a fellow dance enthusiast and raved: 'Now you're talking!'

Gaz, hardly believing his ears, creased his forehead. 'All

of them?' he asked, daring to hope that it might be true after the performance of the previous candidate.

Horse shrugged his shoulders and stuffed his hands in his pockets. 'Well, yeah, I think so.' Registering their sceptical silence, he added: 'Well, it's been a while, mind … and I've got this dodgy hip, you know.' He patted his arthritic right hip, which was still needing a replacement joint after more than two years on the local hospital waiting list.

Not wanting to detract from Horse's initial enthusiasm and keen to see what he really could do, health notwith-standing, Gaz interrupted him: 'Yeah, well,' he said, as if he knew all about dodgy hips. Nodding to his son, he said: 'Stick it on, Nathe,' as the boy stood to cue up the next track. Turning back to Horse, Gaz held his hands out invitingly and said: 'Do your worst, pal.'

Nathan cued up the tape and, as a funky James Brown number filled the room, Horse threw open his arms and spread-eagled his hands in the air in front of him. He began to move, painfully slowly at first, old limbs remembering long-forgotten sequences. The panel exchanged crestfallen looks.

But as soon as the tempo increased and the words started belting out, then very gradually, as the music flowed through his bones, Horse started grooving sinuously around the floor, spinning, twisting, clapping his hands and funking that chicken – much to everyone's surprise and delight.

He rocked and rolled and mouthed the words, lost in his own little world, hands pumping the air, legs and feet pounding the steelworks floor. Gaz and Gerald beat time on their knees, and Dave sat smiling up at the man he'd written off as an no-hoper.

Really warming up now, Horse jumped slickly from foot to foot, clicking his fingers in time and spinning his hands in the air in front of him. There was even a bit of Michael Jackson-style moon walking, before his impressive finale – a loud whoop, followed by a brave, if only partially successful, attempt at the splits – which left him hunched up on the floor, counting the cost of overextending his weary joints.

To enthusiastic and heartfelt applause from a grinning Dave, Gerald, Lomper, Gaz and Nathan, Horse got painfully to his feet and managed a slight bow. He was in.

Next up was a gentle hunk of a plasterer in his mid-twenties, a very good-looking young man called Guy, who sat eagerly in front of the panel, his denim jeans flecked with white plaster, his big builder's boots scratched and worn.

'Me favourite film's *Singin' in the Rain*,' he said with genuine fervour, his hands stuffed shyly under his legs. 'They do that walkin' up the wall thing,' he explained, lifting his arms and using his fingers to imitate walking up a wall. Smiling apprehensively, he added: 'Bloody ace it is, you should see it.' His hands slipped back under him as he waited for a response.

The panel sat silently, waiting for him to carry on. Gerald had inexplicably slid down his chair and was hiding his face behind the newspaper, hissing at Gaz to try and get his attention. 'He plastered our bathroom a few months back,' he whispered. 'Get rid of him!' He was mortified at the idea of someone he knew taking his clothes off in front of him, let alone the thought that word might somehow get back to Linda.

Gaz wasn't in the mood for Gerald's paranoia. This bloke was the best looking they'd had in yet, or even seen in a long time. A Seven at least. 'Shut up,' he murmured. 'You'll be fine.'

Gerald, his nose still deep in *The Mirror*, tried to argue the point. 'He'll blow me cover!' he complained but Gaz didn't seem to be taking his problem at all seriously.

'Shut up,' Gaz repeated. Then, turning to Guy with a frown, he asked politely: 'What walking up wall thing?' He didn't know what this lad was talking about, but it sounded impressive and if he could actually perform such a stunt, it might well become a star attraction for the troupe.

Delighted to have been asked, Guy's face broke into an attractive smile. Maybe an Eight, Gaz thought at the sight of it.

'I'll show you,' Guy offered, jumping to his feet. When he

pulled off his cropped bomber jacket to reveal well-defined biceps bulging from a black short-sleeved T-shirt, Gaz notched him up a point. Nine. Not bad for their third attempt. Even Dave sat up and took notice.

'I'm, er, Donald O'Connor, right?' Guy explained, moving his chair to one side, although not one of them knew who he meant at all. He pointed to the brick wall behind him. 'That's the wall.'

Gaz and Horse nodded their assent. Lomper giggled. Before they could say anything, the young man in front of them had stepped back a few paces, almost to their table, and run full speed at the wall. As they watched in amazement, he somehow managed to get both legs up the wall so that for a split second he was suspended in mid-air and horizontal to the wall. Seconds later, gravity took over, and he crashed flat on his back to the floor, letting out the gasp of the terminally wounded.

'Ouch!' Gaz said for him, as all but Gerald winced at the sight. Gerald, still cowering behind his newspaper, listened to Guy groaning on the other side of the room and wondered what on earth was going on.

Lying spread-eagled on his back, his hands feeling for broken ribs, Guy started to get to his feet. Clutching his chest, he croaked: 'Aye, well, er … it's better than that in the film like, you know.' He attempted a smile.

When he had fully recovered the feeling in his legs and was back standing in front of them, still winded, Gaz decided to take Guy through the finer points of his job application. Puffing on his cigarette, he bobbed his head up and down on his neck, frustrated that his top scorer so far on looks appeared to be completely without talent. 'So you don't sing?' he reminded Guy.

'No,' the plasterer admitted.

'You don't dance?' Gaz was trying not to lose patience.

Guy hesitated slightly as he thought of his attempts at walking up the wall, but finally shook his head. 'No,' he conceded.

Gaz, rapidly losing faith in his hot favourite, half-smiled. 'Hope you don't think I'm being nosy but, er … what do you do?' He took a last draw on his cigarette before stubbing it out directly under Gerald's newspaper barrier.

Guy shrugged his shoulders and nodded. 'Well, er …' he began, unfastening his belt and popping the buttons on his flies. 'There is this.' He let his jeans and boxer shorts slip to the floor in one easy movement and stood up, a self-satisfied look on his face.

The expressions on the faces of the panel – a mixture of awe, shock and respect – betrayed Guy's unique talents. Lomper leaned forward for a better look, Horse dropped his head into his hands with envy and Dave nearly swallowed his tongue.

As Gerald looked around at them from behind his newspaper in puzzlement, a stream of cigarette smoke shot out from Gaz's mouth in a blast and his throat made a strange guttural sound. Gerald wondered what he was looking at. Finally recovering his power of speech, Gaz announced with a gulp: 'Gentlemen, the lunch box has landed.' This was a Ten if ever he saw one.

Gerald, unable to resist a peek, lowered his protective shield. Dropping it to the table when he saw what dangled impressively between Guy's legs, he exclaimed: 'Chuffin' Nora!' completely forgetting his cover.

Recognising him instantly, Guy pointed at him with a smile, giving him a little wave. 'All right, Gerald,' he beamed, seemingly oblivious to the fact that his trousers were still round his ankles and quite unfazed by the reaction he had received. 'Didn't see you over there.' Giving Gaz a thumbs up sign, he grinned and added hopefully: 'Did his bathroom,' as if that would help his application for the job.

Gerald tried to hide behind his newspaper again, but gave up. Unable to recover the situation or take his eyes off the astonishing sight before him, he smiled shyly. 'Hello, Guy,' he said slowly. Lomper, Horse and Dave remained speechless and Nathan's mouth had fallen open in disbelief.

Remembering his son too late, Gaz waved frantically at him to stop looking, calling his name urgently: 'Nathe! … Nathan!' but the boy was transfixed. Blinking suddenly, his brain registered that his attention was being sought and he looked over at his father, forgetting to close his mouth. Gesturing to Guy to pull his trousers up quickly, Gaz lit another cigarette and hoped to God his son wouldn't get a lifelong inferiority complex.

Later that night, Dave stood miserably on his bathroom scales and winced as the needle reached the seventeen stone point and quivered there. Peering at his reflection in the full-length mirror, he lifted his T-shirt and gripped the thick tyre around his waist with both hands. 'I say, Jean …' he called to his wife, who was sitting in bed in her night-dress, reading a magazine.

'Yeah,' she answered absent-mindedly, deeply engrossed in an article on the female G-spot and how to find it.

'Ever been out with a black bloke, like?' Dave called unhappily, running his hand up and down the stretch marks criss-crossing his stomach and examining himself in profile, his rolled-up T-shirt tucked under his double chin.

Jean stopped reading and looked up, her forehead furrowed into a frown. 'You know I haven't, Dave,' she answered, wondering at the question. They'd been to school together, for God's sake. He'd been her first true love. He knew that.

Rocking backwards and forwards on the scales to try and get a lower reading, Dave tried standing on one leg, wobbling furiously all the while. 'But, if you were on't lookout for a new fella, right …' he continued, 'if you were, just saying … would you think about it?' Stepping off the scales dejectedly and pulling down his T-shirt to cover his belly, he wandered into the bedroom.

Jean flicked angrily through her magazine. 'What's got into you?' she asked. He'd been acting very strangely lately, asking her all sorts of weird questions about what she found most attractive in men, which film or sports stars she would give ten out of ten to, that sort of thing. She was getting fed up with it.

Looking across at her from the open doorway, Dave's expression was serious. 'No, would you though?' he pressed, awaiting an answer.

Jean dropped her magazine to her lap, leaned her head back, sighed and studied the ceiling. 'I might do. Yeah,' she said, exasperated. Whatever she said she couldn't win, she knew that of old. 'Is that all right?' she asked, looking across at her husband, wondering if that was the answer he was looking for.

Thoroughly despondent, he padded back into the bathroom barefoot. 'So, it's true then,' he said morosely, his voice flat, examining his figure in profile once more.

Abandoning her magazine, Jean looked around their peach-painted bedroom with its pretty Oriental fans pinned to the walls, its romantic lighting and soft furnishings. It was her favourite room in the house, the one place where she felt closest to Dave, even since he'd started to act strangely. 'I've bloody had enough of this,' she said to no one in particular, shaking her head. To Dave, still in the bathroom, she called: 'What's true?'

Switching the light off against his chubby reflection, Dave called: 'What they say about black blokes.' He padded back into the bedroom in boxer shorts and T-shirt, his jeans draped over his arm and stood by the bed. 'They've got great bodies and that.'

'Well, some of them, yeah,' Jean acknowledged as she picked up her magazine again. Looking across at Dave, who had put down his jeans and was climbing into bed next to her, she added: 'And?'

Dave slid into bed, anxious for his wife not to examine him too closely in his skimpy clothes, slipped the covers over him and lay on his back. 'Nothing,' he answered, his voice even flatter. Pulling his T-shirt up off over his head, he cast it to the floor and flopped back down onto the pillows, the duvet up to his neck.

Jean leaned over her husband, resting on her elbow, and stroked his chest fondly. 'David,' she chided. She only ever called him that when she was ticking him off. 'I don't care if they're black, white or bloody rainbow coloured. I'm married to you. Remember?' she smiled down at her husband, the only man she had ever loved.

'Yeah,' he said, peering up into her eyes for any sign of a lie. Blinking and turning his back to her with a sigh, he called: 'Night.'

Jean snuggled up behind him, her hand slipped up under his arm, caressing the hairs on his broad chest. 'Why would I want anyone else, eh?' she asked, leaning over to kiss his shoulder and pressing him to her suggestively. 'Big man.' She tickled his flesh with her tongue.

'Jeanie,' Dave whined, placing his large hand over her fingers to stop them stroking his chest. 'I'm all done in.' She stopped and looked down at him sadly over his shoulder. Reaching up to turn off his bedside lamp, Dave added softly: 'It's amazing how tiring it is, doing nowt, you know.' He closed his eyes briefly as if going to sleep, but then lay very still staring straight ahead in the darkness.

Jean lay back on her pillows, biting her bottom lip to stop herself from crying. She and Dave hadn't had sex in months. The last few times they did, it was very perfunctory, almost automatic. There was none of the passion they had once enjoyed, no ripping off of clothes or not even making it to the bedroom. She was always being told that, in most marriages, a lot of that sort of thing tailed off after a few years. But with Dave and her it never really had, until now. Even when she'd had her operation, the one that left her unable to have kids, he'd never let her think for one minute that she wasn't still the only woman for him, the love of his life.

Perhaps it was her. Perhaps he didn't fancy her any more. God knows, she thought as she looked down at her ample bosom under her winciette nightie covered in furry little teddy bears, she wasn't much of a catch these days. She no longer even pretended to dress up for him in the bedroom.

But she felt instinctively it was more than that; it went deeper. Dave was a troubled man. She'd forgotten the last time she'd even seen him laugh. Being unemployed had really knocked the wind out of him, he was no longer the jolly fellow she'd married sixteen years earlier, that was for sure. Try as she might, she couldn't get him to open up to her about how he was feeling. All she knew was that he was deeply unhappy, and therefore she was too. But for the life of her, she didn't know what she could do to help. And she didn't honestly know how much more of it she could stand.

Gaz and Dave were on a mission as they walked in through the automatic double doors at Asda the following afternoon. Gerald had told them to try and get hold of some dance videos so that they could learn some basic techniques and pick up a few tips. Nathan had come along to offer what advice he could.

'Go for something classy,' Gerald had advised. 'Something with panache,' although neither of them had a clue what panache meant. Dave thought it was the surname of some French female movie star. Gaz told him not to be so daft, but when Nathan had looked up at him inquisitively, he had announced unconvincingly that it was the name of a fancy Latin American dance step. Dave was still smarting from being called daft.

Gaz wasn't in the mood for Dave's sulks anyway. Only that morning, the big man had informed his friend that he had decided overnight that he simply couldn't go through with it. No dancing, no stripping, nothing. He'd give them every support and do all he could to help in other ways, but he wasn't taking his clothes off and that was final. End of chat. Gaz had heard it all before and took it with a large pinch of salt. Push come to shove, he was confident he'd have Dave where he wanted him. He always had before. But his resistance was far from satisfactory.

Dave decided to try and find Jean, who worked full-time as an assistant in the store bringing in the only real income they had apart from his dole money. Hearing her distinctive laugh somewhere near the household goods section, he strolled casually over in that direction, hoping to see her and apologise in some way for the previous night, although he didn't know how. He stopped behind a rack of compact discs when he saw his wife, hands clasped to her face, giggling conspiratorially with the good-looking young man he knew as Frankie, who was juggling dustpan brushes in front of her. Dave's bottom lip came up to meet his top one and form a grimace.

Gaz, at his shoulder in a flash, watched the scene critically. It was quite obvious that the young man was flirting with Jean and, furthermore, that she was thoroughly enjoying the attention, but he was sure it was no more than that. 'They're just messing, Dave,' Gaz reassured his friend.

Dave picked nervously at a label on one of the CDs and couldn't take his eyes off them. 'You reckon?' he asked, not sounding very convinced.

'Course!' Gaz scoffed, as Nathan joined them, a bag of pick 'n' mix sweets in his hand. 'Just Jean, innit?' Everybody knew that Jean loved a good laugh. She'd always been like that, ever since she was a kid in school. Even years of being married to Dave hadn't diminished her sense of fun, although Gaz knew that it must have really been put to the test lately.

Jean's raucous laughter reverberated across the aisles as Frankie dropped his brushes and she bent down with him to help pick them up, their heads momentarily touching. Dave recalled the conversation he'd partially overheard in the gents' lavatory at the working men's club and wondered if it was true.

Finally dragging his eyes away from the unedifying scene, he looked down at Nathan with a scowl. 'You got any of them mint chocolate jobs, Nathe?' he asked, hopefully.

Nathan scrunched the top of the bag shut with his hand. 'Get lost. You're on a diet,' the boy said, stepping to where his dad was examining video cassettes.

103

Dave looked wounded. 'Don't you start, an' all,' he said, joining them.

Gaz picked up a video of the film *Flashdance* and turned it over in his hand. Sounded about right. Flash and Dance. Bound to have the odd panache step in it and all. Gerald would be well pleased with that. Directing his question at Dave, he asked: 'Right, how much you got then?'

Dave delved into his jeans pocket and pulled out some loose change. Spreading the coins out on the palm of his hand with his fingers he counted: 'Twenty-two … twenty-seven pence.'

Gaz, who hadn't a penny on him, looked down at the change in Dave's hand and shook his head. Replacing the video on the shelf in disgust, he said: 'Four ninety-nine, special offer. We're still a fucking fiver short.' He put it back with a sigh and stared at it with a frown. Twisting his face into an impish grin, he looked up at his friend with a knowing wink. 'Well, you know what this means, Dave.'

It took a second or two for the penny to drop, but Dave finally clicked and shook his head. 'Oh no, come on, Gaz. Why me?' He looked victimised.

Gaz turned to face him with a chuckle. ''Cos you've got an innocent face, love.' Pointing to his own gaunt features, he explained: 'I've got serial killer written on my forehead.' Ready to lead Nathan away, he added pointedly: 'And if you're not gonna dance, you can do summat bloody well useful instead.' As usual he was twisting Dave's earlier offer of help to his own advantage.

Dave had a sudden thought. 'Hey, but, er, what if Jean finds out? She'll throw an eppy. She's only over there,' he moaned, nodding his head at the aisle where he had last seen his wife disappear with that Frankie fella.

Gaz was used to Dave's lame excuses and wasn't having any of them. 'She's miles away,' he said, dismissively. Then, with a hard slap on his back, he added: 'See you later … Good luck.'

Looking down at Nathan, reversing out of the aisle with

his father, quite accustomed to this sort of thing, Dave sneered. 'Give us a pear drop, you,' he said, holding out his hand.

'They're not paid for,' Nathan answered, as if that made any difference, walking off with his father before Dave tried to snatch one from his bag.

Looking furtively around him over each shoulder, Dave turned his attention to the shelf of video cassettes, picking up the one Gaz had chosen with his right hand. Reaching left to select another video with his other hand, he expertly slipped the wanted one under his armpit inside his open jacket while pretending to study the blurb on the other. Returning that one to the shelf as if he was disinterested, he straightened up and peered nervously around him, his left arm clamped to his side to keep the stolen video in place, allowing himself a small smile only when he realised that he had apparently got away with it.

Strolling casually towards the exit, he passed the five-tiered pick 'n' mix sweet counter and, as a reward for his good work, picked up a pear drop and popped it into his mouth. At that very moment, every alarm in the store went off, shattering his calm.

Panicking and convinced – in his dietary guilt – that he must have eaten an alarm-activated sweet, he spat it into his hand and examined it closely, as the bells continued to ring. Dropping it to the floor, he stamped on it, grinding it into the lino. Miraculously, the store fell silent. Dave shook his head in wonderment at such high-tech confectionery and sauntered out of the main doors as every alarm sounded once again, sending him across the car park in a sprint that Linford Christie would have been proud of.

Jam-packed inside Lomper's security office later that night, Gerald, Lomper, Dave, Guy, Horse and Gaz crowded around one of the numerous television monitors as the opening sequence of the stolen video started up, providing the only light in the room. The image that flickered up on the screen showed the former ballet dancer Jennifer Beales, in a full-face welding mask, working on some hot sheet metal, before lifting off her helmet and shaking out her shoulder-length auburn curls.

Dave, who had been in the blackest of moods all evening, suddenly leaned forward in his chair, indignant. 'Hey, what's this?' he exclaimed. 'I didn't go on the nick in Asda for some chuffin' women's "How To" video.'

The rest of the gang ignored him and continued watching the film carefully. Gaz explained the plot quietly: 'It's *Flashdance,* Dave. She's a welder, isn't she?'

Dave frowned and stared at the screen. 'A welder? ... Well I hope she dances better than she welds.' Pointing to the screen with disdain, he added scornfully: 'I mean, look at that, her mix is all to cock.' Guy, sitting the wrong way round on a chair behind Dave, his head resting on his hands, smiled. Horse wondered why Dave was here anyway, if he wasn't even going to dance.

Gaz rounded on his friend angrily. 'Shut up, Dave,' he cried, fed up with all his negative vibes. He'd been nothing but aggro from the start. At least the others were beginning to show a bit of enthusiasm. 'What the fuck do you know about welding, any road?' he added, for good measure, knowing that his remark would hit Dave where it hurt.

Dave was wounded and it showed. 'More than some chuffin' woman,' he sulked, as the welding images continued to flicker on the screen. 'Ah, it's like bonfire night. That's too much acetylene is that.' Pointing accusingly at the screen, he announced: 'Them joints won't hold fuck all.'

It was Gerald's turn to lose his rag. Handing the remote control to Lomper to fast-forward the tape, he glowered at the big man. 'Oh, for Christ's sake, Dave,' he said. 'We're looking for the dancing, aren't we?' He, too, was losing patience.

Guy and Horse, unaccustomed to Dave's dour personality, glanced at each other and then at Gaz, who felt honour bound to explain. 'He's got the hump about Asda,' he said, as if that made everything crystal clear. They nodded and smiled, wishing that it was.

Just at that moment, the tape juddered to a halt in the middle of a dance sequence and Lomper pointed to the screen. 'Hey, cop a load of that,' he said, flicking a switch so that the image leapt at them from all six screens. They sat transfixed as the star of the film, her welding gear discarded, dressed in body-hugging leotard and tights, performed a superb double back flip across a dance floor, followed by a triple pirouette and the splits.

Gerald grinned, triumphantly. 'What did I tell you?' he said, turning to the others with a flourish of his hand. 'She's nifty on her pins is that one.' They watched in amazement as she spun and twisted and leapt and pranced before their very eyes, ending with an upside-down breakdance spin on her back, her knees crossed and toes pointed artistically in the air. 'That, gentlemen ...' Gerald said, tapping the screen, '... is what we are looking for.'

Dave nearly fell off his chair. Pointing to Horse and laughing, he said: 'Oh, aye, I can just see him doing all that twizzling-about bollocks.' Horse looked really hurt.

Gerald shrugged. 'Ah, it's souped-up tango, that is,' he said, imitating the dance movements with his arms. 'Teach any bugger in a week.' Turning to Dave with a smile, he added confidently: 'Even you, mate.'

Dave's top lip curled and he glared up at Gerald. 'Oh, even a fat bastard like me,' he sneered angrily. 'Yeah, I know what I am, so don't take the piss, you.'

Gerald bit his bottom lip while he considered the enormity of such a task. 'All right,' he said, revising his estimate after giving Dave the once over. 'Two weeks.' As all the men in the room stared at each other in astonishment, Gerald chuckled openly. 'Straight up,' he said, nodding his head emphatically. Even Dave felt encouraged.

CHAPTER SIX

It was crunch-time for Dave and he knew it. From out of nowhere this barmy scheme had become a reality and now he and Gaz were on their way to their first lesson with Gerald and the others. Even though he'd insisted he wasn't doing it, Gaz had persuaded him to 'stand in' until a suitable substitute could be found. He'd made it sound so plausible, that Dave would simply be a sort of understudy until another, undoubtedly thinner, Narcissus could be discovered somewhere on the streets of Sheffield. But as the moment of truth approached with the first lesson, Dave was fast losing courage and all his insecurities were crowding in on him.

What if Gaz was lying? What if he never intended to replace him? This could just be a way of getting him so involved that it would be impossible for him to back out at the end. If only he could have talked it over with Jean, asked her advice, but he was afraid to. And besides, she had other ideas for his future.

'I dunno, Gaz,' Dave said, fiddling with a piece of plastic he'd found discarded in the gutter as the two of them turned the corner on the final leg of their journey to the steelworks. It was a route they'd taken together every morning for over ten years in another lifetime and yet here they were, heading for something quite different. 'Jean reckons I should take that security guard job down at Asda.'

Gaz looked askance at him and scowled. 'Oh, Jesus. Security?' he gasped. 'You're worth more than that, Dave.' The salary would be about a third of what Dave had earned as a welder at the steelworks and have none of the kudos.

'She don't think so,' Dave replied glumly, his shoulders

stooped by months of low self-esteem. Softly, he added: 'I reckon there's summat going on with her and that bloke, you know.' He put the piece of plastic in his pocket for safekeeping and stuck his jaw out at the thought.

Gaz snorted. 'The juggling bugger? No, no way.' He was no great fan of Jean and neither was she of him, but he knew she was a good and loyal wife to Dave and he couldn't believe she'd have an affair with a skinny youth half her age. Besides, he'd heard her say as much that time in the club lav. He shuddered now at the memory of Sharon and her amazing party trick.

'It's not as if I'd blame her,' Dave sighed, trying to reason it all out in his mind. He'd been physically and financially impotent for so long now, he couldn't remember the last time he'd satisfied his wife sexually. Emotionally, too, there had been an impasse, as he withdrew more and more into himself, bingeing secretly in his unhappiness, hating himself for it and yet unable to share his despair with Jean. It was a downward spiral and the more he spun towards the vortex, the less he felt able to help himself.

Gaz knew his mate was having problems at home and did his best to cheer him up. 'Well, you could show her, Dave,' he suggested brightly. 'Nobody tells them Chippendales to go and be security, do they? Raking it in, they are.' He still couldn't get that ten thousand quid out of his mind. Better than a lottery win, that was.

Dave carried on walking and considered what Gaz was saying. Seeing that he had him thinking, Gaz cuffed him gently on the arm. 'Two weeks,' he reminded him. 'That's what the man said and he's not taking the piss.'

Dave rubbed his chin and nodded. 'Yeah, it's a thought,' he admitted. What was two weeks between him and terminal boredom at Asda? There were always jobs going there, a couple of weeks wouldn't make much difference.

Gaz stepped in front of him, grabbed him by the lapels of his jacket and shook him. His face inches from his, he cried enthusiastically: 'It's more than a thought! You think of

Jean's face when she sees you dancin' like old fuckin' Flashdance, eh?' He wiggled his hips expressively.

Dave raised his eyebrows, hardly daring to believe what Gaz was telling him. 'Two weeks?' he asked with a smile. 'Just like flashy tits?'

Gaz slapped his arm and stepped away. 'It's what your man said,' he reminded him, walking backwards in front of him, his face hopeful.

'Hey,' Dave called, a grin on his face for the first time in days. 'I can weld better than her an' all.' Gaz laughed aloud and grabbed his mate firmly round the shoulders, pushing him towards his destiny.

Whatever hopes Gerald Cooper had privately entertained about getting his dance troupe into some sort of shape for an imminent public performance were quickly dashed during the disastrous afternoon that followed. Again and again as he demonstrated and shoved and danced his way around the floor of the steelworks, he tried to explain to them the most basic principles of rhythm and timing, and again and again they failed to grasp even the rudiments.

Lomper was by far the worst, a streak of white lard and with about as much sex appeal. Dave was second worst, lumbering about unable to understand any of the directions, but the others didn't have all that much going for them either. Gaz was always at least two steps ahead in a world of his own, Horse – the only one with any real rhythm – seemed unable to work in a team, and Guy appeared to have two left feet tripping him up all over the place, as well as his famous middle leg. It was the most frustrating few hours any of them had spent since they were last down the Job Club trying to type application letters on that confounded computer.

As Gerald watched them form themselves into a staggered row like so many toy soldiers, while several of them moved further forward to make the row even more disjointed, he threw his hands up in the air and raised his eyes to the heavens. If this was punishment for lying to his wife for the

110

last six months, then he had surely done his full penance after more than three hours of this hell.

'Stop! No, No!' he cried, his eyes squeezed shut, his arms flapping at the bedraggled men who were scattered haphazardly about the room like wobbling nine-pins. 'Stop, stop, stop!' His grey fringe flopped forward, his cheeks red with anger; he motioned to Nathan to turn off the Donna Summer hit that had been pounding through the factory and his head for hours. The boy, playing truant and sitting at a giant upturned coil reel acting as a table, hit the switch and put his head in his hands. Perhaps he'd have been less bored in his physics lesson, after all.

'What? What? What?' Gaz cried for all of them. Gerald's bumbling students were no less frustrated than him. Try as they might to understand what he was on about, they couldn't seem to keep together on any of the steps he taught them.

'What?' Horse repeated, his usually kindly face frowning.

But Gerald was fast losing his patience and it showed. Tugging on his red woollen V-neck sweater, his face sweaty, he grabbed Lomper roughly by the arm and shoved him to one side. 'You – stay still,' he said, moving him back to where he was meant to be and pointing to the floor. Manhandling Gaz similarly, Gerald pointed ahead with the instruction: 'And you – go forward, okay?'

'Okay,' Gaz concurred, the palms of his hand held up in the air in a gesture of unarmed surrender. Gerald was really beginning to get on his tits.

Clasping his hands together as if in prayer, Gerald turned to his young musical director, in charge of the portable hi-fi, numb with boredom and wanting to get home to his mum's for tea. All he'd had to eat all day was a bag of cheese and onion crisps and a carton of blackcurrant juice, the debris of which was strewn in front of him. 'All right, Nathan,' Gerald instructed, and the boy pressed the Play button yet again as the dance teacher took his place at the front to watch.

The music blared as Gerald counted: 'One, two, three,

111

four,' slicing his hands through the air in time to the beat. But, to his horror, Lomper rushed forward again with a purposeful stride, hesitated and scurried back two paces as the whole thing fell apart yet again. 'No, no, no!' Gerald cried at the shambles before him, his head in his hands. 'Jesus Christ!' At this rate it would be two years before he got them dancing anything like Jennifer Beales, not two weeks. Being a foreman had never been so hard.

Even Gaz realised that they weren't getting it. 'Oh, fuckin' hell,' he moaned under his breath, staring at his feet, hands on his hips, as Gerald stepped forward again to try and show them what he wanted.

'All I want to do …' he said pleadingly to them all '… is to get you in a straight bloody line!' Staring at the lot of them in utter despair, he screamed: 'What do I have to do?!'

Ashamed, they all stood looking at him and each other in puzzlement, wishing they could at least get something right. Lomper was mortified that he seemed to be the fly in the ointment. He hoped Gaz wouldn't kick him out; these were the only friends he had. Guy felt a fraud, getting in on the act even though he was so hopeless at dancing, just because of his special talents. Dave, convinced that it was his ungainly bulk that was somehow to blame, stared down at his stomach accusingly.

Only Horse looked like he was thinking something through. Finally, from the front of the line-up, he piped up brightly: 'Well, it's the Arsenal offside trap, isn't it?' referring to the defensive play of the Premiere League football team, and their use of the offside rule to trap an attacking player. For the first time that day, the rest of the gang appeared to understand what someone was telling them.

Gerald, watching Horse's lips move but unable to distinguish any language that he understood, was none the wiser. 'You what?' he asked, flummoxed.

Horse stepped forward purposefully. 'The Arsenal offside trap,' he repeated slowly. The rest of the dancers looked up, interested now as he showed them what he meant. 'Lomper here is Tony Adams, right?' he said, pointing to the redhead with his forefinger. 'Any bugger looks like scoring,' he said, moving backwards and looking to his newly-appointed central defender, 'we all step forward in a line and wave our arms around like a fairy.' He demonstrated the movement fluidly.

As the raggle-taggle army nodded in total understanding, Dave responded for them all. 'Oh, well, that's easy,' he proclaimed, thoroughly enlightened and getting back into position as Gerald's eyebrows shot up to meet his unruly fringe.

'Okay,' Gerald said slowly, cautiously hopeful for the first time that day. Turning to his musical director, he called: 'Nathan?' The boy pressed Play and to his and Gerald's complete amazement, the five men before them stepped, perfectly in time to the music, into one straight line and raised their right arms simultaneously in the air.

'Yessss!' they shouted in unison, relieved and delighted finally to have got it right.

Gerald stood looking at them, speechless, his mouth opening and closing silently. Failing to hide his astonishment, he finally blurted: 'Perfect ... Perfect.'

Lowering their arms, they all grinned at each other, ready for the next move. 'Well, you should have said,' Dave commented.

The rehearsals continued apace and very gradually the men started to get the hang of what was required of them. The constant pounding of the music, Gerald's bullying instructions – often shouted at them above the bass beat – and the physical manoeuvres they were forced to repeat over and over again until it almost became as natural as walking, began to have the desired effect. They found themselves humming the tunes constantly in their heads, twitching in their dreams at night in time to the beat, practising their footwork in the bathroom, while sitting on the toilet or waiting for a bus.

Although none of them said anything, each one of them secretly began to anticipate the rehearsals, looking forward to going over the old routines, or moving on to new ones. There was a new spring in their step, something to think about other than being on the dole, and a sense of taking some control of their lives. Without realising it, they were each growing in confidence and stature, dancing their way out of their troubles.

Gaz, the glue that held them all together, put himself through his paces night after night alone in his council flat. Occasionally racked by secret insecurities about his project, he dared not let the others down. To his own amazement, he found himself wanting to please Gerald, to get it right for him in a way that he had never done when he was working under him in the factory.

Lomper, desperate not to get the sack, improved his performance dramatically by practising secretly in his office at night. He fended off his ailing mother's ever-probing questions about where he was and what he was doing by claiming he was putting in extra practice at the brass band. She had always been tremendously proud of his cornet playing.

Dave, no longer bothering to pretend that he wasn't a fully fledged member of the troupe, was on his strictest diet ever – jacket potatoes and baked beans – although that had its own consequences that were not quite so popular with Jean or the others in the troupe. He kept the recording of *Flashdance* at his home and watched it over and over again while Jean was at work, willing himself to acquire some of the dancers' natural skills, to somehow meld mentally with Jennifer Beales while she performed a triple back double flip followed by the splits.

Guy and Horse met secretly and took to hanging around a video store in the city centre, watching every famous dance sequence on celluloid, thanks to Horse's helpful niece, Beryl, who worked behind the counter. Unfortunately, that had to stop when the manager complained that if he saw

Singin' in the Rain on the screens one more time, Beryl would lose her job.

Gerald, his patience tested to the limits with his keen if uncoordinated pupils, found himself reading up on dance techniques and borrowed several 'Teach Yourself' books from the library. He lost weight and built up muscle tone in his quest for perfection. Well, he had to set a good example and he felt full of life for the first time in months. Linda was surprised and delighted by his renewed interest in her sexually, although she did find his nightly demands a little taxing, and resorted to claiming she was suffering from migraines again.

Growing ever more comfortable with each other, making friends and finding common bonds, the unlikely group of men started to meet each other away from the steelworks and their makeshift dance hall. Guy suggested a few of them meet socially on the odd occasion they had enough money to go down the pub, or just play football in the park. The others jumped at the chance, especially Lomper. All of them stopped going to the Job Club. There really wasn't any point.

One Wednesday afternoon, Gerald even agreed to the lads coming round to his house, after Gaz insisted that they needed to meet somewhere private to discuss the next stage in their master plan. Gerald's house was the only option, Gaz insisted, as Jean was on night shift that week and home in the day, Lomper's mum was house-bound, Horse's one-room flat was too small, Guy's shared house too busy, and his own was too cold.

Gerald finally caved in, as Gaz knew he would, although when he unlocked the front door at the appointed time and waved them in, to stop them sniggering at his gnomes and the large ceramic butterflies on the exterior of his bungalow wall, he did briefly wonder at his decision.

'Come on, get in quick,' he told them as they stood, five-abreast, on his doorstep. 'And wipe your boots.' They traipsed in one by one, careful not to leave any mud on the deep, cream, shag-pile carpet as Gerald ushered them through into the sitting room.

It was just as Gaz expected, all pink and frilly and spotlessly clean. Even though Linda only had a part-time job in a city centre boutique, she still kept her cleaning lady on – for appearances' sake more than anything – although she always cleaned the house herself from top to bottom both before the woman arrived and immediately after she left, a fact which exasperated Gerald. Fastidious to the point of being obsessive, Linda had recreated the sitting room from one she had seen in a *Sunday Mirror* magazine, complete with chrome and smoked glass coffee table and a log-effect gas fire.

She was very particular about where her precious ornaments and home furnishing accoutrements were placed, and as the five men wandered in and looked around them awkwardly now, they realised with sympathy that Gerald's wife must be an extremely fussy woman.

Lomper settled happily into an armchair with a copy of *Country Living*, while Guy and Horse sat opposite him, feeling decidedly out of place in such a setting. Gaz examined the drinks cabinet with its fancy soda siphon and cut crystal decanters on a gilt trolley placed directly under a huge and hideous abstract oil Linda had painted herself at night school art classes.

Picking up a delicate china figurine of a ballet dancer from the mantelpiece, Dave held it up to the others and looked at it with contempt. When Gerald followed them in and saw one of Linda's most prized ornaments in Dave's cumbersome grip, he cried: 'Hey, put that back, you'll break it,' and watched anxiously as the big man's hand replaced it with a thud. Gerald would have to check its position later. Linda would know if it had been moved a millimetre.

'I'm just looking,' Dave whined. Turning to Guy, he said: 'Bit posh, innit?' stroking the pink velour suite and glancing self-consciously all around him. Guy sniggered at the sight of

Dave in such a room, his hand clamped to his mouth, and quickly started Lomper off too.

Gaz decided to bring them back down to earth with a bump. Putting down the soda siphon and stepping into the middle of the room suddenly, rubbing his hands together expectantly, he looked around at them all. 'Right then,' he announced. They all looked up at him. 'Are we right?' he asked.

'Right for what?' asked Horse, an uneasy feeling in the pit of his stomach.

'Taking us kit off,' Gaz said with a nod of his head, as if it were nothing more unusual than having a cup of coffee.

As Gerald's face fell, Dave looked equally aghast at being so duped. Both men realised that Gaz had got them here under false pretences. 'Thought you were turning me into a fancy dancer,' Dave said moodily. He hated the idea of stripping in front of the others more than any of them.

Gaz was getting fed up with the lot of them. He'd brought them this far, they were getting the hang of the dancing, but that wasn't the point and he was worried in case they'd forgotten that. 'Listen, ladies,' he said, sarcastically. 'We are strippers, aren't we?' He peeled off his jacket and threw it on the back of the armchair.

Gerald, his hands fumbling with his wedding ring, stammered: 'What? Here? Now? ... In this house?' If he'd known what Gaz had in mind when he said he needed somewhere private, he'd never have agreed to it. He looked over to the bay window with its heavy net curtains and wondered if he should draw the main curtains.

Gaz, unbuttoning his shirt, nodded and glared at the others, daring them not to do the same. They had all known what they were getting into when they started, and now was the time to face the music.

'This is a good area, this is ...' Gerald began again, his expression hopeful but knowing that he'd already lost the argument. He'd come to know Gaz pretty well over the past week or so and he knew that when he set his mind to

117

something, there was no turning back.

Dave, squashed up against the fireplace, cocked his head to one side and looked up miserably. 'Gaz …' he pleaded, hands in his jeans pockets. 'I dunno …'

But Gaz was having none of it. Slipping his shirt from his shoulder to reveal a grubby grey T-shirt, he rounded on them angrily. 'If we can't get us kit off in front of ourselves, what chance have we got in front of all them lasses?' he asked, flexing his wiry frame. There was a pregnant pause before he added, forcefully: 'Tops off!'

As the rest of them looked at him and then each other warily, he beckoned them with his hands and insisted: 'Come on!' There was no question of refusal.

Guy was the first on his feet and, with a shy smile, he quickly removed his denim jacket before starting on his shirt. Dave, down in the mouth, watched Horse and Lomper do the same. Gerald, who looked as if he might be sick, slipped his blue blazer from his shoulders.

All eyes were averted as each man dealt with his own embarrassment and started to shed his clothing. Dave, the only one still fully clothed, realised that he couldn't possibly get out of it. Telling the others sulkily, 'Well, no looking – and no laughing, you bastards,' he reluctantly took off his jacket and started to untuck his T-shirt. He wished he'd worn his longer boxer shorts.

Gaz, topless now, stood guard as Lomper peeled off his anorak, and Horse, standing next to a pink plastic standard lamp in the shape of a bamboo tree, dropped his coat to the floor. Gerald, his woollen cardigan slipped off most unwillingly, stood next to Gaz, his face like thunder. 'I used to have a proper job, me,' he said, unbuttoning his shirt.

Lomper, hesitant in the middle of the room and struggling to pull his Marks & Spencer's patterned sweater over his head, looked around him. 'I ask you, what are we doing?' he complained. 'What are we doing?' But he carried on taking off his shirt and vest, as the others did the same.

Soon, all six men stood topless, facing each other silently.

Everyone stared at everyone else, shyly at first, but then openly assessing each other's bodies. Guy's physique was the most impressive, his pectorals very pronounced, and even Horse looked good for his age. Gerald, tanned and lithe, held his stomach in, and Lomper, white as white, underlit with blue veins, was surprisingly flabby on his chest. Dave, his rolls of fat forming a thick canopy over his belt, looked around him guiltily, his arms folded high across his hairy chest, wishing that he'd taken that security job.

'And the kegs,' Gaz said, suddenly breaking the silence, nodding at their trousers. He lifted his leg to remove his shoes.

All five men took a deep breath, but no one dared argue. Dave, eyebrows raised, reached down and undid his shoe laces, a complaining expression on his face. Gerald, his eyes closed for the shame of it, undid his belt too. Guy whipped his jeans off as smoothly as he had done before and stood to attention in tight green underpants as they all took another peek at his impressive bulge.

Gaz, the second to be undressed, studied the others critically. He was wearing bog-standard white boxer-shorts, but, to his left Horse, his trousers round his knees, stood up to reveal the most extraordinarily baggy white long johns, all the way down to his ankles. The bulge in the groin area was so insignificant it could hardly be seen at all. To a man they stared openly at him.

'Horse by name, horse by nature, eh, Horse?' Gaz teased, his eyebrows arched.

'Oh, shut it, you!' Horse spat, mortified that his secret was out.

Lomper, in turquoise ribbed boxer shorts and black socks, stood shyly in the middle of the room, his hands across his chest to hide his nipples, but nobody was looking. They were too busy studying Gerald in his Y-fronts. 'Hey, how come you're so brown any road?' asked Guy.

'No reason,' Gerald said, defensively, his eyes lying.

Guy beamed at him knowingly. 'Someone's got a sun-bed,

haven't they, Gerald?' he sang. The others looked up hopefully at the suggestion.

Gerald bristled visibly. 'It's Linda's, and no you bloody can't,' he retorted, through clenched teeth. 'And don't even think of asking.' Guy beamed at him, regardless.

Dave, silent in the middle of the room in his green boxer shorts, looking around at the rest of them, felt even more wretched. 'What am I gonna do about this?' he asked no one in particular, stroking his huge belly.

Gaz eyed it experimentally in profile as the rest of them considered it from all angles. 'Well, it's not too bad,' he said, leaning forward. 'From the front, like.'

Gerald, remembering something Linda was always going on about, put his hands on his hips, straightened his neck and proclaimed with tremendous gravitas: 'Fat, David, is a feminist issue.'

They all looked across at him in amazement. Dave finally spoke for all of them. 'And what's that supposed to mean, when it's at home?'

Taken aback slightly, Gerald shrugged and said: 'I don't bloody know, do I? ... But it is!' All but Dave smiled.

Dave, still studying his bloated gut, whimpered: 'I try dieting.' There was silence as they all looked down at his stomach with scepticism. 'I do try,' he added. 'Seems I've spent most of my fuckin' life on a diet.' Glancing around at his colleagues, he explained: 'The less I eat, the fatter I get.'

Lomper, a beanpole by comparison, his hands flat on the small of his back which had the effect of forcing his stomach out, piped up: 'So stuff yourself and get thin.'

Feeling sorry for the big man, Guy told the redhead: 'Oh, shut up, saggy tits!'

Lomper, pulling on his nipples to raise his non-existent pectorals, complained: 'They're not!' and examined himself critically for the first time, as Gaz and Horse studied their own chests to see if they could be classed as sagging.

Gerald, still stinging from his recent embarrassment, offered another of Linda's words of wisdom. 'This mate of

Linda's had this plastic stuff put on her at this posh health club,' he said, demonstrating a wrapping technique with his hands as they all listened, interested. 'And she lost stones, it were like magic. It, oh, what's it called now?' he said, trying to think of the technique. 'Anyway, it's like, er, cling film,' he concluded.

Gaz concurred with a nod. 'I've heard of that,' he said, trying to be supportive. He remembered reading about it in some women's magazine in the dentist once – clear plastic film wrapped in layers round and round the body to make the skin sweat and so reduce the fat.

'Cling film?' Dave cried, outraged. 'I'm not a chicken drumstick, Gerald!'

The six of them fell into a general chatter about the various slimming techniques they'd heard of and which ones might help Dave. Just as Gerald was about to offer some more pearls of wisdom, the doorbell rang, its musical notes chiming throughout the house. All the blood drained from his face as he stood in just his underpants and socks in his living room with five virtually naked men, on a wet Wednesday afternoon.

'You can't just take stuff,' Gerald said angrily, as two strapping blokes in black leather jackets pushed into his empty living room and pointed to the gleaming new television. The owner of the hire purchase company had called in the loan on Gerald and had sent his 'boys' to repossess a few items.

'Sorry, mate,' the burliest of the two men said, unplugging the video and manhandling the television off the side table while Gerald buttoned up his shirt.

'But I only owe him a hundred and twenty quid,' Gerald complained, doing up the last button. He was indignant. He'd spoken to their boss the previous week, promising to settle his account soon, and now this. What if Linda had been home?

'Aye, that's all these'll fetch, secondhand,' one of the

leather-clad bruisers answered with a wry smile, heaving the full-size television into his arms.

'They're not secondhand,' Gerald retorted, outraged. He'd paid good money for them less than a year ago. They'd hardly been used. Linda was always out, spending, and he had only started regularly watching television recently with his new-found interest in sport.

'They are now, mate,' said the larger man, a smirk on his face, helping to lift the television towards the door. He was pleased there was no real resistance from the owner, as there often was in situations like this. At this rate, they'd be out of here in no time and down the pub just in time for opening.

Glancing up, however, the smile dropped from his mouth, and his eyes widened to saucers. Standing in front of them, a few paces behind their intended victim, Dave, Horse, Lomper, Gaz and Guy – still stripped down to their underpants – looked as menacing as anything the two men had seen in their long history of repossession work. They stopped mid-stride and stared up at them in terror.

'Put down and piss off,' Dave said gruffly, standing at the front of the pack, his huge arms held at his side like a gunfighter ready to fire as he took one pace closer to them.

'Fuckin' hell!' cried the younger of the men, hurriedly depositing his end of the television and heading for the door.

The other did likewise, never taking his eyes off the big man in case he made a grab for him as he shuffled past him sideways. 'Er, I think there's been a mistake,' he stammered, a bead of sweat trickling down his cheek. 'We'll just check with the office.' Reversing at speed, the two men were gone, out through the doorway like greased lightning. The front door slammed behind them. They'd seen the male rape scene from the film *Pulp Fiction* and they weren't hanging around to find out if these boys had too.

Gerald beamed a wide grin at his protégés, his shirt tails flapping. 'Cheers, lads,' he said, as the rest of the gang stood around big Dave and patted him on the shoulder.

Smiling warmly back at them, Dave looked dead chuffed.

'Hey, it's not bad this stripping lark, is it?' he said, as they all burst into uncontrollable fits of laughter.

With Horse translating Gerald's complicated dance instructions into common football terminology, the gang progressed remarkably and really started to cook. Every day they awoke in their respective beds, feeling excited about the hours ahead. Meeting in the middle of town, they'd march up the street towards the steelworks together six-abreast, feeling glad to be alive for the first time in ages. Nathan, too, shared their excitement, skipping off school with his father's approval, to help stop and start the music, watching their transition from caterpillars to butterflies with satisfaction.

Gerald returned all the Teach Yourself dance books to the library and swapped them for football manuals. He started watching Premiere League games on the salvaged television for the first time – much to Linda's consternation – taking notes about the tactics used so that he could turn them to his advantage.

Very gradually, this group of men, many of whom hardly knew each other and who might otherwise never have met or had anything in common apart from losing their jobs, started working together as a team, forging bonds of friendship and loyalty forgotten since the days of full employment. On the dole, it was every man for himself and don't let the buggers see you down. Now, they began helping each other out, offering advice and encouragement when one of them couldn't get something right; praising each other heartily when they could. Although they didn't realise it, they were regaining their lost self-esteem and reinventing themselves in a world where roles had shifted and deeply-held beliefs had been overturned.

Gaz, the man who had lit the fuse and was watching it burn, felt the changes in himself too, although he didn't really understand them. He had never suspected when he started on this crazy scheme that there would be so many beneficial side-effects. The most surprising of all was his improved relationship with Nathan, as the boy proudly watched his father struggling manfully with tricky dance steps and stripping manoeuvres, knowing that he was only doing it for him. There were no more complaints about wanting to do 'normal' things, or Gaz's flat being too cold. It seemed the lad wanted to spend as much time with his father as possible, making up for the lost years of his earlier childhood. Gaz didn't really understand what had brought on this change, but he was extremely grateful for it.

Back at the rolling mill's makeshift dance floor once again, Nathan watched his father, heart in his mouth, as he sat poised to turn the music off. With Gerald standing in front of them, giving them every encouragement, the men were tentatively going through the entire dance routine they had just finished learning. Gaz, far left in the line-up, was concentrating so hard his tongue was rolling around inside his cheek. Music reverberated around the mill, and the men reached the finale with a single movement that did, indeed, resemble a football line-up. Gerald was very pleased.

Taking a break for a cigarette, Gaz sat down near Nathan and watched as Gerald joined the line-up to take the rest of them through their paces to the tune of *The Stripper*. Their dance teacher was undoubtedly the most co-ordinated of the lot, Gaz realised, as he watched the oldest of them lead the others by example.

'Dave and Lomps up the wing,' Gerald was saying. 'One, two, three, four … Left touch line, three, four … Right touch line, three four … Offside trap. One, two, three, four.' The music pulsed through the room and the men kept good time, forming a perfectly straight line at the front.

Gaz drew on his cigarette and reached across to the pile of security guard outfits that Lomper had 'liberated' for them. As Lomper was busy concentrating on his steps, Gaz picked up one pair of trousers and ripped them right the way down the side seam, closely examining the stitching.

Gerald knew the hard part was coming up. 'Now the belt … ' he encouraged, '… three, four …' he shouted. With a flourish, he whipped his belt from his trousers in a single movement, slapping Guy, to his right, smartly in the face with a loud smack. Guy, his hands to his head, groaned and fell backwards.

Gerald, unaware of the injury he had caused, carried on regardless, calling out his instructions as Gaz and Nathan watched the whole thing fall apart in front of their eyes. 'Now the shoes, three, four ...' Gerald called, hopping on one foot as he, Lomper, Horse and Dave pogo'd around on one leg, trying to take off their shoes with one hand at the same time as somehow keeping in line. Guy, his hand still clutched to his face, attempted to remove one of his trainers, but, his sight impaired, he lost his balance and fell against Gerald.

Undaunted by the complete disarray, Gerald continued bellowing his instructions above the rousing music: 'Now the socks ...'

But Horse hadn't even got his left shoe off yet. 'Hang on, hang on,' he called above the music, half-leaning over a doubled-up Dave. 'Hang on, I can't get me ...' He rocked unsteadily on one leg, trying to undo his laces. Gaz shook his head with a smile and ripped open another trouser seam.

'Three, four ... Carry on ...' Gerald urged.

Dave tugged insistently at a reluctant sock, but at that moment Horse crashed into him, knocking him sideways. Dave stomped back on Horse's foot, Lomper fell flat on his back and Guy staggered towards the wall, still rubbing his injured eye, wondering how he was supposed to dance half-blinded.

Nathan, shaking his head, pressed the Stop button to end their pain. 'That were crap,' he announced, his expression comical. He was fast becoming their biggest critic.

Gerald, unused to being chastised, spoke for them all, as he looked around for his left shoe. 'Well, give us a chance,' he said. 'I bet even Madonna has difficulty getting her shoes and socks off,' although he wasn't sure she ever wore any.

Guy, still staggering around and in some pain, yelled at

125

Gerald: 'You could've had me eye out!' He couldn't see out of his right eye at all for the tears coursing down his cheeks.

Gerald was contrite. 'I'm sorry, aren't I?' he said, without much humility.

Lomper, looking up from his position on the floor, suddenly noticed that Gaz had ripped his uniforms to shreds. Indignant, he got to his feet and rushed at him. 'Hey what are you doing with them, you great bugger?' he asked, his face reddening, his fingers outstretched. 'They're bloody borrowed, them.' There'd be hell to pay if his supervisor ever found out he'd 'liberated' the uniforms from the old stores. Gaz had promised him they'd be returned in exactly the same condition when they'd finished.

Gaz, a roll-up stuck to his bottom lip, the smoke from it closing one of his eyes, explained patiently: 'We can use them for the show. It's what them Chippendales do.' The brief image he had in his mind of the American dancers was of them on stage at the working men's club dressed in what he guessed were US firemen's uniforms, all polished buttons and crisp blue serge. Horse, Dave, Gerald and Guy, still redressing themselves, stopped what they were doing to listen.

Pointing to the split seams and holding them together in his hands, Gaz added: 'They put Velcro down the side, and then ...' he separated the seams with a flourish, '... all is revealed.' Seeing that Lomper was far from satisfied with the explanation, he promised: 'I'll sew 'em back up after.'

Lomper was unimpressed. 'Oh aye,' he scoffed, 'and where did you learn to be an ace sewer then?' He could just imagine the state they'd be returned in if some clumsy bloke was in charge of the stitching.

Before Gaz could answer or come up with a reasonable excuse, Nathan responded for him. 'Prison,' the boy said matter-of-factly. He didn't realise the full import of what he had said until there was an awkward silence and those in the room who had no idea that Gaz had ever served time exchanged silent glances.

Gaz, looking up with a sigh, threw the trousers to the floor and nodded his head at them all as an admission of guilt. Okay, his secret was out. It wasn't the end of the world, although he'd much rather people didn't know about his shady past, least of all people like Gerald. Information like that could seriously undermine his authority, especially when it came to the crunch and he needed them to believe in him.

'Cheers, Nathe,' Gaz said sarcastically, inhaling on his cigarette. The boy bit his lip and wished he'd kept his mouth shut.

CHAPTER SEVEN

Alan Rotherfield had known Gary 'Gaz' Schofield since they were young kids and he had saved the younger and much wilder boy from a bloody-nosed punch-up in the school playground. If Alan hadn't intervened then the scrap of a boy from the rough side of the city would have been pulverised by a gang of older boys who were after the few coins he had been given for his lunch money.

Even after he'd pulled the battered Gaz out from under the rugby scrum of kicking feet and arms, the boy was decidedly ungrateful. He'd sworn at Alan for intervening, claiming he could fight his own battles. Alan didn't doubt for one minute that this angry young lad could, but at six against one, the odds had been a bit too highly stacked against him.

In all the years since, Gaz had never once thanked Alan, or even mentioned the incident again. But the blunt Yorkshireman knew that it was there somewhere between them, a thin thread of camaraderie that meant neither one would ever do anything willingly to harm the other. They had certainly never been best mates – Dave Horsfall had been the closest Gaz would ever get to that – but they'd grown up together, shared more than a few drunken nights, and had a common bond. Or so Gaz thought.

Now the gnarled-faced manager of the Millthorpe Working Men's Club, Alan had led a full and varied life. He had worked his way through four wives, a £20,000 bingo win and two drink-driving bans. He'd fled England for Spain for a while to run an English pub in Marbella, had spent time inside for fencing stolen goods, had six children from his various marriages, and was currently shacked up with Patsy, a former hooker and part-time stripagram.

But, despite a past as chequered as a Grand Prix flag, he was a stickler when it came to procedure. These days he did everything strictly by the book. Times were too hard for favours, which was exactly why – friendship or no friendship – he was not going to let his club out to that wild-card Gaz without a hefty down-payment first.

'Oh, come on, Al, it's me,' Gaz remonstrated, Nathan at his side, as the pair of them watched the bald-headed manager systematically unloading crate after crate of beer in through the back door of the red-painted club. Gaz had just collected Nathan from school and persuaded him to accompany him to see Alan in the hope that the boy's presence would soften the club manager. But to no avail.

'Which is precisely why it's a hundred quid up front ... half price,' Alan's throaty voice called from the back of the open-sided lorry. Stepping down with yet another crate of beer, his multicoloured shirt unbuttoned to the waist, he explained: 'If I give you club for nowt, you don't turn up ...' he placed one crate on top of the other onto a metal trolley and dusted his hands off, '... or come back on your word, I'm left with an empty club on a Friday night.' He gave Gaz a look which said he was hard up enough without losing business like that.

Gone were the golden days of working men's clubs in cities like Sheffield; when there was one on every corner and you had to queue at the door to get in of a weekend. Alan's father, from whom he inherited the job, used to clear over a thousand quid a night in the 70s, and that was when a thousand quid was a lot of money. He and his staff couldn't pull the pints fast enough, while the punters were still lined up at the door.

Nowadays, he'd be happy if he made five hundred a week. There was far too much competition from the city's discos, swanky nightclubs and rave warehouses for his liking. The club, which had been the beating heart of the steel community, was deserted most nights – apart from the odd

Darby and Joan meeting, bingo leagues and occasional visits by the likes of the Chippendales or the sensual men and women dancers in the Ann Summers Roadshow.

Despite the club's long-established name (reduced to the initials WMC on the billboard outside), most of Alan's customers these days were women – the blue rinse variety at that – and they weren't big spenders. He knew several old dears who could make a glass of dry sherry last a fortnight. There weren't enough working men left around Millthorpe even to pay his electricity bill, let alone finance their own club.

The establishment had suffered as a result. It was in desperate need of a makeover, a lick of paint for starters. The sound and lighting systems wouldn't have looked out of place in a museum, they were so antiquated, and the 'special effects' were confined to a huge mirror ball hanging from the ceiling with dozens of its little glass tiles missing, and some fancy scalloped gold curtains that Patsy had brought home from a closing down sale at one of her strip clubs.

Alan had no idea what Gaz wanted the place for – he wouldn't tell him – but he knew the lad of old and he didn't trust him to bring in the minimum number of customers he'd need before shutting the club to non-ticket holders on a Friday night. Shaking his head at him, his gold medallions jangling on his hairy chest, he stood firm.

'Well of course we'll turn up,' Gaz whined pathetically. 'I haven't got hundred quid.'

Seeing the pleading look on his face, Alan softened slightly. 'Well, if you tell me what you're up to, it might help,' he said, glancing at his fake gold Rolex before stopping for a moment and raising his right eyebrow at Gaz quizzically.

Gaz and Nathan looked at each other and shook their heads. 'I can't,' Gaz said. 'It's top secret.' They'd already decided not to tell Alan, just to fly post the area and wait for their salivating audience to arrive in their droves waving tenners. Gaz was sure Alan wouldn't let him have the club if he really knew what he was up to and he wouldn't really blame him.

Hurt at not being trusted enough to be let in on the secret, Alan straightened his back and lifted an empty beer barrel into the back of the van. 'Sorry, kid,' he said, shaking his head once more and walking off towards the cellar. His shining bald pate was the last thing they saw disappearing down the steps.

Gaz was desperate. He didn't know who else to turn to. He'd thought it out every way, but he still couldn't think of any other method of getting the money he needed to book the club. Reluctant as he was to go down this particular path, knowing the risks involved, he felt he had no other choice. Besides, Nathan had assured him it would be all right.

Pulling open the door to the clothing factory, he took a deep breath and stepped inside, his son hard on his heels. Climbing the stairs to the first floor assembly line, they looked feebly around at the scores of female machinists working at their tables, sewing ready-cut bits of cloth inside bras for linings, making up skimpy T-shirts and fixing string straps to summer dresses.

Not one of them looked up when the two strangers walked in and started playing around with a huge reel of string, unravelling it and wrapping Nathan up like an Egyptian mummy. They were all too engrossed in their work, chewing gum furiously and listening to the local Hallam FM blasting out through loud speakers to drown the dreadful din of the whirring machines.

Mandy spotted the pair of them from her glass box of an office, and hurried across the shop floor, clipboard in hand, wondering what they could want. Nathan should be at her house doing his homework by now, having let himself in with his key and made himself something to eat. Gaz wasn't even meant to see him until Saturday. He really was the limit.

With a loving smile for her son, Mandy called out: 'All right, love,' as the boy quickly unravelled himself from the rope. Mandy stroked her son's hair affectionately.

'Hi, Mum,' the boy said, flashing her a cheeky smile. He seemed so happy she decided against bringing up the subject of his homework and why Gaz had, once again, extended his visiting rights to the boy on a whim.

Turning to her ex-husband, Mandy's voice hardened. 'What d'you want?' she asked, her arms clasping her clipboard to her blue woollen cardigan defensively.

'All right, Mand?' Gaz grinned, hands flapping, wondering how to begin. He looked drunk or intoxicated with something, she didn't know what. She stared at him silently. 'I'm gonna get you all your money … our money,' he began, beaming at her, before nodding at his son and correcting himself: 'Nathan's.'

She saw the same strangely exhilarated look on her son's face as he nodded his agreement at his mother. Mandy stood watching and waiting. She knew Gaz wouldn't dare darken the doors of the factory unless he really wanted something.

'Well, you, you know …' Gaz stammered, losing faith rapidly under his ex-wife's icy stare, '… for … for definite this time.' His head bobbed up and down so vigorously, she thought it might drop off.

Mandy closed her eyes and flicked back her head. 'Yeah right,' she said. She'd heard it all before. In fact she'd been listening to Gaz talk like this for most of her life, and where had it got her, him or Nathan. Nowhere. 'That all?' she asked. Her tone was brusque, her chin tilted up, still waiting and wondering what he had really come for.

Gaz nodded back. 'Yeah, yeah,' he said, deeply uncomfortable and wishing he could vanish into thin air. Nathan glowered at him and thumped him on the arm. It had taken the boy ages to persuade his father to come here; he wasn't going to let him back down now. 'Well, no, er …' Gaz started again, still fumbling for words. With a sudden flash of inspiration a maxim from one of the posters at the Job Club leapt into his head. 'The thing is, Mand,' he explained, 'you have to speculate to accumulate … In business, like.' Nathan took a step closer to his father to provide moral support.

Mandy's mouth opened slightly and she almost stepped back with the realisation of what he was asking. 'Oh, I'm not sure I'm hearing this,' she said, her eyes narrowing to slits.

Gaz held up his hand to reassure her. 'I'm gonna get you the whole lot,' he promised, moving closer as she backed away. Holding out his hand and pinching his forefinger and thumb together to demonstrate his point, he added: 'I just need a tiny little bit.'

Mandy, her cheeks burning, glared at him. 'You want some money?' she asked, utterly amazed at his nerve. She'd been subbing him all these years and now, even now, he wanted more?

Gaz clicked his fingers together and pointed at her, as if she'd hit the nail right on the head. 'Yeah!' he said, still beaming, willing her to agree. Nathan had the self-same stupid expression on his face.

Mandy eyed the two of them in amazement and set her jaw. 'Right, I need someone in packing section,' she said, eyeing Gaz defiantly. 'Two fifty an hour. You can start now if you like.' She stood facing the pair of them, calling their bluff, ready to lead Gaz to the relevant section. 'Are you coming?' she asked.

Gaz and Nathan, the smiles wiped off their faces, stared blankly at her and then at each other. Gaz swallowed hard, his Adam's apple bobbing in his throat. The light disappeared from his eyes.

Stepping back towards the exit, Nathan reached up and grabbed his father's limp hand. 'Come on, Dad,' he said softly and pulled him towards the door.

Nathan had never been more determined in his life as he was later that afternoon when he asked his father to meet him in town, after he'd nipped home to get something. Mystified, Gaz had met him at the tram garage and followed him into the main shopping street, only to realise at the last minute what the boy had in mind.

'Nathe, Nathe!' Gaz called, following him through the glass doors and into the post office, minutes before it was due to close. 'You can't do this, kid,' he pleaded, 'it's your savings.'

But the twelve-year-old marched up to the counter determinedly and turned to face his father. 'I can. I just need your signature. It says in book.' He waved the account book at his father and the woman cashier behind the glass partition window. Sliding the book across the polished wooden counter, Nathan told the cashier: 'I'd like to take me money out, please.' But before she could take it, Gaz snatched it back and held it in his hand.

'Well you bloody well can't have it,' he said under his breath, twitching. To the perplexed cashier, waiting to lock up, he called back through the glass: 'You're all right, love, it's, it's sorted.'

Nathan snatched the book back and passed it under the glass partition once again. 'It's my money – I want it,' he insisted, his father's stubbornness in his eyes. To the cashier, he gave the instructions: 'A hundred pounds, please.' She opened her cash drawer in anticipation and studied the pair suspiciously.

Gaz squirmed. Nathan was right, it was his money, it had been accumulated over the years, ever since he was a baby. Gaz had sent him what he could when he could, although he'd had to bend over backwards proving to Mandy that none of it was from the proceeds of crime; Nathan's grandparents had given him the odd cheque at Christmas and birthdays; and he'd earned some money doing a paper round in the school holidays. Now he wanted it and, as soon as his dad signed for it, he could have it.

Gaz grabbed the book from the perplexed cashier's outstretched hand and tried to reason with his son. 'Well, when you're eighteen, you … you can walk in and get it yourself, can't you?' He didn't have much idea of right or wrong but holding the book to his chest in both hands, he felt instinctively that there was something terribly immoral about taking the money from the boy. He could just imagine what Mandy and Barry would have to say if they found out, and – with that thought – he gripped the book even tighter and blocked his son's path. The cashier sighed and looked at her watch.

Nathan was losing his patience. Snatching it from his father's hand, he told him accusingly: 'You said you'd get it back.' He stared up into the steelman's face silently, waiting for an answer.

Gaz scowled at him and shook his head. 'I know,' he admitted. 'But you don't want to listen to what I say.' It was a terrible admission to have to make, but he knew it was true, especially when it came to money. He gazed down at his son fondly, amazed that he had even listened to him.

Nathan blinked twice and peered up into his father's eyes, his innocence shining from him like a halo. 'You said so,' he said quietly. He paused. 'I believe you.'

Gaz's forehead crumpled into a frown. 'You do?' He felt his heart pounding in his chest and the sensation of raw emotion rising up through his stomach.

'Yeah,' the boy nodded, his simple faith written all over his face.

'Blimey, Nathe,' Gaz whispered, astonished and proud all at the same time. It was the first time anyone had shown any real faith in him since Mandy had said 'I do' at the Rotherham Registry Office nearly twenty years earlier. He felt now like he did then, overwhelmed by the love of another human being, a rare experience for him.

Smiling down at his son, genuinely moved, Gaz made himself a promise. Whatever it took, he would get Nathan his money back, and the maintenance arrears, so that the slate could be wiped clean. He knew he didn't deserve Nathan – he'd hardly even deserved Mandy and he'd lost her already. He was more determined than ever to prove himself to the lad, to live up to his high expectations and make him proud.

Standing to one side, his eyes misty, Gaz allowed the boy to push the account book under the glass partition for the final time. The cashier waited a few seconds before snatching it, hanging onto it this time in case they changed their minds again.

* * *

The days not spent rehearsing were to be filled with fitness training, football-style, in the local park high on a hill above Sheffield in an area incongruously called The Manor because it once was the site of a baronial manor house.

Gerald, now a football groupie, had seen footage of Glen Hoddle taking his England team through their paces – sit-ups, stretching, warm-ups, the lot – and the ex-foreman had decided that his lads' routine should be none the less taxing. He told them all to meet him at the park the following morning at nine o'clock for their first session.

Dressed in a previously unworn blue and white striped tracksuit that Linda had bought him four years ago, and with a whistle on a string he found in a local junk shop, he tracked back and forth down the line of puffing men, whistling and shouting encouraging instructions.

'Very good, one, two, three ... Come on, come on,' he yelled at Lomper, who – still wearing his grey anorak over trousers and a shirt – was struggling to complete five arm and leg scissor-jumps. Guy, superfit and lithe next to the redhead, was on his second set of twenty without hardly losing a breath. Horse and Dave jumped up and down next to him, puffing and rubbing their aching backs. Gerald joined in to show them how easily it could be done, although he found it a lot harder than he let on.

Next came the sit-ups. Dave, collapsed on the ground, his hands clutching his stomach, was breathless and blotchy after just two. Gerald knelt at Lomper's feet, urging him on as he managed five. 'Great ... and one for luck,' Gerald smiled as the young security guard pushed himself to the limits. Guy, on his tenth sit-up, laughed cruelly at the rest as they struggled on.

After a brief rest period, Gerald had them at it again; all lined up in a row this time, face down for twenty press-ups each. This time he joined the end of the line and found it just as gruelling as they did. Dave thought his heart would explode in his chest, Lomper felt sick but started to get the hang of it with Guy's help, and Horse worked through his hip pain to keep up with the rest. On the count of twenty, all five men flopped to the ground in perfect unison, in a horizontal offside trap line-up that Tony Adams would have been proud of.

The training over, the fun could begin, and after a quick swig of water or, in Lomper's case, a cup of sweet tea from his ubiquitous flask, they stood around in a huddle discussing their dance routines, and practising the odd step, giggling like schoolgirls on an outing. They wondered what Gaz could be up to. He'd said he was going into town to organise 'something vital' to their scheme, and they speculated what it could be. Dave was genuinely concerned; the way Gaz had been behaving lately, he was afraid to let him out of his sight. He knew he needed money and he feared he might have gone back to his bad old ways.

Refreshed after their break, the new sports addict among them suggested a knock-around game of football. Within minutes of Gerald throwing the ball onto the pitch, every one of them had forgotten the pain they had been in moments earlier, as they pushed and shoved, dribbled and kicked, tugging on each other's clothes and mercilessly disobeying the rules, the competitive spirit in each of them coming to the fore. Guy successfully tackled Lomper mid field and even Gerald scored a goal.

It was a brilliant afternoon; they hadn't enjoyed themselves so much in ages. The infectious communal gloom that had descended over them during their long days at the Job Club had rendered them incapable of even considering something as enlivening as an occasional game of football to brighten their lives. What was the point? had been their universal cry, as they slouched in their chairs, smoking their heads off and playing cards for matches.

Only now, with their new-found zeal, did they realise how flat their lives had previously been by contrast. Not only did they no longer work hard physically down at the steel works, they had stopped working their bodies in other ways too – at sports, riotous nights at the working men's club, even in bed with their wives and lovers. As they collapsed together in a sweaty heap at the end of their kick-around, their muscles twitching from the activity, the men caught their breath and reflected happily on what a difference the last few weeks had made.

Gaz hadn't wasted his afternoon. It was time to make plans, he had decided, and slipped off to visit to an old mate from prison who now worked at a city centre print shop and who would do him a nice little favour. By the time Gaz walked out of the shop two hours later, a box of specially printed paper tucked furtively under his arm, he was ready to push the lads that one step closer to the edge.

Even Dave was impressed with the name Gaz had come up with for the strip group – after finally rejecting his first idea – and the graphics of the posters Gaz had printed looked almost professional, having been laid-out by Nathan on the school's computer using its desk top publishing software. In bold black and white lettering, the posters read:

MALE STRIPPERS
PRESENT

HOT METAL

WE DARE TO BE BARE!

WOMEN ONLY
MILLTHORPE
WORKING MEN'S CLUB
FRIDAY MAY 25TH 8.00P.M.

Arming Gerald with a pot of paste and a brush, and Lomper with the posters, Gaz and his unlikely cohorts took to the streets and surreptitiously began sticking them up on every bus stop, post box, lamppost and corrugated iron fence they could find. Five hundred posters had been printed up for free, and five hundred posters, Gaz insisted, would be on display by the end of the afternoon. It wasn't like when he and Dave had delivered free newspapers, dropping a few through some letterboxes and tipping the rest into a skip. This was genuine.

It was less than a month since Gaz and Nathan had watched the Chippendales do their worst, and the intervening weeks had been filled with a great deal of hard work, determination and training. But now they were ready – or at least Gaz had insisted they were. They had to be, he'd booked the club, using Nathan's money. It had taken them a little longer than Gerald had promised, but then even he couldn't perform miracles. In ten days they were on.

Just as they had worked so hard at the rehearsing and training, with equal enthusiasm they took to their fly posting task, each one contributing in some small way. Gaz would choose the spot, Lomper would unpeel another poster from the roll, Horse would hold a corner here, Dave a corner there, while Gerald pasted it on and Guy provided the ultimate quality control. And as they stood back and admired their handiwork, the men tried to quell the butterflies in their stomachs and look forward to their big night with something like anticipation.

'It's not straight that, Lomps,' Guy said critically, tilting his head at an angle as Lomper haphazardly positioned yet another to the outside wall of a derelict pub, already thick with old posters. The others crowded around him to confer.

'Give over, it's only a poster,' Lomper countered moodily, but he nonetheless corrected his mistake and slid the poster back into position, as the rest nodded their approval.

Hearing giggling behind them, the men turned to see two local women, Sheryl and Louise, stomping towards them, arm in arm, high heeled and dangerous. 'Christ all bloody mighty,' Gaz exhaled at the sight of the two women, both of whom he was ashamed to admit he'd known carnally over the years.

Standing a few paces behind him, and feeling suddenly

defensive, the group shuffled together to cover up the still-dripping poster on the wall. Greeting the women jauntily, Gaz called: 'All right, sweethearts?' although he and Dave had already mentally awarded them only two out of ten and neither would ever fall into the category of their sweethearts.

'Gary the Lad,' Sheryl said flirtatiously with her nasal twang and a flicker of her pencilled-in eyebrows, stopping a few feet in front of them. Her mouth full of gum, her shoulder length blonde hair hooked back over her ears, she winked at the man she'd once shagged behind the gymnasium changing rooms at school, and several drunken times since. 'What are you up to then, Shifty?' She was a sight in her shiny jungle-print leggings and bright orange stilettos.

Gaz, hands stuffed in his pockets, looking as cheeky as hell, ducked and dived with his shoulders as he answered rhythmically: 'Bit of this – bit of that – bit of the other.'

Smelling a rat, Sheryl's eyes narrowed. 'M-mm,' she responded. Louise, her red hair fresh out of a bottle, her huge silver earrings dangling on the shoulders of her mauve denim jacket, reached forward and snatched a rolled-up poster from Lomper's trembling hand. The two women unfurled it and eyed it archly, their jaws almost dropping to their well-endowed chests.

'Ah, just a bit of advertising for some mates,' Gaz faltered.

'Oh, aye,' Sheryl winked, not buying that for a second, her elbow leaning on Louise's shoulder. 'And, er, who's gonna come and see *your* mates.' She laid special emphasis on the final two words, making it clear that she wasn't fooled for one minute. Serious now and reminding Gaz of the competition he was up against, she added: 'We had the real thing up here the other day, you know.'

Gaz, the gauntlet thrown down, reached for it foolishly. 'Well, *us* mates are better,' he bragged, his head swaggering on his shoulders, his tongue in his cheek.

The two women glanced around critically at the motley crew behind Gaz. Recalling the sight of the oiled-up hunks they'd thrown their knickers at the previous month, they chuckled openly, tickled by the suggestion. 'Better?' Louise asked, her jaw chewing gum eighteen to the dozen. 'How's that then?'

Gaz, his mouth flapping furiously as he searched for inspiration, shrugged his shoulders and stuttered: 'W-well ...' as the two women waited, staring him out. Suddenly finding his voice, he announced: 'Well, this lot go all the way.' His expression was triumphant.

Gerald, at the back, nearly swallowed his tongue. 'Stark naked?' he asked, incredulously.

Half-turning to his colleagues for reassurance, Gaz said: 'Don't they, lads?' but he turned back to the women quickly before they could answer.

Sheryl couldn't believe her ears. Mouth agape, she blinked at Gaz. 'The full monty? You lot!?' Louise bayed loudly at her side. Gaz nodded proudly as the men behind him looked aghast. 'Hellfire! That would be worth a look,' Sheryl agreed. Tottering off on her six-inch heels, Louise clamped to her side, still laughing, she called: 'See you there then.'

Louise added: 'Ta-ra,' before erupting once more into an explosion of laughter.

As Gaz watched them disappear down the hill, he froze to the spot, hardly able to bear to turn and face his colleagues, knowing what they would be thinking. Suspecting that at that very moment they were probably advancing on him to a man, murderous expressions on their faces, he tried to sound conciliatory. 'Keep your hair on,' he called, before turning round to face them. Sure enough, their faces were like thunder.

Dave's lips were pursed, his voice clipped. 'No way. No and never, in that order, kid,' he said, as the others nodded angrily.

Horse, who was trying to hang on to what little dignity he had left, pushed forward crossly. 'Excuse me,' he raged, his hand pointing to Gaz and then himself. 'No one said anything to me about the full monty.'

Gerald, Lomper and Guy crowded in around him.

Gaz shrugged his shoulders helplessly. 'Well you heard 'em,' he reasoned, his tone pleading. 'We've gotta give 'em summat your average ten bob stripper don't.'

Horse, finally admitting what was really bothering him, looked around him furtively and blurted out: 'Yeah, but – me willy. I mean to say.'

Lomper interrupted, his voice two octaves higher than normal. '*Your* willy?' he exclaimed, his freckles reddening. '*My* willy!'

Guy, standing behind him, listened to all these frightened men and tried not to laugh. At least he'd have something to be proud of.

Gerald, recovering himself at the back, shook his head slowly from side to side. 'A laughing stock. Totally,' he warned Gaz, the sudden realisation of what he had got involved in dawning on him.

Gaz continued to argue his point. 'Well, they're coming, aren't they?' he indicated to the two tarts still chuckling audibly down the street.

'Aye, with a pair of scissors,' Lomper offered dolefully. Looking up, he added: 'They know it's us, you know.' He wondered what his mother would have to say if she ever found out.

Gaz nodded. 'Yeah and by closing time every bugger in Sheffield's gonna know it's us, whether we do it or whether we don't.' Gerald and Dave paled, the visions of their respective wives finding out chilling their blood.

Gaz wasn't finished. Adopting his most persuasive tone, he reminded them curtly: 'We can either forget it, go back to the fuckin' Job Club, or do it and just maybe get rich.' The mention of the Job Club silenced them all. Gaz nodded for emphasis. 'And I tell ya … folks don't laugh so loud when you've a grand in your back pocket.' He stood defiantly in the face of the improbable strippers he'd somehow roped into his foolhardy scheme three weeks earlier.

'Now are you in, or are you out?' he demanded as a final

punch-line, throwing his shoulders forward with the challenge. It was ultimatum time.

For three days, the gang mulled over what Gaz had said. For three days and three long nights. Each had a long list of reasons for packing it all in and each had all but decided to throw in the towel. First and foremost, there was the ignominy – much more of a factor for those whose wives and families knew nothing about it, than for the others.

For the rest the personal embarrassment factor was the one that kept them in a cold sweat at night – Horse with his less than generous attributes, Dave with his unsightly flab, Lomper with his puny body and saggy tits. Only Guy and Gaz didn't give a toss about either factor. They were both good-looking fellas, young, free and single, in it purely for the money. Or so they thought, until they realised how much they had come to rely on the camaraderie of the others, how much they hated the idea of going back to the way they were before they started on this caper. A thought that also came into the heads of the others time and again, despite their best efforts to keep it out.

With rehearsals cancelled and all bets off, the men lived miserably in their own little worlds for a few days, feeling quite bereft without the daily highlight of meeting at the steelworks, of learning a new step and improving their techniques. Life was a much duller place without their dance sessions. Depression crept back into their psyches and they quickly lost the spring in their step.

Gathered together for the first time since Gaz's ultimatum, the men took their places silently in the regular fortnightly queue for their unemployment benefit payments down at the city centre dole office. Giving each other no more than a nodding acknowledgement, their shoulders hunched, their demeanours downcast, they waited their turns as they moved gradually up the ever-lengthening queue.

Gaz stood apart from the others, in a separate queue, as if to sum up his isolation from them. Glancing across at Guy,

Dave, Lomper, Horse and Gerald, a few places apart from each other in the line next to his, Gaz wondered how he could ever have expected them to be strippers. They resembled nothing more than the unremarkable members of an average bus queue.

Guy, their best asset but really no more than a moonlighting plasterer, was an utter nutter over his walking up the wall thing. Everywhere they went, he hurled himself bodily at walls, trying in vain to perfect the technique. It was only a matter of time before he fractured something. He might well qualify as the Lunch Box of the Year, but what did that mean with two legs in plaster?

Dave was a fat bastard, which wouldn't have mattered to anyone, except that he was so miserable with it. His insecurities about his weight, combined with his ongoing marital grief, had sucked the spirit out of him, and it was all Gaz could do sometimes to stop himself from head-butting him. He'd been against the idea from the start and Gaz was stupid to think he'd ever persuade him to follow through on his initial commitment.

Horse was an enigma: a man with something to prove, although Gaz didn't know what. He was a nice enough bloke, but he needed a replacement hip, wore ill-fitting clothes and often seemed to suffer from a complete sense of humour failure. It was more a case of funky turkey than chicken. This bird was well past its sell-by date.

Lomper was also a mystery, a fresh-faced young lad apparently devoted to his sick mother but who had tried to kill himself. The only one of them with a job, albeit part-time, he'd latched onto them like a heartsick puppy, afraid to be left alone once they'd rescued him. Gaz had made allowances for his complete lack of co-ordination, looks and talent and yet now the redhead was telling Gaz he couldn't go through with it. That was a bit rich.

As for old Twinkle Toes Gerald, Gaz knew he was trying his best but anyone could see he was a man on the edge. Unemployment had hit him harder than any of them, and it was only a matter of time before Linda discovered his dark secret and his Walter Mitty world was blown apart. He was middle-aged, middle management and middleweight. How Gaz ever could have considered him an attractive stripping prospect, he didn't know.

Drawing deeply on his cigarette, Gaz dragged his eyes away from his former fellow dancers and rolled his head around on his neck, easing the tension in it. Listening to the radio announcer tell the uninterested audience that heavy rain was causing problems for drivers on the Pennines, he scoffed. As if any of this lot gave a toss. As if he did. It was all bollocks.

'But now back to the music,' the disc jockey said cheerily. 'Here's another disco classic from the 70s ... It's Donna Summer with *Hot Stuff*.'

Gaz raised his eyebrows to the heavens. Why was it, he thought, that at the end of a relationship it was always the songs that provided the most painful reminders of how things might have been?

The familiar opening chords blared out across the room as the social security staff, trapped in a 70s time-warp, turned the radio up – anything to take their minds off the thankless task they called work. Gaz closed his eyes and listened to the beat with the familiarity of one who had danced to it over and over again in his waking hours and in his dreams.

Glancing across at the adjacent queue once more, he blinked and wondered what was different about the men he had just been watching. Their backs straightening as they waited, oblivious to him and to each other, Gaz was amazed to detect the faintest stirrings in them as the music built.

As the lyrics boomed Gaz watched Gerald and Guy smile privately to themselves in their places in the queue, remembering their routines. Gradually, slowly, almost imperceptibly, they began moving to the music.

It began with a shoulder twitch from Guy and a hand gesture from Lomper – barely noticeable rhythmic spasms –

as they stood reading a newspaper over the shoulder of the man in front. The stranger, a middle-aged former steel hand with a greying ponytail, frowned behind him at the two men, only to look forward and see Horse and Dave in front of him doing exactly the same. He frowned again and buried his nose in his paper.

Dave, who was yawning heavily while he queued, didn't even realise his buttocks were squeezing involuntarily – first one, then the other – in perfect time to the beat.

Only the trained eye would have noticed. The morose men queuing between the would-be dancers certainly didn't, preoccupied as they were with their own thoughts. But Gaz watched, fascinated, grinning to himself. It was like trying not to giggle in church. The urge to dance was bubbling in them all, and as the song progressed and got under their skins, their movements synchronised irrepressibly. Still only the smallest of gestures, they were cooking with suppressed energy – energy that dancing together had given them – and a new purpose to their otherwise miserable existences. Whatever happened after this, Gaz smiled and realised that he was responsible for that.

As the song reached its climactic chorus, each of them found himself involuntarily performing a tamed down version of the pumping action, thrusting his hips backwards and forwards, his fists clenched at the waist and pulling back. Not surprisingly, this did catch the attention of two of the men in the line-up, those directly in front of the 'pumpers', and they each stepped a pace forward, uncomfortably peering behind them with a look that was far from cordial.

Gerald, his mind transported to another place, the music coursing through his veins, suddenly found himself at the front of the roped-off queue, ready to approach the cashier's window and collect his money. Oblivious to anyone else in the room as the music rose to its crescendo, his inhibitions snapping, he started dancing, actually dancing in the middle of the dole office while Gaz watched open-mouthed.

Behind him the entire gang – their right feet moving backwards and forwards in perfect time on the grubby carpet, looked up admiringly as their troupe leader broke into a double-shimmy and a full 360 degree twirl, before slapping his UB40 on the counter with an exhilarated grin.

Gaz was equally euphoric at the sight. The gig was back on.

CHAPTER EIGHT

The distinctive musical chimes of Gerald's front doorbell disturbed him from his afternoon nap. Casting his *Daily Telegraph* to one side, he rose to his feet from his armchair and padded to the hallway in his socks. He hoped to God it wasn't Linda home early from her shopping trip to Saltaire, or he'd be done for. Telling himself not to be stupid, he realised that she would always use her key.

Cautiously, he peered through the frosted glass door and gave a sigh at the sight of the outlines on the other side of it. The figure at the front of the group of four men rapped his knuckles urgently on the glass, sensing that Gerald was there. The ex-foreman opened the door with reluctance.

Standing in front of him in the pouring rain, dressed in Hawaiian shirt, Bermuda shorts and dark sunglasses, was Guy, smiling hopefully, a bottle of suntan lotion held in his hand. Dave, Lomper and Horse were huddled round behind him, coats zipped up against the weather, sporting cheesy grins.

'No!' Gerald said firmly, slamming the door in their faces. He knew what they wanted and he'd already told them they couldn't. It was bad enough having the gang taking their clothes off en masse in his living room, without leaving their sweaty imprints all over Linda's sun-bed.

But Guy knocked even more insistently on the glass, his face squashed up against it. 'Gerald, come on, mate. Just an hour?' he pleaded, desperate to get his body tanned if he was going to be showing it off to half of Sheffield shortly. The rest of the team shuffled forward behind him, making it clear that they weren't leaving until they got what they came for. Afraid that the neighbours might be looking, Gerald weakened. He let them in on the condition that they were gone exactly one hour later, and that they didn't touch anything they weren't meant to.

Within a few minutes Guy, his protective goggles on, was luxuriating on the expensive full-size sun-bed that took up most of Gerald and Linda's spare bedroom. Hanging on the wall opposite were two of Linda's hand-stitched 'Come Dancing' dresses, all pink and white sequins, with feather boas to match. Dave hardly even noticed the glamorous outfits, he was too busy admiring Guy's physique yet again, wishing he had a body like his. The last time he'd had legs that thin, he'd been three. Sulkily, he leaned against the sill of the bay window – its curtains firmly drawn by Gerald – picked up a girlie magazine he'd found hidden in the bottom of Gerald's wardrobe and flicked through the pages distractedly.

Horse, still wearing the grey suit that appeared to be his only outfit, with the sole addition of a burgundy sweater to keep the chill off his kidneys, was cycling gently on an exercise bike next to Dave, listening to the music playing on a radio. Lomper took himself through his dance steps yet again, without much effect. No matter how hard the redhead practised, he always ended up looking like a majorette, marching in front of a brass band.

Peering across at the magazine with a grin and trying to ignore the ache in his hip, Horse said: 'Hey, you get some fit birds in there.' From his tone, it was obvious that he was a regular subscriber.

Lomper stopped dancing and leaned over to take a look at a double-page spread Dave had the magazine open on. 'Nah, her tits are too big,' he scoffed, turning back to his task, his legs pumping up and down in time to the music. Dave looked up at him, amazed at his comment and his new-found confidence these days. This was hardly the suicidal, freckle-faced young chuffer he'd dragged from his smoking car.

'Yeah?' Horse asked Lomper with a frown, taking

another look. 'Didn't know they could be.' He'd always been a bit of a breast man, himself, and even Dolly Parton seemed perfectly in proportion to him.

Completely unfazed, Lomper rummaged through a stack of cosmetics on Linda's dressing table and picked up a tub of something in order to scrutinise the label. 'Anti-wrinkle cream?' he read, as Gerald walked in, still very anxious that they might be discovered, even though all the curtains in the house were drawn and the security latch was firmly clicked into place on the front door. He reckoned that even if Linda came home unexpectedly, he'd have time to get the lads out of the back door before he had to release the catch.

'Hey, can fellas use this an' all?' Lomper asked, unscrewing the lid on the foul-smelling cream and wondering if it would help uncrease his saggiest bits.

'D'you mind, you?' Gerald chided, switching off the radio lest the neighbours hear and grabbing the tub from Lomper's hand. Screwing the lid back down, he placed it carefully back where it belonged. Left a bit, right a bit. There. It had to be in just the right place or she'd know.

Dave, contemplative as ever and still flicking through the magazine, offered a salutary thought. 'Well, I just pray they're a bit more understanding about us, that's all,' he said, sourly, peering down at the big-breasted woman with the near-perfect figure.

Horse stopped pedalling and looked at Dave. 'You what?' he asked, a bead of sweat trickling down his face from his exertions.

Dave pointed to the centre-spread as Gerald, Lomper, Horse and Guy stopped what they were doing and paid attention. 'Well, they're gonna be looking at us like that, aren't they?' Dave commented. There was silence in the room, so he continued. 'I mean, what if next Friday, four hundred women turn round and say: "He's too fat",' pointing to himself with his thumb, '"He's too old",' indicating Horse, 'and "He's a pigeon-chested little tosser",' pointing to Lomper, who puffed up his chest defensively. 'What happens then, eh?' Dave looked down at his stomach, unhappily, as Guy lifted his goggles and sat up on the sun-bed to listen.

Horse, who had stopped mid-pedal, looked aghast. 'They wouldn't, would they?' It had never really occurred to him, or indeed to any of them, what the women in the audience might actually be thinking. They had simply been concentrating on getting them in through the door and separated from their cash.

'Why not?' said Dave. 'He's just said her tits were too big.' He pointed an accusing finger at Lomper, who was sticking out his chest and examining himself critically in the mirror.

Still stinging from the earlier rebuke, Lomper shrugged. 'That's different, we're ... blokes,' he said by way of mitigation, realising how corny it sounded even as he said it.

'Yeah ... and?' Dave challenged him. Surely even someone as naive as Lomper didn't think that being a bloke gave them the slightest advantage these days.

Gerald, leaning in to look at the centre-spread, swallowed hard at the thought and suddenly felt very generous to the female gender. 'I think she's got nice tits actually,' he offered, blushing and thrusting his hands into his trouser pockets hastily.

Lomper, apologetic for what he'd said earlier, added mournfully: 'I never said owt about her personality, like. I mean she's probably quite nice if you get to know her.'

But Dave refused to let him off so lightly. Shaking his head at him, he said: 'No, and they won't say nowt about your personality neither ... which is good, 'cos you're basically a bastard.' As his words sank in, they all listened in stunned silence. The thought of several hundred pairs of eyes assessing their physiques making them shudder collectively.

'Bollocks to your personality,' Dave added. 'This is what they're looking at, right?' He patted his stomach. 'And I tell you something, mate,' he added, directing his comment to Lomper. 'Anti-wrinkle cream there may be, but anti-fat bastard cream there is none.' He straightened the magazine in his hand with a heavy sigh and pretended to read.

There was an uneasy pause as each one contemplated his own shortcomings with horror. Lomper twirled a ringlet of red hair round and round in his fingers wondering if pigeon-chested and saggy meant the same thing. Horse sat speechlessly on the exercise bike, contemplating desperate measures, and Gerald looked as if he had aged five years.

Only Guy didn't appear to be that bothered and, hoping to fill the awkward silence, he got up in one fluid movement from the sun-bed and reached into his towelling beach bag next to him. 'Here, lads,' he said, pulling out a cluster of tiny garments and throwing one to each of them.

Dave caught his skimpy red leather G-string in his hand and looked down at it fearfully. 'Oh, Mother,' he cried. It looked like a pair of toddler's swimming trunks.

'Bloody hell!' echoed Gerald, recoiling from the objectionable item in his hand as if its very touch would burn his flesh. Lomper and Horse examined theirs as if they were incomplete specimens from a zoo, turning them over and over in their hands, willing there to be more to them than that.

Guy looked almost apologetic. 'Well, Gaz said he wanted something a bit flashy, you know,' he said, softly, recalling Gaz's very specific instructions as to what Guy was to pinch from his cousin's swimwear store. 'Hey, it's top of the range. Real leather, like.'

Dave was unimpressed. 'Yeah, but ...' he began, sniffing it suspiciously. What it was made of wasn't the issue at all. It was how little of it there was that worried him. He didn't even undress in front of his wife unless wearing boxer shorts almost up to his armpits. This was shameful in its skimpiness.

Lomper, looking down at the £19.99 price tag still attached to the label, shook his head. 'Well, you don't get much for your money, do you?' He clearly thought the price was scandalous. Guy smiled at him. He sounded just like his mother.

Horse had paled visibly. 'What day is it again?' he asked,

the lump in his throat making his Scouse voice even huskier. He held his G-string across the palms of his upturned hands like some sort of sacrificial offering.

'Monday,' answered Gerald, holding his garment up to the light with disdain.

'And when are we on?' Horse asked, knowing the answer, but not wanting to hear it.

'Friday,' Gerald reminded him. With a gulp, he added: 'Dress rehearsal tomorrow.' They all looked at him, in mortal trepidation of the thought of what the next four days would bring.

Now a pale shade of green, Horse lowered his head slowly to study the G-string in his hands, before whispering: 'I think I'm gonna be sick.'

A few hours later that night, in a telephone box in a city centre side street, Horse cradled the receiver furtively near his mouth, while he looked around him watching for any passers-by who might be listening in.

Losing his patience with the woman assistant at the other end of the line, he hissed into the mouthpiece: 'How can I read the instructions? There wasn't any.' Listening to her response, he added: 'No, well maybe there's a part missing.' Delving into a green plastic bag, he pulled out a highly complicated rubber contraption with bits dangling off it and held it in his hand. Going through a checklist as she read the various items out, he dubiously fitted together each part, starting with a large plastic sheath in the shape of a penis. 'Yeah, got that,' he said, studying it from all angles in the light from the single bulb. 'If that's what you call it.'

The sheath was attached to a long plastic test-tube, which in turn was attached to some sort of syringe and a rubber hand-held pumping device. The combined package had cost him nearly twenty quid from a mail order catalogue and yet he was sure something wasn't right. He'd been using it three times a day since he'd bought it a week earlier and so far it hadn't made the slightest difference.

Agitated with the assistant now, who he felt wasn't fully appreciating the seriousness of the situation, he spoke stealthily into the receiver: 'Yeah, well, if it's all there, how come it's not working?' He examined the contraption once more and listened carefully to what she had to say. He thought he could detect the faintest hint of sarcasm in her voice.

'What d'you mean in what sense?' he asked, exasperated. 'It's not working in the sense that it's not working.' Lowering his voice slightly as a couple passed by the telephone box on the other side of the street, he whispered: 'No, I can't speak up!'

Asked to explain himself further, Horse lost his temper completely and, forgetting where he was, began to shout. 'Nothing's happening!' he complained. A passing dog cocked its leg against the telephone box and started barking at him outside. 'You know what I'm saying?' Having to spell it out for her, he shouted: 'Nothing's getting bigger!'

This was a matter of life and death as far as he was concerned. There were just days to go before he was about to be made the laughing stock of Sheffield. All his life, ever since his father had jokingly given him the nickname 'Hoarse' as a teenager – because his voice had broken to become permanently husky – he had silently enjoyed the inference his name had when people (especially women) assumed it was spelt the other way.

Without any foundation, word had got out that he was fantastically well-endowed – well, all black men were supposed to be, weren't they? And he'd never actively sought to shatter the illusion. Of course, the women he had slept with had been dismayed at first, but he had never had a disappointed lover, priding himself on having other attributes in bed that endeared him to them and he had persuaded the women not to betray him. When he had first applied for the stripping job, he had had every intention of stuffing his underpants with something impressive to keep the myth going at the same time as earning a few bob.

That was until Gaz the Mouth had told the world and his wife that they were going the full monty. Now, faced with the dreadful day of reckoning, he had gone to the most desperate lengths imaginable to improve his assets – making enquiries about the possibility of emergency surgery on the NHS; tugging and stretching; even attempting weightlifting with tiny makeshift dumbbells, before finally succumbing to the astonishing advertising claims of the very latest high-tech penis enlarger.

Listening one last time to the advice the woman at the mail order company had for him, Horse frowned in indignation and dismay. It was clear she wasn't going to be able to help him further at all. A note of desperation in his voice, he pleaded: 'Well this is an emergency, is this.' There was a snort of derision, followed by a click on the other end of the line.

Three miles away, across the city, Dave emerged from his bathroom in his boxer shorts, a strange expression on his face. Meeting Jean's steady gaze as she lay in bed, waiting for him, he pulled his T-shirt off and climbed in next to her, rolling over towards her with a kiss. Delighted at the unexpected attention, Jean rubbed his arm fondly and pulled him towards her, returning his kisses passionately, her mouth hungry for more. Dave slid his hand under the bedclothes and climbed on top of his wife, kissing her tenderly at first, and then more fully as his passions aroused. He buried his face in her neck, kissing her shoulder as she rubbed her hands up and down his broad back, urging him on.

Quite suddenly, he stopped moving, his head still hanging down by her neck, and she felt his lust for her slip away. Raising his head, he looked down at her, her pupils enlarged, her lips moist from his kisses. She gazed into his eyes with such love that he was almost moved to tears. Swallowing hard, she asked softly: 'What's the matter, big man?', nudging the tip of his nose with hers, willing him to continue.

But, despite all his best intentions, the spark had gone from his eyes and, shaking his head, he whispered: 'I'm sorry.' Jean let out a sigh as Dave rolled off to sit on the edge of the bed. His head bowed, he clenched his hands into fists at his side and tried to compose himself, his breathing laboured.

Trying desperately not to cry, Jean called his name gently and reached out to stroke her husband's back. But the touch of her fingers was like an electric shock through him and he jumped to his feet and walked out of the bedroom without another word. 'Dave?' Jean called, her eyes blinking back the tears, watching him go. But he could no longer hear her.

Three streets away, in Gaz's dingy council flat, the pounding rhythm of Donna Summer's *Hot Love* was driving the neighbours mad. It had been on constant replay for the past two hours. The woman downstairs had taken to banging on the ceiling with her walking stick, but to no avail.

Inside his living room, Gaz was oblivious to anything but his dance routine, going over it repeatedly, backwards and forwards across the threadbare carpet as if in a trance, checking and rechecking himself, making sure he had got it right. Left shoulder forward twice, then the right shoulder; left foot forward three times, right foot forward, one, two, three; pelvic thrust, hands clenched into fists. Then the footwork again and a final spin before starting the whole thing over again, his mind racing.

However ebullient Gaz may have appeared to the rest of them, he was secretly full of uncertainty about what he was doing and why he was doing it. He had privately considered throwing in the towel more times even than Dave.

Ever since he was a kid, he'd been on the offensive – initially to hide the pain of his miserable childhood and later to fend for himself in the private hell that became his family life. This whole scheme had been born out of the same kind of aggressive attitude. Gaz wasn't one for going under just because he lost his job, and although some of his moneymaking ideas were bordering on the insane, at least he was still coming up with ideas in the first place, while the rest of them sat around examining their navels.

But all of those little capers of his had been essentially private – a personal thing between him, Nathan and Dave. He may have bragged about them down the Job Club, but the actual execution of the plan was always done on the sly. This was different, this was about as public as you could get, and Gaz wasn't sure he was ready. It was not that he was ashamed of his body, or even afraid to take his kit off in public. It was the thought of all the lads down the pub taking the piss and the certain knowledge that from Friday onwards, his lifetime reputation as someone with a bit of street credibility would be out of the window.

It wasn't only himself he was thinking of either, for a change. There was Nathan too. What would the kids at school have to say about a lad whose old man took his clothes off for a living, even if it was just the once? Nathan had already had problems with bullies at school – problems Mandy had begged Gaz not to get involved with – and he worried about how this might affect their son.

As if on cue, Nathan appeared in the doorway of the kitchen in his pyjamas, having just finished the cheese sandwich he'd made for his supper before going to bed. Watching his father dance around the living room with the critical eye of an expert, he shook his head disapprovingly as the chorus finished fractionally after Gaz did. 'You're ahead,' he said flatly, as Gaz turned in surprise.

Not in the mood for such an observation, Gaz stopped dancing, stomped over to the stereo and turned it off with a black look. A barely audible cheer rang out from the flat downstairs. 'Oh, give us a break, will ya?' Gaz complained, spinning round to confront his son angrily. Nathan, contrite, shrugged his shoulders and stood in the doorway awkwardly. His dad had been in a funny mood all evening and the boy didn't really understand why.

Gaz realised he'd been unnecessarily short and was sorry. 'All right, kid?' he said, walking over to where he stood and tousling his hair like he always did. In that single action, repeated constantly by both his parents – but never by Barry – Gaz and Mandy conveyed their unspoken feelings to the boy. With his mum it generally just meant 'I love you'; but with Gaz it meant that plus a dozen different things – 'Sorry'; 'I've been an idiot'; 'I need your help'; 'Don't tell your mum'. Nathan peered into his father's wide eyes now and mentally added another new meaning to the list – 'I'm Scared'.

Dropping to his knees suddenly in front of his son with a rare show of vulnerability, Gaz looked up into Nathan's face, a pleading expression on his own. 'Tell us straight,' he said. 'We're not just making the biggest arses of ourselves in known universe, are we?' As Nathan averted his gaze, half-smiling, he resisted the temptation to reach out and ruffle his father's hair in return.

Her eyes bruised from crying, Jean stood in her night-dress and dressing gown at her bedroom window and pulled the net curtains to one side. In the small back garden below, there was a light on in the shed and she could see someone inside moving around. It was the silhouette of a large man. Her forehead creased into a frown.

Inside the shed, dressed in a T-shirt and sweat pants, Dave sat down heavily on a wooden box and looked around him sullenly. A naked light bulb swung overhead. Surrounded by garden tools, clay plant pots and an assortment of rusting car parts that he'd never got around to using, there was hardly any room for him to squeeze in beside the lawnmower that didn't work and the broken deck chair.

Pulling aside an old Pirelli calendar, he retrieved a Mars bar hidden behind it. Undoing the wrapper with the expertise of a chocaholic, peeling it back so that it formed a neat holder to keep any telltale chocolate off his fingers, he took a bite and chewed furiously on it. He stared into the far distance, dwelling glumly on Friday.

A hundred times he'd started to tell Jean, to share his anxieties about the big event with her, but a hundred times he'd imagined the look in her eyes, the way she'd throw her head back and laugh in his face, that raucous howl of hers that could be so hurtful. He imagined her telling Frankie and the others down at Asda, imagined himself becoming the butt of jokes throughout Sheffield, eventually losing her to some lithe young lover who could satisfy her every need. In his mind's eye, on the basis of this one imaginary conversation, he had devised a pessimistic scenario in which she had left him, got a divorce, remarried and was living happily somewhere else.

When they'd first met, things had been so different. He prided himself on being the larger than life character, the one with the belly laugh who they all crowded around in the pub. Jean had been attracted to that in him, his sense of humour and easygoing nature. He'd even done a turn or two as the compere at the Millthorpe Working Men's Club, taking to the stage like a natural – introducing acts, announcing prizes, cracking jokes. He had been elected social secretary for the steelworks five years running, organising the Christmas parties, the summer picnics, all the dances. He was the life and soul.

He could hardly bring himself to believe how low he had sunk since then. In a few days' time, for the sake of maybe a hundred quid, or possibly even less, he was going to be standing on the stage of the club once more, after an absence of several years. Only this time, instead of wearing a dickie tie and a sparkling jacket lent specially to him by Alan, he would be captured in the spotlight stripping his clothes off like some cheap tart, wiggling and wobbling all over the stage in the most farcical, pathetic display of ugly white flesh that had ever been seen. Dave Horsfall. Your host for the evening.

Putting down his chocolate bar, and wiping his mouth with the back of his hand, he reached his arms over his head and tugged at the back of his T-shirt. Pulling it up over his head, he draped it on a nearby watering can and sat, topless, for a few moments, miserably contemplating the vision of his forthcoming performance. Reaching over to the workbench, he picked up a giant roll of cling-film that he'd pinched from the kitchen drawer on his way out of the house.

Still chewing on his mouthful of toffee and caramel, his expression pensive, he loosened a small piece of the clear plastic film from the roll, held it with the flat of one hand to his dimpled belly button and wound the roll around his back and then around his front, squashing the hairs on his chest flat and squeezing the flesh tight under his nipples.

He repeated the process with difficulty until he had encircled his huge stomach three times. Tearing the cling film off with his fingers, he tossed the roll back onto the side, picked up his Mars bar and sat, chewing it, fully chicken drumstick'd, and wishing he'd asked Gerald how long it would take before the pounds were meant to fall off him.

Dave was still considering asking Gerald that question the following morning. The two of them were keeping a prearranged rendezvous in town for their regular monthly interview with social security officials wishing to know if they had managed to find any work yet.

The 'job seekers' were seen in batches, not based on anything simple or dignified like the alphabetical order of their surnames, but on the code numbers by which they were known at the dole office. Gerald and Dave happened to share the same three digit prefix. The interview was a futile process, a complete waste of time for all concerned, but under a new Government initiative to catch out the dole cheats, it was a necessary if tedious formality.

Waiting together at a bus stop after their respective interviews, the pair had decided to go home and get their gear first before meeting up at the steelworks later for the dreaded dress rehearsal. Hunched into his jacket, Dave sat on a wall by the bus shelter on a unseasonably cold and misty Sheffield morning, the fog stretching into the far distance. The sight did nothing to lift his mood as he tried to coax some life into a roll-up and wondered if microwave cling-film was more effective than the regular brand.

A troubled-looking Gerald sat next to him, his own mind spinning with unanswered questions. Suddenly plucking up the courage to speak, he turned to his companion and asked, half under his breath: 'Dave, mate, er, can I have a word? … In private like.'

Dave frowned at him and looked around. They were in the middle of bloody nowhere waiting at a bus stop that neither the bus driver nor any other passengers seemed to know existed. They couldn't be more private. Shrugging his shoulders, he said: 'Yeah – suppose so.'

Looking decidedly anxious now, Gerald spoke with urgency. 'Dave, you won't tell anyone, will you?' he asked. What he wanted to say was 'You won't tell Gaz, will you?' but he thought Dave would know what he meant.

Seeing how serious Gerald's expression was, Dave resisted the temptation to make a joke. 'No,' he faltered. 'Your – er – your secret's safe with me.'

Gerald took a deep breath and studied his shoes as he tried to find the words to say what it was he needed to say. 'When I were about twelve …' he began. Dave sighed and prepared himself for a long story; '… our school took us for – for swimming lessons.' He looked at Dave with meaning, as if he must already have the gist, but Dave looked blankly at him so he carried on. 'Mixed classes,' Gerald said, his eyes widening. 'You know – boys, and, er – and girls.' His eyebrows arched expressively at the final word. Dave nodded but remained silent.

Shutting his eyes to the memory, Gerald shook his head ferociously from side to side. 'Oh, it were terrible, Dave,' he went on, suddenly standing over him, his words coming in short bursts. 'I were there … standing at the side of the pool in me trunks … with all these pretty lasses standing around …' He opened his eyes even wider. Dave still looked blank, so Gerald spelt it out for him, coming closer to whisper the final part: '…in bikinis,' he said, twisting his mouth into a strange shape.

Bracing himself against the thought, he pursed his lips and

leaned in towards Dave's ear conspiratorially, his eyes darting right to left as he stared into Dave's meaningfully. 'And well I ... I got, er,' he began, tightening his clasp on the wrought iron railing behind him. 'Well I ... I got a stiffy.' His description of his childhood erection was spoken hurriedly and half-whispered.

Dave's expression hardly changed. He sighed slightly and looked up at Gerald with a frown. 'What did you do?' he asked softly, his expression one of admiration rather than pity.

'I jumped in the deep end, didn't I?' Gerald said, much louder now, shame written all over his face. 'I nearly fuckin' drowned.' Failing to get a response, he knitted his eyebrows together and held his hands in front of him as if in prayer. 'But what if it happens again?' he asked, grabbing Dave's sleeve desperately. 'Think of that, eh? – In front of four hundred women!'

Dave looked up at his companion sadly. Thinking of his own experiences with Jean the previous night, he spoke Gerald's name and peered up into his eyes, willing him to understand and to leave the matter alone. Finally, with a hint of bitterness in his voice, he said quietly: 'You're talking to the wrong man.' Without another word, he got to his feet, stuffed his hands in his pockets and started walking up the road, a picture of wretchedness.

Seated and bemused on a battered sofa in the middle of the steelworks rolling mill was Horse's mum with two equally ancient old ladies in tow. Feisty West Indian grandmothers, they had lived through a lot of experiences in their time, but they'd never been invited to something quite like this.

Tired of waiting, Horse's mum took out her knitting and started on the sleeves for her baby granddaughter's summer cardigan. Her younger sister Leticia sat next to her with her handbag clamped to her knees and asked for the fourth time how much longer it was likely to be. Daphne, the third sister, sat silently intrigued as various men appeared and disappeared at the window of a derelict control room in front of them, nervously watching what the women were up to outside.

Currently occupying the window was Horse, who gulped nervously and stepped back into the room to be confronted by Gerald. 'I thought you said it were just your mum,' the ex-foreman said, terrified at the thought of performing in front of three women. To him it represented three times the chance of getting an erection, although he was relieved at least to see that they were all well past their prime.

Horse shrugged. 'Well, it's family, isn't it?' he said, 'What can you do?' Gerald knew little of the close-bonded networking of West Indian family life and didn't really understand what Horse meant. He didn't know how he remained so cool when he had claimed earlier that the idea of taking his clothes off in front of his Auntie Leticia filled him with dread. Gerald had an aunt like that and he'd have swum the English Channel and back again rather than strip in front of her.

At the sound of footsteps approaching outside, Horse's mouth fell open. He and Gerald swung their heads towards the window in unison and gasped. So much for keeping their cool. Joining the older women on the sofa was an astonishingly pretty young woman in denim jacket, black miniskirt and black leather boots, an expectant grin on her face.

'Who the hellfire's that?' Gerald asked, his voice up an octave, his sweaty hands pressed against the glass.

'Oh, no,' Horse groaned. 'It's Beryl. My niece.' He tossed his security guard's trousers to the ground and turned back to the room where Gaz, Nathan, Lomper and Guy were all waiting around in various stages of stupefaction, Gaz the only one showing real stress.

Sitting on the edge of a table, his legs swinging, Nathan looked around the room glumly. Lomper and Guy were to his left, at the other end of the room, discussing the finer points of their routine. Gerald had hardly heard a word they'd said. His face was pressed against the window despondently, wondering how he could possibly keep calm in the presence of such an attractive young woman. Horse was sitting with his head in his hands, losing his bottle fast. There was only one man missing and everyone was fed up with waiting.

'Where's Dave?' Nathan asked finally, speaking for them all as Gaz stopped pacing and turned his head. Throwing down his cigarette, he strode towards the door. There was no point waiting any longer. He was bloody well going to go and look for him.

Fifteen minutes later, after getting no reply at Dave's house, Gaz had a brain wave and headed for Asda. Marching through the automatic sliding doors, he jogged down the crowded aisles looking right and left until his eyes fell on a large man in a security guard's uniform standing by the pick 'n' mix, juggling pear drops. At first sight, Gaz sighed with relief – at least Dave had his stripper's uniform on – but as he drew closer, he realised with dismay that the badge on his shirt bore the name Asda.

Dave, unaware of Gaz bearing down on him from behind, chuckled as he perfected his juggling technique. He was pleased with himself. This was only his first day at work and he was already doing it almost as well as Frankie.

''Ere, Dave!' Gaz called, as the big man picked up some chocolate bonbons and tried juggling them. The wrappers made it difficult and he had dropped several on the floor by the time Gaz reached him. 'Dave!' Gaz shouted, his arms outstretched in indignation. Dave stopped mid-aisle and turned to face his friend. 'What you doing?' Gaz asked, pointing to his outfit.

'What does it look like?' Dave asked, not in the mood to be bullied.

Gaz poked him in the stomach and spoke through tight lips. 'We're on in three days' time. Where the fuck are you?' he asked, spoiling for a fight.

Dave stiffened defensively. 'I'm here, working ... earning,

that's where. Not pissing about,' he said, a strange look in his eyes. With a quick nod of his head, he added: 'End of chat,' before turning on his heel and walking away.

Gaz sighed and followed him along the aisle, two paces behind, calling his name. 'Dave, come on Dave,' he whined, but his pleading was getting him nowhere. Dave carried on walking, shaking his head No.

Passing a rack of smart jackets, Gaz had another bright idea. 'All right then!' he announced, as Dave stopped and turned to see what he was up to. 'Oooh, very nice!' Gaz said, holding the jacket up in front of him for size.

Dave threw back his head with a sigh. 'Gaz, please, don't,' he pleaded, seeing what was coming and hoping that Gaz wasn't thinking what he thought he was thinking.

Lifting the jacket off the rack, Gaz held it up very deliberately in front of Asda's newest security recruit and grinned. Standing just five paces from Dave, he challenged him. 'Come on, Mister Security Guard,' he said, 'do your job.' There was a wicked twinkle in his eye, and he had turned to run before Dave could grab him.

'Gazza,' Dave called, heading after him at a trot.

Back in the rolling mill, Hot Metal's first ever audience, who had been expecting a show half an hour earlier, began a slow hand clap to indicate their growing impatience. The sound of it did nothing to calm Horse's nerves. His fellow dancers were disappearing one by one, first Dave, then Gaz. It was like something out of an Agatha Christie mystery and he was fast losing courage.

Gerald held his hand to his mouth anxiously as he watched the women through the window. 'Horse, mate,' he called to the man sitting dejectedly on a chair. 'Get out there and tell 'em there's been a bit of a delay,' he urged.

Horse shook his head in despair. 'Well, they won't wait for ever, you know,' he pointed out, wondering what he'd say this time. Just as he spoke there was a loud crash and a groan. Guy had hurled himself full speed at the wall again, still trying to perfect his wall-walking routine, only this time he'd got one leg far too high and dropped like a stone, head first, to the floor. Lomper shook his head and helped to pick him up.

The football training and the dieting had paid off. Dave was far fitter than he had been in weeks and as he chased after Gaz as fast as he could through the aisles, his fingertips outstretched, he almost had him. But the slippery bastard was too quick for him. He ducked and dived his way around the store, side-stepping bewildered customers, skipping over counters, under railings and finally past the garden furniture and towards the main double doors.

Goading his pursuer, Gaz added insult to injury by turning his head to see where Dave was and yelling back at him: 'Keep up, you fat bastard!' just as he ran through the doors, setting off the familiar alarms. Turning to check Dave's progress behind him was his biggest mistake. By the time he'd turned back to see where he was going, he was too late to avoid a head-on collision with a moving snake of shopping trolleys being returned from the car park by a junior member of staff.

With a yell of pain, Gaz hit the barricade full in the ribs, rolling over the top of it and falling awkwardly onto the ground beyond. In seconds Dave was upon him, leaping the trolleys as if they were hardly there, angrier than Gaz had ever seen him.

Grabbing the injured thief forcibly by the lapels and dragging him to his feet, Dave shoved him hard against a second row of trolleys, winding him still further. 'Don't ever call me a fat bastard, all right?' Dave spat, shaking him, his face so close to Gaz's that he could smell the pear drops on his hot breath. Shouting in Gaz's face, Dave repeated: 'All right?'

Looking up at him pleadingly while still clutching his ribs, Gaz begged: 'We need you, Dave.' The routines were all very precisely worked out on the basis of six dancers. God knows what would happen if one of the 'central defenders' didn't play. Besides, Dave was his mate, the one who'd been there for him from the start. He wanted him at his side when he swallowed what little pride he had left and took to the stage at the working men's club in a few days' time.

Dave, fighting to catch his breath, stared long and hard into Gaz's eyes, his mouth turned down as he struggled to control his emotions. Releasing his grip finally, he pushed him away and shook his head. 'I can't,' he told him. Registering his friend's disappointment, he repeated: 'I just can't – all right?' Picking up the stolen jacket from where it had fallen on the ground, he turned away and headed back into the store.

CHAPTER NINE

The waiting was really getting to Gerald. Rocking backwards and forwards on his seat in the steelworks control room, he looked constipated as he tried to focus his mind on the matter in hand. Dressed in his uniform now, and twisting his security guard hat tighter and tighter in his hand, Gerald asked his colleagues for their advice.

Guy, sitting on the table next to him, nursing a bruised leg after his latest jump at the wall, couldn't help but smile when Gerald told them about his problem. Lomper, pacing the floor in front of them, fiddling with the buttons on his uniform, was silent. Only Horse, sitting the other side of the table, was doing all he could to comfort Gerald.

'Listen, just think of the most boring thing you can come up with,' he encouraged. 'That should keep well in order.' Lomper and Guy nodded their agreement. Nathan, who hadn't initially understood what they were on about, was now riveted to the conversation with an astonished expression.

'Like what?' Gerald asked, frantically trying to think of something that wouldn't give him an embarrassing erection in front of the ladies waiting outside on the sofa.

'Double glazing salesmen?' Guy suggested with a wry smile.

'Gardening,' Horse advised. 'The Queen's Speech?'

'*Dire Straits* double album,' Guy ventured, enjoying the game. Nathan, standing by the window, listened in wonder. As a young lad who'd only just discovered such delights, he hadn't realised, up until this moment, that having an erection could be a problem.

Gerald still looked deeply troubled, so Guy tried again. 'Nature programmes?' he said, thinking of all those boring documentaries about frog spawn and amoeba.

Gerald awoke from his concentrated reverie. 'I like nature programmes!' he protested, still rocking backwards and forwards on his hands and thinking of the many happy nights he'd spent with Linda watching David Attenborough talk them through the finer points of wildlife in the Serengeti.

'Aye, but they don't give you a hard on, though, do they?' Guy scoffed. Registering the ex-foreman's silence and the guilty expression in his eyes, he erupted into laughter and asked incredulously: 'Do they?'

Horse, Lomper and Guy chortled in unison at the realisation that nature programmes did indeed give Gerald a stiffy. Nathan's eyes widened in disbelief. He'd have to try that one. 'Blimey, Gerald,' Guy said, genuinely impressed. He might pack a mean lunch box but even he didn't get sexually aroused by the sight of a newt giving birth in the village pond.

'Ah, shut up you,' Gerald chastised them. 'It's not funny … It's medical.'

Their hilarity was interrupted by the back door opening and Gaz walking in, his face as long as a wet weekend. Horse and Guy smiled at him hopefully, but Gaz shook his head briskly. 'He's not coming,' he told them, as they looked at each other nonplussed. Seeing the apprehension in their eyes, he knew it was time to whip up some enthusiasm. Head up, he announced: 'It's all right, we can do without him.' Horse clapped his hands together authoritatively to wake them all up. Unzipping his jacket and throwing it onto the back of a chair, Gaz quickly slipped out of his clothes and into his uniform. Game on.

To the thumping, foot-stomping beat of Gary Glitter's *Rock and Roll*, the door to the control room opened and the five surviving members of Hot Metal marched out onto the steelworks floor with a flourish. Horse was first, hat on, head lowered, then Lomper, followed by Guy, Gerald and

finally Gaz. Guy and Gaz were the only ones without hats –
Lomper was still trying to purloin a couple more – but all
wore their security guard jackets and trousers, over an
assortment of T-shirts, shirts and vests.

Averting their gaze from that of their astonished audience,
sitting to attention on the sofa in preparation for the show,
the men formed a straight line in front of the women and
began swaying from side to side nervously in time to the
music.

Nathan, controlling the stereo, yanked up the volume
quickly at Gaz's nodded instruction, and – extremely
tentatively at first – the men began parading in a slow circle
in front of the giggling women. Only Lomper looked like he
was enjoying himself – beaming at them with his dimpled
smile. Gerald's lips were taut across his mouth, as he tried to
recall the finer details of the last Queen's Speech, and Gaz's
tongue was so deep in his cheek it looked like he was eating
a giant gob-stopper.

With the music pumped up, the Gang really began to
cook. All the weeks of rehearsals and closely-supervised
training had paid off. Gaining confidence, they jumped to
their left in perfect unison, watching each other to keep good
time, remembering each step that had been drummed into
them by Gerald, translated into football-speak for them by
Horse and honed in the privacy of their own homes.

Eyes raised now and beginning to enjoy themselves, they
flirted openly with the women before them, as each of them
began to slink and slide, strutting their stuff in perfect
formation. Gaz fluttered his eyelashes sexily at Horse's
mum, who stopped knitting and stared back, before being
nudged by her sister, Leticia, sitting open-mouthed and
wide-eyed next to her. Guy winked at Beryl and she grinned
back. Horse, once he'd overcome the fact that these were his
nearest and dearest watching him, quickly got into his stride
and gave them his winning smile. Even Lomper managed to
look a little seductive, as one by one they peeled off their
jackets and started taking off their shoes.

It was going much better than they had expected, they were keeping good time and playing to their audience beautifully. Nathan, tapping his feet in time to the music, sat next to the stereo grinning openly. Gerald was so busy remembering his steps and watching the others to make sure they were in time, he didn't have a thing to worry about. Even when Beryl winked coyly at him, he was delighted to find himself staying flaccid.

Outside the factory, the thumping 70s beat rebounded off the walls of the empty buildings, reverberating and making it sound ten times louder. Tucked away on the edge of a vast industrial estate that had once formed the heart of the cutlery capital, the steelworks was a normally desolate and uninhabited place.

But for the single policeman whose lonely beat included this patch, there was never anybody about. PC Walter Henry didn't even bother to walk the estate normally, but today he had decided to take a look after one of the night watchmen at a neighbouring factory had reported hearing some strange noises in one of the deserted rolling mills.

Reaching the huge peeling sign that read 'Millthorpe Steelworks' on the side of a building, PC Henry stopped and listened. Wasn't that music he could hear? Not the works brass band whom he knew sometimes practised here, but pop music? Gary Glitter to be precise, unless he was mistaken. This warranted a closer inspection.

By the time the second verse had come to an end, Gaz, Guy, Lomper, Horse and Gerald were taking turns to shimmy towards the front of the dance floor in pairs, back to back, hands interlocked, chins down, eyes fixed on the squirming women. Lomper and Guy first, then Gerald and Horse. Gaz had to do the routine on his own, without Dave, but he blustered bravely on.

While the others struck various poses behind him, Guy slid on his knees to the space directly in front of Horse's mum, her knitting still clamped firmly in her hands, and gave her his most seductive pout. Peeling off his shirt, as the others did the same behind him, he arched his eyebrows at her, as she took a sharp intake of breath and wiggled hers back at him. She'd been a widow for twenty-two years and yet there were stirrings within her she thought her body had forgotten. Leticia saw the expression on her sister's face and nudged her hard in the ribs once more.

Stripped down to their trousers, to the growing delight of their audience, the men twirled their shirts over their heads and started to remove their belts. Even Nathan was impressed as he watched his father flick his shoulder seductively at a blushing Beryl.

Lomper, rubbing his hands bawdily over his chest, was in a world of his own; Horse stood behind him thrusting his hips backwards and forwards at his aunt, who looked as if she was thoroughly enjoying it; and Guy rolled over onto his stomach to perform a slow, sexually-loaded press-up that had Horse's mum glowing crimson and clicking furiously away on her needles.

Gerald was the first to whip out his belt and flick it backwards and upwards ostentatiously and without injury. Unfortunately, his trousers started to slip down a little prematurely and he lost his rhythm momentarily as he struggled to hold them up. The others removed their belts without problem and the four women, hunched together on the sofa now, transfixed, were grinning from ear to ear in delighted anticipation.

Adopting the tactical defending manoeuvre they had learned, so that the troupe stood a few feet away from each other, two at the front and three at the back, each man dropped his hands to his thighs and grabbed a handful of trouser leg as the music rose to a heart-thumping crescendo. On the count of a specific beat, they yanked their arms upwards and forwards with a great flourish, ripping the flimsy Velcro binding apart and tearing the trousers off to reveal their tiny red leather G-strings, barely covering anything in front and with the thongs wedged high up between the cheeks of their buttocks.

The women were more than astounded. Horse's mum, shocked and delighted all at the same time, dropped several stitches. Beryl and her aunts fell against each other, hands to their faces, laughing breathlessly and Nathan almost jumped to his feet to applaud. They were marvellous as they formed a tight, bare-cheeked circle for their final routine.

The only person who seemed unimpressed was PC Henry, standing in the open doorway, his chin dropped to his chest in surprise. No one had heard him come in, the music was turned up so loud, and he had witnessed the last few seconds' performance in astonishment. Never in twenty years in the force had he come across anything like this, least of all in a steelworks.

Guy spotted him first and, grabbing Lomper by the arm, legged it through a back door. Nathan gulped hard and slammed his hand down on the Stop button, as Gaz shook his head in disbelief. Horse, frozen mid-step, tried to cover a nipple with a hand, while Gerald, standing almost bollock-naked in front of a law enforcement officer, jumped to attention in front of him, his hat clamped firmly to his groin to conceal his increasingly excited state.

The red-haired social worker adopted her most sympathetic smile, tilted her head and leaned towards Nathan as if she wanted him to share a secret with her. 'So, your daddy dances in front of you, does he?' she asked softly, as the boy sat stony-faced in the interview room of Millthorpe police station, being studied by another member of the Child Protection Team.

Peering through the glass door at his father in the charge room outside, dressed only in a grey blanket and leather G-string, flanked by Horse and Gerald, Nathan looked back at the expectant faces and answered with a frown: 'When he's rehearsing,' as if that explained everything. The woman nodded sagely before giving her male colleague a meaningful look and scribbling something onto a pad. There was more to this than met the eye.

Outside, Gaz watched his son through the glass door with

173

paternal concern, as two of his partners in crime shivered next to him, pulling their thin blankets further round their shoulders. Police officers and members of the public wandered in and out of the room, barely giving them a second look, although Gerald felt as if each one was boring into him with their eyes.

Gaz, the only one apparently unaffected by the humiliation of their arrest and handcuffing, the ignominious transportation to the police station and subsequent herding into the charge room from a meat wagon, told Gerald over his shoulder: 'We were dancin' all right then and all.'

Gerald, utterly miserable, couldn't believe what he'd just heard. Here they were, nothing more than common criminals, about to be banged up for all they knew and all Gaz could think of at such a time was their dancing ability? Gerald was beside himself with embarrassment. He'd never even had a parking ticket before. He took a bottle of scotch to his local police station every Christmas Eve. He was a former chairman of the local neighbourhood watch scheme, for God's sake, and now – thanks to this no-good scally from the works – he was standing in a police station naked but for a red leather G-string and under arrest.

Rubbing each foot alternately on the back of his calves, he complained: 'My feet are freezing,' while the station sergeant at the desk in front of him – apparently completely unfazed by the sight before him – dropped two sweeteners into his mug of tea from a height and, with great deliberation, opened a new report book.

'Right. Name?' the sergeant asked Gaz, his pen poised above the pad. Gerald raised his eyes to the heavens and felt like crying.

'Gary Schofield,' Gaz replied matter-of-factly, turning back to keep an eye on his son. The station sergeant scribbled on the first page and then flipped open a separate charge sheet, looking up at Gerald expectantly.

'Gerald Arthur Cooper,' Gerald whispered, trying not to say his name too loud.

'What?' the bald-headed sergeant asked with a frown, unable to hear him.

'Gerald Arthur Cooper,' Gerald replied, clearing his throat and almost shouting his name. He wished the ground would open up and swallow him whole.

The sergeant nodded at Horse, standing silently at the end of the desk. 'Barrington Mitchell,' Horse said quietly, leaning forward to speak, as his companions looked at each other in surprise.

'Barrington?' the sergeant repeated. Horse nodded, hoping that the lads now understood why he chose to use his nickname instead. 'That one "r"?' the sergeant asked.

'No, two,' Horse replied, as the sergeant duly corrected his entry.

Lomper and Guy were grazed, bruised and shivering with cold by the time they had vaulted over thirty-odd garden walls and fences to reach the back garden of Lomper's house. En route and still giggling at the ridiculousness of their situation, they'd pulled a dressing gown and a sheet from a washing line to provide limited cover, almost getting caught by an irate househusband in the process.

Now, as they scrambled up onto the kitchen roof to try and climb in through Lomper's bedroom window, they were starting to suffer badly from exhaustion and exposure.

'Come on, Lomps,' Guy encouraged as he held out his hand for Lomper to pull himself up onto the roof from the guttering. Lomper reached up and his sheet half-slipped off his shoulders, leaving him once again dressed only in the skimpy red G-string he'd just crossed Sheffield in on a freezing cold May day.

Gary the Lad knew all about the Old Bill and he had told Horse and Gerald to leave all the talking to him. 'I know what I'm doin', I've been here before,' he had reassured them. 'Just keep your mouths shut and let me use me charm on them.'

Reluctantly bowing to his greater expertise in the matter, well aware – thanks to Nathan – that he had been in prison before, they listened carefully. He had told them all about 'Smiler', the sarcastic nickname he gave to the dour-faced Yorkshire police inspector who would be interviewing them. He said he'd known him since he was a lad, and knew exactly how to handle him. 'He was a plod on the beat when I was fresh out of school and nicking cars,' Gaz boasted. 'I was one of his first arrests. We go back a long way.'

Deeply sceptical that such a dubious connection would be of any help to them whatsoever, the two men had agreed unwillingly, but as they sat either side of Gaz now in their blankets, facing the uniformed police inspector in an interview room, they wondered at their decision.

'Told you,' Gaz was repeating. 'Robbing pipes, that's all.' Gerald and Horse looked sideways at Gaz and then at each other, wondering how they had ever got involved with such a man in the first place.

The police inspector wasn't swallowing it. When it came to Schofield, he rarely did. 'Gary, my friend,' he said wearily. 'No bugger robs pipes in the buff.'

Gaz grinned and shook his head as if he was trying to explain something to a child. 'We do,' he said, shrugging his thin shoulders. 'Don't get your clothes dirty, do you?' It was logical, if nothing else.

The inspector folded his hands together in resignation. 'Oh, well, don't fret, gents,' he told them with sarcasm. 'There's a right good laundry in Wakefield Prison.'

Horse's mouth fell open and Gerald, drawing his blanket protectively to his neck, was aghast. 'Eh?' he said, looking up. He knew he should have had a quiet word with the inspector, like he wanted to. Man to man, the officer would surely have realised that a person of his standing couldn't possibly be involved in anything smacking of impropriety. But now this, the unbearable humiliation of being arrested and the prospect of a prison sentence to come. His life was over.

Just then, the door opened and one of the South Yorkshire Constabulary's finest – PC Henry – appeared, three video tapes in his hand. Placing them on the table in front of the inspector, he explained what they were. 'Security camera tapes off the front desk.'

The inspector picked them up and studied them quizzically. 'What happened to the security guard?' he asked, as the three blanketed men huddled closer to each other in silence.

Lomper was the first onto the ridge tiles outside his bedroom window, trying to push the old Victorian sash up as high as it would go. He knew he should have got those cords replaced before now. Balancing on the roof of the kitchen below, and hoping that none of his neighbours in the redbrick terrace were in, he hoisted his left leg up onto the windowsill, still clutching the sheet he'd managed to retrieve a few minutes earlier.

Trying to get a foothold, the sheet slipped from his shoulders yet again, this time lost for ever. Guy, dressed in a fetching peach satin knee-length dressing gown, wobbled barefoot on the peaked roof next to him and urged him on. Helping him get his legs up and through the small gap afforded by the faulty sash window, Guy sniggered outside as Lomper landed headfirst with a crashing thump on the bedroom floor, his naked buttocks covered in angry red marks where he'd scraped and scratched them, his black nylon socks still on his feet.

'Ssssh, sshhhh,' he whispered to a giggling Guy whose head appeared at the window behind him. 'Be quiet. Come on, ssshhh!' Guy was almost incapable with laughter, so Lomper grabbed his muscular forearms and started to drag him in through the window. Unable to get a grip on anything with his feet, Guy almost slid back down the roof, but Lomper, a fistful of satin in his hands, yanked him further inside, ripping the flimsy garment to shreds as he did so.

Wiggling his legs around furiously outside the window,

trying to get the momentum he needed to slide inside, Guy nearly wet himself laughing as the motion of sliding his lower half in over the windowsill pulled on the special quick-release catches of his thong, leaving him with nothing much more than a torn dressing gown on.

With the added momentum of Lomper clamped around his thighs, pulling him, Guy fell through the opening all of a sudden, knocking the dressing table with his feet. It tottered dangerously, sending bottles of aftershave and deodorant crashing to the ground. Giggling uncontrollably now, all Guy could manage was: 'Oh, no!' as Lomper, still entwined with Guy's limbs, tried to scrabble to his feet to save the fallen items.

'Sssh, be quiet, me mum,' Lomper chided to an incapable Guy, as he manhandled him into an upright position too, holding onto his bare arms.

'Oh, I've always wanted to meet your mum,' Guy sniggered, a little too loudly, as Lomper pressed a finger to his lips urgently to make him be quiet.

'Ssssh,' Lomper tried once more, lifting his friend gently to his feet, Guy's hands pressed for support around Lomper's thong-clad hips.

Abruptly silent, they suddenly found themselves standing facing each other, inches apart and all but naked. There was an unexpected pause, as they stared deeply into each other's eyes, transfixed.

Finding himself sympathetic to Gerald's medical problem, Lomper reluctantly slid his hand from where it had been supporting Guy's arm. Unwilling to let him go, Guy reached up and gently touched Lomper's hand, keeping it in position, as the two of them half-smiled at each other, their breath hot on each other's faces.

For Guy, this was nothing new. He'd 'come out' years ago and had enjoyed a number of relationships with both men and women since, although none of them with much meaning. But for Lomper it was quite different. The virginal redhead, who had spent his whole life deeply confused about his sexuality, and so terribly ashamed of his secret feelings that he had almost killed himself because of it, closed his eyes with the relief of someone who finally knew what he wanted. He was Home.

By the time the video recorder had been found and the first of the tapes inserted and played, several employees of Millthorpe police station had found some excuse or other to make their way to the third floor interview room and watch.

While Gaz, Gerald and Horse sat uncomfortably at a table facing the television screen, the inspector on the other side, a group of uniformed male and female officers crowded in at the open doorway, giggling collectively as they watched the entire dance routine, captured for posterity by the security cameras.

'I can't believe what I'm watching,' the inspector remarked with feeling, unable to prise his eyes from the screen, echoing the view of everyone else in the room. For him, this was even more astounding, seeing Gary Schofield – the local Jack the Lad he'd known since his youth – performing a clearly well-rehearsed striptease with a bunch of the unlikeliest-looking men he had ever seen. Maybe he was getting too old for this job. He'd never seen the like.

Gerald, his circumstances momentarily forgotten now that his professionalism was being called into question, studied the screen with the eye of an expert. He hadn't expected to be so impressed. Gaz was right, they had been dancing well together, with one exception. Nudging Gaz now and pointing to the screen, he commented critically: 'You're always ahead there.'

Gaz sneered. 'You're always bloody behind, more like.' It wasn't his fault the rest of them couldn't keep up.

Gerald was fed up with Gaz's inability to dance in time with the rest of them. It ruined the line-up completely and made them appear straggly. He'd tried everything – placing Gaz in the middle, on the end, two men along, but nothing had worked. If only he'd thought of videotaping them earlier, now he could show him exactly what he meant at last. 'Oh, bloody look ...' he complained, leaning towards the inspector and reaching out for the remote control from under his blanket. 'Excuse me, can I borrow this for a second?' he asked, picking it up anyway as the inspector's mouth fell open.

There was more sniggering from the doorway as Gerald rewound the tape to run the opening sequences again. Turning on the crowd of officers, he shouted impatiently: 'Look, shut up will ya?' They fell instantly silent. Then to Gaz, Gerald said: 'Watch!' as he pressed the Play button.

In respectful silence, the ten or so people in the room watched the sequence again; this time all eyes were focused on Gaz, the dancer to the far left. Just at the point where the men were swivelling their hips, about to take their jackets off, and had to do a full 180 degree jump to the right, Gaz was clearly seen jumping two or three seconds ahead of the others. He made the rest look as if they were following him in some sort of sloppy Mexican Wave.

Nodding his agreement as he watched the routine closely, the inspector – a stickler for precision himself, ever since his days in the police cadets – piped up: 'He's right. You're ahead.'

Gaz, hardly able to believe that this was happening to him – that Gerald was now in cahoots with the Old Bill on the question of his dancing ability – shook his head in indignation. 'Go bollocks!' he said to the inspector, who looked decidedly hurt.

Once it had been ascertained that the arrested men had being doing nothing more criminal than stripping their clothes off to music, they were given a caution and told to go home. There was no law against what they had done: they hadn't broken into the steelworks and the boy appeared to be physically unharmed. Gaz told Gerald and Horse confidently that it was no more than he had expected, although neither of them believed that his so-called 'charm offensive' had had anything to do with their unexpected release.

Carrying in a pile of their clothes, a uniformed officer entered the reception area where they were waiting, still in their blankets. Gerald – in pink cotton boxer shorts – jumped on the pile, sifting through it eagerly, grabbing his own clothes and handing a pair of trousers to Horse and some jeans to Gaz, who was busy remonstrating with the duty sergeant at the desk.

'What d'you mean I can't bloody see him. He's me son!' Gaz shouted, standing barefoot in white Y-fronts and a grey T-shirt, his neck veins throbbing. 'I haven't even been charged.' Pointing to the interview room, he added: 'Ask "Smiler" in there. No charge.'

The sergeant shook his head. 'Sorry – social services have requested an interview with you,' he told him. 'Have to make an appointment.'

Before he could head butt the officer, the door to the charge room opened and Mandy was shown in by a WPC, her expression one of motherly concern. She was breathless, having run from her minicab outside, and, glaring at her ex-husband, who was quickly trying to get one leg into his jeans, she turned to the sergeant. 'I've come to pick up my son,' she said, a catch in her voice, as Gaz frantically readjusted his clothes three steps in front of a shamefaced Horse and Gerald, doing much the same.

Looking askance at Gaz, whom the boy's mother had completely ignored, the sergeant faltered: 'Oh, right, er … just a minute, Madam.' He could see there was no love lost there.

Gaz, still with only one leg in his jeans, hopped pathetically towards his ex-wife and tried to reason with her. 'Listen, Mand. He's – he's fine,' he said. 'We've not been charged or owt.'

Mandy rounded on him, her eyes on fire. 'So, this is your great money-making enterprise is it, Gary?' she asked, scathingly. 'Pornography?' God only knows what he'd been doing with her son. She was beside herself. She had been ever since the police had called her factory and told her the

181

scantest of details. A woman police officer had said only that Nathan had been found with five half-naked men in a deserted steel mill, dancing to music instead of being at school, like he should have been. The social services had been called, the WPC added, and Nathan had been taken into temporary custody.

Mandy had spent the next fifteen minutes in a cold sweat, waiting for a cab, then rushing over to the police station as fast as the driver could take her. What on earth was Gaz up to? Was it her fault in some way? Should she have lent him the money, like he asked? She had nearly driven herself crazy with all the terrible thoughts spinning round in her head. And worse was still to come. Barry would go berserk.

Gaz laughed in her face at her suggestion that they had been doing anything pornographic. 'Oh don't be daft,' he told her. 'We're trying to get you your money, that's all!'

Mandy's voice came out of her mouth in a shrill screech. '*My* money!' she cried. '*Nathan's* money!' So, she knew about that now and all, Gaz realised, swallowing hard and feeling guilty all over again for so callously pilfering his son's post office savings account.

Breaking the impasse, the door to the interview room opened and the sergeant returned. 'Here he is,' he said cheerily, leading Nathan in, a policeman's helmet cocked jauntily on the boy's head. The social workers watched carefully through the window, ready to take notes. It would be interesting to see the child's behaviour responses to both parents, they thought.

'All right, Dad?' Nathan asked, beaming at his half-dressed father. This was better than school, any day. Apart from the weirdos asking questions, that was.

'All right, kid?' Gaz replied hollowly, a dreadful feeling in the pit of his stomach.

'Yeah, fine,' Nathan grinned. Wait till he told his mates at school about this. More cautiously, Nathan smiled at his mother and ran over to her. 'Hi, Mum,' he said, wary of her strange expression.

Removing the helmet from his head, Mandy placed a hand firmly on her son's shoulder. 'Come on, love,' she told him, so relieved to see him and realise that he was all right that she could have cried. 'We're going now.'

'Come on, Mand,' Gaz pleaded, stepping towards her, the waistband of his jeans in his hand. There was something in her eyes which was really bothering him.

But as she rounded on him, her cheeks flushed, her eyes glistening, he knew he should have left it alone. 'Unemployed ... Maintenance arrears of seven hundred pound ...' she began, her voice breaking up. 'And now you've been arrested for indecent exposure.' Holding Nathan defensively to her side, she added: 'Still think you're a suitable father, do you?'

Gaz was genuinely wounded by her remarks and could think of nothing to say. Nathan recognised his expression and turned to his mother. 'He is trying,' he pleaded.

Gaz shot his son a grateful look. 'See?' he reasoned, as if that made all the difference.

Mandy hung her head sadly. 'Bit late for that,' she told her son, her stinging comment aimed directly at Gaz.

Gaz, really hurting now, bent double to get his jeans on and hopped after her as she turned towards the door. 'Hang on a minute,' he said, still hoping to win her round. This was important. He had to try and make her understand.

But, abandoning Nathan by the door, Mandy turned back to him, raging inside. 'Look at yourself, Gary,' she said, her voice cracking, her eyes darting down to where his jeans were suspended, half way up his thighs, his Y-fronts exposed. 'Just ... look ... at ... yourself.' Seconds later she had gone, taking Nathan with her. Gaz held his breath. It was history repeating itself.

By the time Gerald turned the corner into the street where he lived, he was just about ready to drop. It had been the second worst day of his life. The first had been the day he was made redundant from Harrison's and he'd walked the streets all day, trying to summon up the courage to tell Linda when he got home.

Walking into their warm bungalow that night, she'd smiled from the kitchen and asked him if he'd had a good day, as if everything was normal. Checking his watch, he'd realised that, by sheer coincidence, he had walked in through the front door at 5.45 p.m., dead on cue, even though he'd been officially unemployed for over four hours. If he could do that the next day, and the day after that – until he managed to get himself another job – he might never have to break the bad news to her after all. Six months later his plan was still working.

Tugging nervously on the hem of his quilted anorak now, in the hope that Linda was out shopping somewhere or having her hair done when he got home, he peered through his front conifer hedge and froze at the sight before him.

Parked in his driveway was a large removal van. Walking to and from it, carrying various items of furniture and personal possessions, were the two repossession men he and the lads had seen off previously. Breaking into a run to try and stop them, he faltered when he spotted Linda on the doorstep, her face hardened, as the men manhandled her precious exercise bike into the back of the van, knocking over one of the garden gnomes in the process. Picking it up and clutching it to her bosom, Linda's expression hardened still further.

Slowing his pace, and with his head hung low, Gerald knew the game was finally up. With a sigh, he passed the *Quicksteps* house sign and shuffled slowly up the garden path towards her. With a nervous laugh, the younger of the two repossession men nodded a hello. 'All right, mate?' he asked, hoping the owner of the house was alone this time, but Gerald ignored him.

Peering into Linda's taut features, Gerald's eyes admitted that the situation was hopeless. 'So?' she said, her voice clipped.

'Yeah,' was all he could manage with a sigh, his shoulders stooped.

'And this has been going on how long?' Linda's false pink fingernails tightened around the gnome's head.

It was the moment of truth Gerald had been dreading. Whitening, he looked to the sky as if trying to calculate how long, before finally stammering: 'Er ... about six months.' In a way, he was relieved it was over. It had been a terrible strain.

Blinking hard, her expression murderous, Linda stared daggers at him and found herself unable to speak. Gerald couldn't bear to look into her eyes and hung his head. Finally, she told him curtly: 'I can cope with losing the sun-bed ... car ... television.' Glancing across the street at the net curtains twitching in the window of every house opposite, she added: 'I can even cope with the shame of everyone watching this.'

Her jawbone jutting out, she clenched her teeth and spat her next words at her husband. 'But six months, six ... bloody months!' With that, she held up the gnome in her jewel-encrusted fingers and hurled it to the ground with a smash, '... and you wouldn't say to *me* ... to your *wife*.' Beyond words, she stopped and gasped to catch her breath.

Unable to respond and looking down at the shattered gnome, in a thousand pieces at his feet, Gerald shook his head sadly and pointed. 'I thought you liked them,' he said.

Steeling herself, and blinking back her tears, Linda glared at him and said coldly: 'No, Gerald – I never liked them.'

CHAPTER TEN

Gaz had never felt so low. Lying on his back on his tatty sofa in his depressingly lonely flat, he inhaled the smoke from his cigarette and blew it out into perfectly formed rings above his head. He hadn't fully appreciated how seriously Mandy would take this latest escapade until she had rounded on him in the police station like that.

Somewhere deep inside him, Gaz had always hoped that there was still a chance with Mand, that one day – given the right circumstances – she would come back to him and he and Nathan and her would all be a family again, like they had been once a very long time ago.

There had never really been anyone else in his life apart from Mandy. Of course there were the countless numbers of women he'd shagged, from the brassy barmaid to Mandy's sister Jenny (not that Mandy knew about that one). But none of them had counted for owt, he had only truly loved one woman – his childhood sweetheart and the mother of his child.

Even when she shacked up with boring Barry, he hadn't been that bothered. Sure, he'd been jealous all right. He'd bloodied Barry's nose that time to prove it, but he knew that Mandy was only with him for the money and the security for Nathan that he could offer her. Gaz was convinced that Barry knew, in his heart of hearts, that Mandy didn't love him, could never love him or any man after giving her heart so completely to Gaz once before.

Rightly or wrongly, Gaz had genuinely believed that if his luck changed, if he were to win the lottery or one of his money-making schemes really paid off, then she'd come running back to him and all would be forgiven. She was a mother first and foremost, and what mother wouldn't want her son to be living in a happy family unit, his natural father permanently on tap? It was only a matter of when.

But the confrontation in the police station the previous day had put paid to all of that. For the first time in his life, he had seen something in her eyes that he had never seen there before – contempt. It was the look of a woman who could hardly believe she had ever had anything to do with someone like Gaz in the first place. Above all, it was the expression of a wife who had fallen out of love.

Gaz just had to face it. It was over. And not only did that mean that he, Mand and Nathe would never play happy families together again, it meant that she really was serious about this custody thing and, if she won, he might never see his son again. The idea was almost too painful to allow space in his head. Not just for his sake, either. For Nathan's. God knows, the boy needed his father.

A knock at the front door of his flat shook him from his gloomy thoughts. Jumping to his feet, he stubbed out his cigarette and smoothed down his dishevelled clothes. He never knew his luck, it might be Mandy come to say she was sorry and to bring Nathan back. Yeah, and pigs might fly.

Standing in the doorway instead was Gerald, eyes half-mad, his hair wild, soaked to the skin from a recent rain shower, a half-eaten bag of vinegar-smothered chips in his hand. 'They've taken me sun-bed. They've taken everything,' he announced, his voice slightly slurred and higher-pitched than usual. A man on the edge.

Watching him staggering in the doorway, his suit carrier draped over his shoulder, Gaz wondered how Gerald had got away with his ruse for so long. That Linda must have been a right stupid cow if she couldn't see straight through this one. You could read Gerald like a book. Trying to make light of the situation, Gaz nodded at the limp food parcel in his hand: 'Kept hold of your chips, though,' he commented, but the ex-foreman looked right through him with the eyes of someone who had just sunk three large brandies on an empty stomach.

'House repossessed … wife thrown me out …' he continued in a rambling, absent-minded sort of way. Now that he actually said it, heard the words fall from his mouth, it didn't sound so bad. He'd been dreading it for so long, lying fitfully in bed at night, fearing this day, and he'd allowed it to become even more frightening in his imagination than it actually was in real life. Now it had happened. Linda couldn't trust him any more, she said, she needed time to think.

Gerald had picked up the afternoon post, thrown a few things into his bag and fled, grateful that he was still alive to tell the tale. Free of his wife for the first time in thirty-two years, he felt shaky but strangely liberated, positively light-headed with freedom, although he suspected that this was just a temporary feeling and he would soon be missing the woman he'd shared most of his life with.

Waving an opened envelope at Gaz with an almost hysterical look as he was ushered in, he had more news. 'Guess what?' he asked, with a snort, indicating the letter that had been waiting for him at home on the doormat. Gaz shook his head, unable to imagine what the envelope could possibly contain. 'I've just been offered that job.' Gerald's face was triumphant. This was all that he had been waiting for.

'Congratulations,' Gaz answered, his expression dead-pan as he closed the door. Looked like he had a new flatmate. One with a job too.

In the wake of Gerald's unexpected arrival into his home and inspired by the new-found independence his flatmate was enjoying, Gaz decided to confront the issues bothering him head-on. He was going to fight for Nathan, do all he could to win him back, and stop Mandy and Barry taking control.

Gerald was proud of him. He said so. He also promised to do all he could to help Gaz in his legal battle. His brother-in-law was a solicitor, he told him enthusiastically, but then stopped himself when he realised that Linda's side of the family probably wouldn't be jumping over themselves to help him or his mates right now.

Gaz thanked him but told him not to worry. He didn't need a solicitor, he was going to deal with this in his own way. Mandy was a reasonable woman and as long as she could see that he and Nathan were okay, that they were getting along better than ever before, then he felt sure she wouldn't block his access to the child. If he played his cards right, and somehow got her all the money he owed, then it would never even get to court. Barry would be happy the minute he got his hands on the seven hundred quid and the pressure would be off. Gaz just had to win them round to his way of thinking.

Loitering by the school gates later that day, kicking a football up against the wall, Gaz waited anxiously for the bell to sound and for the children – or one child in particular – to emerge. With nothing better to do and nowhere else to go, Gerald had accompanied him. He stood, hands in pockets, watching Gaz dribbling the ball, considering how much his life had changed and how surprisingly relieved he was that it had.

Within a week, he was going to be working, earning again, after months of uncertainty. He'd stay with Gaz until his first pay cheque, then get himself somewhere to live, make something of himself, and maybe start the long and difficult process of wooing Linda back again. She had her faults, and she'd made the last few years of his life hell with her high spending and social climbing, but if they could get through this and still see some sort of future together, then he had every hope that it would be a bright new start.

The school bell duly sounded and the children scurried from the building like ants. Spotting his son through the railings, Gaz's face lit up and he called his name, 'All right, Nathe ... Fancy a kick about in't park?' He kicked the ball towards him hopefully.

His rucksack over one shoulder, the boy's face brightened when he saw his father. Smiling and waving his hello, he nodded enthusiastically at the suggestion, delighted that they could still spend time together. It was a very confusing time for the twelve-year-old. He loved both his parents – he didn't even mind Barry that much – but now it seemed there was a new frostiness when his mum spoke of his dad, and he was afraid that she and Barry might stop him seeing his dad altogether.

Just as he reached Gaz and Gerald, Nathan heard his mother's voice and turned to see her and Barry hurrying up the street towards them from Barry's smart new car parked a few hundred yards further down. 'Nathe!' Mandy called, a note of urgency in her voice. Rushing up the hill, she reached out and placed an arm protectively around her son. 'Hiya,' she said, a little too breezily. 'All right, love?' There was the mandatory hair ruffle.

With Barry standing behind her, his hand squeezing her shoulder, Mandy glared at Gaz. There was that look again in her eyes, coupled with anger. 'You shouldn't be here!' she said breathlessly, relieved to have got to the school in time to rescue her son.

The muscles in Gaz's jaw tightened. 'Says who?'

Barry interjected before Mandy could answer. 'Read the lawyer's letter, why don't you?' he said with a sneer, Mandy still clamped firmly to his side. His manner said he'd just about had enough of Gaz and his irresponsible ways. This latest escapade with the strippers was the final straw for Barry. He'd put his foot down and made Mandy agree to a full-scale legal battle, backed by the social services, and he wasn't going to let Gaz wriggle out of it this time.

Gaz considered decking Barry but realised it would only make matters worse. Studying his mud-spattered shoes, he shivered as he recalled the terrifying jargon of the letter that had arrived by special courier that morning, with its talk of sole custody, supervised access and its instructions not to try and make contact with the 'ward'. That was his son they were talking about, he had shouted to no one in particular, crumpling the letter into a ball and hurling it across the room while Gerald made him a soothing cup of tea.

Nathan registered the sorrow in his father's eyes and stepped towards him with the start of a smile. Mandy freed herself from Barry's clutches and held on to her son fearfully, as if she was afraid that Gaz might snatch him away from her. He was so desperate at the moment, she didn't know what he might do.

Nathan's voice broke the uneasy silence. 'We're going swimming, Dad. Do you wanna come?' Mandy grimaced at his question.

Gaz looked from Mandy to Barry and back to Nathan, but avoided his son's steady gaze when he answered. 'I can't, kid,' he said, his eyes smarting. Raising his eyebrows in a half-hearted attempt at levity, he explained: 'Haven't brought me trunks, have I?'

Nathan, hesitant, turned to his mother, his eyes like saucers. 'We can go and get 'em, can't we, Mum?' he asked, hoping that was the answer.

Before Mandy or her lover said anything that any of them might regret, or which broke Gaz's heart, he interrupted. 'I can't, love,' he said to Nathan softly, his nostrils flaring, his face taut. He was incapable of saying anything more.

His heart pounding in his chest, Nathan looked suddenly frightened. 'Why?' he asked, shifting from foot to foot and eyeing both parents alternately.

'I just … I just can't,' Gaz whispered. 'Sorry.' He stared at the ground, the tears gathering.

Nathan eyed his mother warily as she stroked his shoulder. 'He's not allowed, is he?' he asked, his voice very small. He'd heard all the talk of lawyers' letters and court action, but until this moment he hadn't fully appreciated what it meant.

Mandy, close to tears herself and wishing there could be another way, stared long and hard at Gaz, the man she had once loved so much she thought she'd die of it. Rubbing their son's head and pulling him gently away, she whispered: 'Come on, love.' Her chest heaving as she struggled to control her own emotions, she took the boy's hand and led him slowly back to the car, glancing back up at Gaz wide-eyed as Nathan climbed into the back.

No longer able to hold back the tears, Gaz stood, his mouth twisted in pain, watching them go. Gerald, standing a few feet away, leaning against the school railings, noticed that he was trembling. Pushing away from the wall and placing an arm around his shoulder, the older man turned to lead him away, patting him hard on the back.

Gaz dropped the football to the ground and kicked it angrily against the wall, abandoning it where it lay. Wiping his nose on the back of his hand, he stared over his shoulder at the Rover disappearing down the street, his son's tearstained face pressed up against the rear window.

Dave was on his twentieth circuit of the store, watching for shoplifters, willing someone to nick something or do anything to relieve the dreadful boredom. His feet hurt from the tight black shoes he'd been issued and his trousers were straining at the waistband after all the canteen nosh he'd been enjoying since he started at his new job. If he carried on at this rate, he'd be the size of an elephant within a year, but the boredom, coupled with the enticing, subsidised food, were conspiring against him.

If he heard one more 'Ping Pong ... Staff Announcement' from the woman with the sinus problem who had obviously been to the British Rail School of Incomprehensible Announcements, he'd commit a murder. He'd perfected his juggling skills as far as he could go; he'd eaten more pear drops than his teeth could handle and had come to the conclusion that 'Wankie Frankie' was no threat to Jean at all. There was little left to do, except wait for his weekly pay packet and his gold watch.

Mentally awarding an eight out of ten to the male half of a young couple he followed down the Snacks & Biscuits aisle, he was suddenly aware of someone calling his name. 'Dave,' the voice whispered from behind a stand displaying

192

ladies tights. 'Dave! – Oi, you deaf git.'

Dave, recognising both the voice and the insult as Gaz's, turned, half-expecting to be badgered into rejoining the troupe again. 'Oh, what do you want?' he said, his hackles up and ready. 'I've told you, I'm finished with it.'

Gaz looked unusually glum. 'We're all finished, Dave,' he said, his shoulders hunched, his hands stuffed in his pockets, as he recalled the dreadful events of the previous two days. 'I'm a bloody marked man now.'

Dave softened and nodded with a frown as the two men ambled along the central aisle. 'Sorry about your Nathan. It's a bad one that.' Gerald had come in to the store to tell him all about their arrest and the subsequent legal action against Gaz, suggesting Dave pay Gaz a visit to cheer him up. But Dave had resisted, afraid of being roped into one of Gaz's tricks again, or of being dissuaded from his new line of work. He'd promised Jean he'd give it a go.

Gaz shrugged his shoulders as if he didn't care, but his eyes said differently. 'Anyway,' he began, changing the subject rapidly and still strolling. 'It's about Lomper.'

'What does that pasty-faced chuffer want?' Dave asked, stopping. He'd never really taken to the redhead, ever since he'd called him a bastard for saving his life. And, like an elephant, Dave had a long memory.

'His mum died two days ago,' Gaz informed him.

Dave faltered, sorry for calling him names. 'Ah … Poor lad. I'm sorry.' He knew how much Lomper's mother meant to him. From the little the redhead had given away about himself, it seemed he'd been caring for her for years, sacrificing any life he might have had. It became a full-time job when his dad died and, as an only child, he'd been left to do everything from the cooking to giving her baths. He got a small carer's allowance, but it barely supplemented the part-time job at the steelworks and his dole money. Dave knew her death would hit him hard.

Gaz nodded. Dave watched his face and realised that he hadn't just come to tell him the sad news. There was something more. Sensing Dave's curiosity, Gaz looked hopefully into the big man's face and pleaded: 'You couldn't borrow us a jacket or summat for the funeral, could you?'

Dave threw his head back in indignation. 'Gaz ...' he began, protesting.

'Oh, come on, Dave. It's not for me, it's a funeral,' his friend said, pleadingly, pointing to his tatty leather jacket. He made it sound so straightforward, so logical. Ever since they were kids, they'd 'borrowed' things they needed from shops like this – clothes, household items, whatever they needed – returning them to their racks a few days later. No one was the wiser, it wasn't exactly stealing and the goods were hardly used.

As ever, Dave gave in. Looking over his shoulder to make sure his supervisor wasn't watching, he nodded reluctantly. 'What colour?' he asked with a sigh.

Gaz cocked his head to one side and looked askance at the friend who never failed to amaze him, even at times like this. 'Orange,' Gaz said, blinking furiously.

Dave nodded with resignation and started heading towards the clothes aisle. Stopping suddenly, he repeated: 'Orange?'

Shaking his head in exasperation, Gaz spelled it out for him. 'Black, for fuck's sake,' he hissed. He wondered about Dave sometimes, he really did.

'All right,' said Dave, glancing around furtively again. 'Look, I'll meet you by doors.' He nodded his head at the automatic double doors the two of them had escaped through so many times before. Gaz sauntered over to a garden furniture display near the exit, and, innocent as anything, sat down on one of the white plastic chairs under a garden umbrella as if he was considering buying it for his patio.

A few minutes later, he saw Dave walking fast towards him, two jackets in his hand, holding one out to Gaz. It was top of the range, wool and cashmere mix, a proper blazer, the label still attached to the sleeve. Gaz was impressed. 'Nice one,' he said, slipping it on. Watching Dave slip into the other jacket, its label similarly attached, he was puzzled. 'You've got some time off?' he asked.

'Nah … that fuckin' pick 'n' mix were driving me crazy,' Dave said with a wink, about to walk from the first proper job he'd had in years. 'Besides, it's a funeral.' Pulling on the collar and not even bothering to rip the label off, he looked at Gaz doing likewise and asked: 'You ready?'

'Ready when you are,' Gaz replied with a nod, the old sparkle back in his eyes. Their heads held defiantly high, the two men turned and marched side by side through the automatic doors, not even breaking their stride as every alarm in the store started ringing. Increasing their speed to a run with a yell, they sped off through the car park and down the hill, free again and roaring at the top of their voices.

Lomper knew that as soon as the vicar had finished the final lines of his funeral address at the graveside, it was his cue to play *Abide with Me*, his mother's favourite hymn, on his cornet. She had always loved it; it had been played at his father's funeral and she had made her son promise then that, when her time came, he would play it for her.

In the wind-buffed silence that followed the vicar's words as the mourners stood on the hillside cemetery overlooking the city, Lomper twice raised the instrument to his trembling lips, but found himself unable to play. Wiping his mouth violently on his sleeve and blinking back the tears angrily, he tried again. Shaking his head, he dropped the instrument to his side as the vicar, the entire steelworks brass band standing beside him and his five friends eyed him pityingly.

Close to tears himself, Guy stepped shyly from the mourners and walked over to Lomper. Whispering something in his ear and squeezing his shoulder, he urged him to play. The redhead in the black suit and tie smiled wanly at his friend and put the cornet to his lips for the third time. Thinly at first, and then with increasing confidence, the mournful tune floated across the graveyard, welling as the rest of the steelworks band – in full blue and gold dress uniform – joined in.

Lomper closed his eyes against the flood and remembered the words his mother so loved to sing:

'...When other helpers fail, and comforts flee
Help of the helpless, Oh abide with me...
Change and decay in all around I see
O thou who changest not, abide with me.'

He always knew this day would come, that she would leave him to join his father. He'd expected it for years, but now that she was gone he could hardly bring himself to believe it, or to come to terms with the realisation that his work as a full-time carer was over. He was free now, free to live his life at last, to fall in love, to be with friends. Thirty-three years old and this was the first time in all those years that he had been alone.

Not that he was alone, he realised. His mother's timing had been perfect, as if she knew somehow. She had waited until he had found himself, found someone else to share his life with and – the very same day, almost to the hour – had breathed her last, reassured that he would not be entirely bereft.

Guy, his hands clasped in front of him, his eyes blinking away tears, watched Lomper with loving pride as he played. He knew how hard this had been for his friend, how much his mother meant to him, and he was glad he'd persuaded him to go ahead with it, to keep his promise. Next to Guy, Gaz, Dave and Horse hung their heads in respect as the coffin was lowered into the grave where Lomper's father was already buried. Gerald stood erect behind them, remembering his own mother's funeral, mournful for the young Lomper. Thrown together by their common goal to earn some money, unexpectedly bonded by the friendship they discovered, they now found themselves united in grief for one of their number. This was not a day any of them would forget in a hurry.

Once the formalities were over, Gaz and Dave wandered down the hill for a cigarette, the band members and their fellow mourners following. Only a red-eyed Lomper, comforted by Guy, was left at the grave, admiring the floral tributes and reluctant to leave. Puffing away on their cigarettes as they leaned against Lomper's Austin Princess parked by the cemetery chapel, Dave and Gaz, in their smart new jackets, kept looking back up the hill.

'They bloody are, you know,' Gaz told his friend, his eyes wide as he peered over Dave's broad shoulder surreptitiously, trying to get a better view of the two men at the grave. 'They're holding hands!'

Like Dave, he was still in the Dark Ages when it came to homosexuality. Although he knew it went on, it was never flaunted in the social circles he mixed in and he had certainly never seen two grown men publicly displaying such affection. Despite himself, he was quite shocked. He had always thought he would have been able to tell if someone was gay, but he'd worked, even danced alongside Guy and Lomper and never even had a clue. The thought made him quite uncomfortable.

Dave, his testosterone bristling, peered round over his shoulder, trying not to stare. 'They're never!' he exclaimed, as taken aback as Gaz. He too felt somehow threatened by it, although he had no idea why.

'Straight up!' Gaz reassured him.

Dave, his face sullen, flicked the ash from the end of his cigarette. 'I never even hold hands with ruddy ladies, me,' he said. Then, with a sudden thought that he might be mistaken for someone who was gay if he didn't, he added: 'Maybe I should.'

Dragging his eyes away from the two men as they left the graveside and strolled together down the hill towards them, Dave shook his head in wonder. 'Well, who'd have bloody thought it, eh?' he said. He too had always imagined that a gay man would be easy to spot – overtly camp, some sort of cross between Liberace and Julian Clary. He'd been the first to express his shock when he found out that Rock Hudson was gay, but Guy and Lomper? He was flabbergasted. 'Ah well – there's nowt as queer as folk,' he commented drily.

Turning to face Gaz as they both suddenly realised the double meaning of his words, the two men erupted into a fit of uncontrollable giggles, Gaz nearly choking as the freshly-inhaled smoke in his lungs burst from his mouth. Dave, his hand held to his face to hide his laughter, repeated: 'Eh, Gaz, I said there's nowt as queer as folk,' thoroughly pleased with himself as the two of them bent double and let out a couple of raucous belly laughs.

Registering the disapproving looks on the faces of the vicar and funeral attendants, Gaz nudged Dave hard on the arm. 'Shut up, Dave,' he chided, sniggering. 'It's supposed to be a bloody funeral,' he added, still unable to repress his own laughter.

Beside himself with mirth, Dave spluttered an apology but was incapable of much more. Looking up to see the vicar and coffin bearers frowning at the inappropriate laughter, he gave them a big, friendly smile.

Guy had always been keen on keeping fit and just because the gig was off, didn't mean his training stopped. He didn't get a body like his by lying around on the sofa all day, watching telly and eating chips, like Dave. He liked jogging best, and on Friday morning he got up early and slipped his shorts and sweatshirt on quietly, so as not to wake Lomper, who'd hardly slept a wink after his mother's funeral.

Setting off up the hill from Lomper's terraced house, he contemplated how much his life had changed recently. Had it not been for the chance sighting of Gaz's advert down the Job Club he'd never have met all the lads, or Lomper specifically. In the past few weeks, he felt he had grown enormously in confidence and stature. Naturally good-looking, he'd never had a problem scoring lasses – or, later in his life, lads – but there had never been much meaning to the encounters. Now, with Lomper, there was the hint of something long-term and serious, and for the first time, he welcomed it.

The morning air was damp and he pulled his sweatshirt hood up against the chill as he climbed the hill. Whatever happened next, he was ready for it. Lomper still had a lot of grieving to do. Guy was his first ever boyfriend, first ever relationship in fact, and he was still feeling his way – literally, in some instances. The poor lad didn't really know what he wanted from life. He'd only just been cut free from his mother and although he was physically older than Guy, emotionally he was years younger. Guy knew he'd have to go gently.

Despite the uncertainty, and the disappointment of not being able to get full-time work, the last few weeks had been the best for Guy for a long time, and he looked forward to the future with anticipation.

Reaching the top of the hill at a trot, Guy spotted a group of teenage girls sitting on a bench chatting animatedly as he approached. He tucked his chin into his chest and carried on. Just as he drew level with them, one of them squealed in delight at her friends, recognising him. 'Hey look,' she cried. 'Who's that? It's that guy.' Guy frowned momentarily, wondering what she could mean. Running past them as they giggled uncontrollably, one of them wolf-whistled and called: 'Show us your pecs!' Gaining courage, another shouted: 'Let's see your knob, boy!'

Blushing, he turned mid-jog and flashed them an embarrassed smile. Still puzzled, he ran on down the hill, too far away to hear the first girl turn to her mates and say: 'They were together in the paper, weren't they?'

Later that morning it was Horse's turn to go through the perfunctory social security interview that ascertained whether or not he should continue to be entitled to unemployment benefit. The outcome was always the same – his payments were always approved, because there was simply no work in Sheffield for a former furnace hand in his mid-fifties with no other skills and worsening arthritis in his joints.

No matter how hard they tried to retrain him under the Training for Work scheme – and he'd been on five courses to date (learning everything from hotel and catering to car mechanics) – the jobs simply weren't there at the end of the courses, or, if they were, the employers only offered three-month contracts and the money he ended up with was less than what he would receive on the dole.

Arriving at the usual counter to sign on after the interview, he handed the hard-faced clerk his Job Seeker's Allowance Book and watched as she punched his number and other details into the computer in front of her. It would only take a couple of minutes, he knew of old. She would have to go through the formality of asking a few questions, he would nod and answer them, and his latest dole cheque could be collected two days later.

The bespectacled woman with dark lank hair appeared to be utterly bored and didn't even looked up. This was hardly the most inspiring of jobs, Horse supposed graciously. 'Have you been actively seeking work over the last fortnight?' she asked him, automatically.

'Yeah,' Horse replied, equally mechanically, his hands leaning on the counter. It was a familiar ritual. As soon as it was over, he'd go and get some breakfast.

Still not looking up, the woman asked the next question: 'Have you done any work, paid or unpaid, over the last fortnight?' Tapping away at the keyboard, she waited for his response.

Horse knew his lines off by heart. 'No,' he said, waiting for her to input his answer into the system as usual.

But the woman paused. Peering up at him over the top of her glasses with just the hint of a seductive smile, she said softly: 'That's not what I've heard.' Horse frowned and wondered what she could mean.

Now free from all dietary constraints, Dave helped himself to another slice of thickly-buttered white bread and dipped it into the remnants of his fried egg. The all-day breakfast was, in his opinion, the greatest British culinary invention since, well, the hamburger. As he sat in his favourite café, tucking into his second breakfast of the day, he thanked God he didn't have to squeeze into a tight red leather G-string any more.

Wiping the juices from his plate with the last slice of bread, he crammed the dripping wedge into his mouth, licked his fingers and pushed his empty plate away. Still chewing, he took a cigarette from his pack, placed it in his mouth, lit it and leaned back to rub his belly with the satisfaction of a fully sated man.

Looking up for the first time since his heavily laden plate had arrived four minutes earlier, he spotted something across the café that made the food in his stomach turn to lead. A young man with a ponytail sitting a few tables away was holding up a copy of the Sheffield *Star* while he read the inside pages. Plastered all over the front pages in lettering three inches high the banner headline read: 'STEEL STRIPPERS EXPOSED'.

A few streets away, Gerald Cooper scurried from his local newsagent's, their entire stock of the Sheffield *Star* under his arm. Thirty copies. And this was the fifth newsagent he had visited. It had all but cleaned him out. The shop owners had all thought him very strange.

Glancing right and left, and realising there was nothing he could do about the newspaper billboard outside which read 'STEEL STRIPPERS BUST', he strolled casually across the shop's forecourt as if he was heading home, but stopped abruptly at a large plastic bin, dumping the entire pile of newspapers in it.

Damn the police for giving the details of their arrest to the press, he cursed under his breath. That was the last bottle of scotch they were getting from him at Christmas. Hurrying off down the hill, anxious not to be associated in any way with the lurid headline, he headed for the next corner shop.

* * *

Lomper's brass band had practised in the empty rolling mill every Friday since the plant closed down, initially hoping that it might one day reopen, but ultimately staying together for the hell of it. Although it was a bit dank and gloomy in the deserted factory, the acoustics weren't bad and they could make as much noise as they liked without disturbing the neighbours.

Grieving for his mother terribly, but bolstered enormously by Guy's constant presence, Lomper sat on a chair on the front row, surrounded by his fellow players as he cleaned his mouthpiece in preparation for the practice. The band had been invited to play at a school concert next week and he certainly needed all the practice he could get. He'd missed several rehearsals recently and was quite rusty.

The conductor, a stocky former furnace hand who was a bit of a hard task master, had been waiting long enough. Delighted to see Lomper in the front row, he tapped his music stand with his baton, and called: 'Come on, you lot.' On his instruction, each band member raised his instrument to his lips, ready to play, their music sheets spread out on stands before them.

'*Slaidburn*,' the conductor reminded them. It was one of Lomper's favourite pieces of music, a haunting melody named after the Lancashire dales. He studied his music sheet and inhaled.

'One, two, three, four ...' the conductor counted them in and waved his baton to indicate that the band should begin. Lomper began reading off the notes and playing accordingly, but was taken aback to find his contribution making a discordant sound against that of the other players. Perplexed, he stopped playing and hastily checked his music sheet, wondering if he'd somehow started on the wrong page.

Looking up at the conductor with embarrassment, he was surprised to see a cheeky grin on his face. Glancing around, still confused, he saw several fellow band members winking at him knowingly and turning their instruments to face him

202

as they carried on playing. Then, all of a sudden, everything clicked into place. Listening for the first time to what they were playing, Lomper heard the distinctive opening notes of the classic striptease tune, *The Stripper*.

Putting down his instrument coyly, the redhead blushed scarlet as he sat listening to their teasing with a shy smile on his face. Looking up at his grinning conductor, he mouthed the words: 'Is this you?', getting an expressive eyebrow wiggle in response. Flustered, he crossed his legs and arms defensively across himself, giggling and waiting for the practical joke to end. His secret was out.

CHAPTER ELEVEN

Gaz was not looking forward to the difficult task ahead. He was en route to the working men's club to face Alan and break the news to him that the gig was off later that night. Not that he expected Alan to be surprised – the women were hardly clamouring at the door to see the likes of Gaz and his mates bollock-naked. Alan would almost certainly earn more out of the evening by opening the doors to his regular punters as usual. But he knew the hard-faced businessman wouldn't see it that way. He'd regard Gaz's news as a betrayal, a personal affront after he'd done him a favour by letting him have the club half price in the first place. There was going to be a large piece of humble pie to eat and Gaz wasn't hungry.

There was worse news to come for Alan. As if cancelling the gig at the eleventh hour wasn't bad enough, Gaz was going to try and invoke the Old Pal's Act to try to get him to give him back his hundred quid. It was Nathan's money, not his, and he knew he should never have let him take it out of his post office account in the first place. That was just one of his many regrets over this whole escapade.

But if he could at least get that cash back for the boy, then he might gain some credit with Mandy and stand a better chance in the forthcoming custody battle. It was his last hope. There was no other way of appeasing her right now, least of all clearing his maintenance arrears. He might even have to accept that job she offered him at the clothing factory, just to show her that he was at least trying.

Lost in his miserable thoughts as he crossed the street towards the club, Gaz rounded the corner to see two men approaching, deep in conversation. Nodding a hello to the blokes he vaguely recognised from the works, he carried on past them, oblivious at first to their silent, mocking faces. It was only when he heard them laughing and turned to see them performing a little dance in the street behind him that he realised that they were singing the tune to *The Stripper*. Hitching their T-shirts up with a wiggle of their hips, the men chuckled in delight and shouted: 'Get your dick out!' This was all Gaz needed. Shaking his head, he shouted: 'Go get shagged,' and stalked off down the street.

Still smarting from the experience, he decided against the confrontation with Alan, unable to stomach his teasing right now. If those lads knew about their little caper, then Alan surely did and he'd never hear the end of it from the big fella. Turning left instead of right towards the club, Gaz promised himself he'd go and see him next week, once the dust had settled and he felt better able to face him. Alan would soon realise the gig was off when nobody showed. Nathan would just have to wait for his money.

Hearing the persistent hoot of a car horn, Gaz turned to see Alan pulling his ageing Ford Escort up to the kerb next to him. He swore out loud and tried to skip past him, but Alan was out of his car like a shot, his arms outstretched, his face twisted into a smirk. 'Hey, Patricia the Stripper!' he called in a phoney French accent.

'Bugger off,' Gaz sneered, hands in his pockets sullenly. This was just the sort of thing he'd been trying to avoid.

Alan looked genuinely hurt. 'Where have you bloody been?' he asked, leaning against the open driver's door. Gaz hung his head and didn't answer. Alan was suddenly troubled. 'Well, what's going on?' he asked, leaning on the roof of his car and squinting into the sunlight. 'I've had to buy in twenty barrels. I've not heard a word from you.'

Gaz shook his head and faltered. 'Yeah, well I hope they're sale or return,' he said sarcastically.

Alan was silent as he tried to take in what Gaz was telling him. Finally, incredulous, he told him: 'You're joking ...

You're bloody famous!' The lad couldn't possibly be calling the gig off now, a few hours before show time.

'Yeah, don't remind me,' Gaz winced. If this was fame then he didn't want any part of it. He'd have to lay low for a few weeks, pretend it hadn't happened and wait till it all blew over.

'Yeah,' Alan nodded enthusiastically. 'I've sold two hundred-odd tickets.'

Gaz froze, his heart in his mouth. Head craning forward on his scrawny neck, he asked: 'How many?' His eyes flickered while his brain went into overdrive as it tried to work out exactly how much money that would bring in.

Guy, Horse and Lomper sat morosely at a table in the smoke-filled Job Club, all the spark gone from their eyes. This was it, then. This was their life. Back to the bad old days of sitting around filling in mock job application forms and playing cards. Half of Sheffield, it seemed, had heard about their desperate plan and now that even that was cancelled, they couldn't help but fear that people would think even less of them than if it had gone ahead. It was almost too horrible to contemplate.

Dave sat slightly away from them at the computer screen, staring angrily at the keys, trying to find the letter 'k' without success. Why the hell they didn't place the letters alphabetically, he didn't know. This bloody job application was going to take all day. He was seriously questioning the wisdom of walking out of the Asda job. It was all Gaz's fault. All of it.

The door opened and Gerald walked in, wearing a smart silver-grey suit, briefcase in hand. He was grinning broadly and lapping up the attentions of Luke Marcus, the Job Club manager, who had hardly ever been in such a situation before – bidding farewell to a long term customer who'd got himself another job.

'Well done Gerald. All the best,' Luke said again, patting him enthusiastically on the back. This would look bloody marvellous on his report, a fifty-three-year-old foreman back at work within six months. He could almost smell promotion.

Gerald nodded and smiled. 'Thanks,' he said, and meant it. Regardless of what the rest of them thought of the Job Club, it had at least kept him from going mad all those months. It had given him a warm, dry place to go, a sense of purpose and the chance to improve his typing and computer skills. Many of the staff were genuinely trying to help the men who shuffled in and out each day, although their help was largely unappreciated. If it wasn't for the Job Club, though, his old mate from Harrison's wouldn't have known how to contact him about the interview and, albeit indirectly, thanks to Luke he had got the job. He was genuinely grateful.

Luke coughed to attract the attention of the men sitting in the room. 'Example for you there,' he said, his patronising tone more pronounced than usual, as Gerald freed himself from the insistent handshake of the man the rest of them so loved to hate and walked shyly towards those he had come to consider his friends.

Dave swivelled round on his chair to face Gerald and smiled up at him. Giving him a half-hearted wolf whistle, Horse winked at him encouragingly. 'Nice suit, Gerald,' he said, as their former dance teacher chuckled and nodded, feeling more than a little embarrassed at the new purchase, bought on a whim that morning. He had been to see his new boss for lunch and had come to the Job Club straight from the works to say goodbye to the lads. Now he was here, it felt a little uncomfortable.

'Well, I best be off,' Gerald said, almost reluctant to part company with the people who had come to mean more to him than he cared to admit. He felt like a paroled prisoner being released back into the community after a lengthy sentence – eager to be free but afraid to walk through the prison gates for fear that it wouldn't feel as safe and comfortable as the place he had just spent so much time, or the people be as kind as the fellow prisoners who had become his friends.

Turning to them one last time, he added: 'You never know, there might be a job in it for you boys ... I'll see what I can do.' They nodded their thanks, knowing full well that there was little chance of Gerald getting them anything in the industry they no longer recognised as their own, but grateful for the thought all the same.

Gerald turned to the door to leave but before he could go, his path was blocked by Gaz, twinkling at them in the doorway. 'All right, lads?' he asked, striding in and grinning cheekily. Dave frowned slightly in recognition of the expression he knew usually meant trouble.

'All right, Gaz?' Guy responded quizzically, not the only one among them wondering what had stoked up Gaz's fire as he swaggered into the room.

Gerald greeted him warmly with 'Gareth', his pet name for the man he used to detest but to whom he now owed so much.

Unable to contain himself any longer, Gaz patted Gerald's arm and blurted: 'We're on!' Seeing the blank look on all their faces as he paced a small triumphant circle round the Job Club, he shouted: 'We're bloody on!'

'You what?' Lomper asked, not sure what Gaz meant.

'We've sold two hundred tickets!' Gaz exclaimed as Guy and Lomper hugged each other excitedly.

'Oh, what?' Guy exclaimed, delighted. Horse beamed up at Gaz and gave him a congratulatory nod.

'That's two grand already!' Gaz said, translating it into hard cash for them, a mathematical feat that had taken him most of the journey on his way over from the club.

Gerald interjected. 'Oh, it's a bit late for all that, Gaz ... I mean ... I mean, fresh start, you know.' He opened his arms to show off his new suit meaningfully.

Gaz stepped up to him and fixed him with his eyes, a fire burning within. 'One more time, Gerald,' he tempted, his arms swinging casually by his sides. 'You've got the rest of your fuckin' life to wear a suit, man.'

Horse, swept along by Gaz's enthusiasm, nodded. 'Come on, Gerald,' he said, indicating that he was in.

'Aye, go on, Gerald, eh?' said Guy, winking at him.

'Come on, Gerald,' Lomper encouraged, hopefully.

Gerald, weakening in the face of such unity, shifted uneasily from foot to foot and considered the possibility. Dave watched him with the same anxious expression on his face.

Gerald swallowed hard and thought about what Gaz was saying. He was right. He'd been wearing a suit all his life and he probably would for the rest of it. This dancing caper had been the one time in his life when he'd been really free of all that, the responsibilities, the constraints of his marriage, his position, his so-called 'standing'. He'd had more fun in the past three weeks than in years.

Now – for a while at least – there was no more reputation, no more Linda, no neighbours to give a toss about. Just a bunch of lads he'd grown inordinately fond of. Men like him struggling to find themselves. How could he let them down now? After what seemed like an age to the rest of them, his face broke into a grin. 'Just once,' he announced.

'Yes!' Gaz cried, shaking a victory fist at the rest of them.

Gerald nodded. 'That's all … Just tonight.' He grinned back at their smiling faces and shared their excitement. Why the chuff not? he thought. He could do what he liked for a change and to hell with the consequences.

Congratulating each other breathlessly, Gaz turned to see Dave watching them out of the corner of his eye. Stepping over to him, he asked softly: 'How about it, Dave?'

Dave swallowed hard and thickened his neck. 'Haven't you grown out of all that yet?' he said ebulliently, as if he was somehow above all that. Secretly he was terribly torn. He wished he had the courage to do what Gerald was doing, to be a part of it with the rest of them, but his embarrassment and insecurities crowded in on him and he gave Gaz the most scornful expression he could muster.

'Come on, mate,' Gaz whispered, wishing Dave would put away that enormous chip on his shoulder and join in the fun.

But Dave just shook his head. 'No. Sorry, lads,' he said, and swivelled round on his chair to get back to his typing and hide the sadness in his eyes.

In less than twenty minutes Dave had fled the Job Club and was hurrying home. It was more than he could stand, listening to the rest of them talking excitedly about the gig in a few hours' time, planning a quick rehearsal at the steelworks first, to remind them of steps they now felt slightly rusty about. Dave longed to be home, locked away behind closed doors with his misery. He wanted to see Jean, to tell her all that he was feeling inside, to lift the lid on the great bubbling cauldron of emotions inside his head. Although he knew damn well he wouldn't.

Putting the key in the lock of his front door, he turned it and stepped inside, relieved to have reached sanctuary. Sitting on the floor in the hallway was a single suitcase. Jean's. Dave frowned, his face puzzled. She shouldn't even be home from work yet. What could it mean? Was someone ill? Her mother hadn't been well for a while. Did this mean bad news?

'Jean?' he called, concern in his voice. There was no reply. 'Jean, love?'

Climbing the stairs to their bedroom, he walked in to find his wife, her jacket on, sitting on the edge of the bed, her back to him. 'There you are,' he said, unsure of himself. He was no mind reader but he could tell immediately that there was something wrong.

Without turning, Jean tossed a bottle of men's aftershave over her shoulder and onto the bed. It was some nicked stuff Gaz had given him a few months back but he'd only worn it once, the previous week when he had tried it to see if it made him feel any sexier. 'Should've guessed when you started wearing tottie lotion,' Jean said, her voice strained, the muscles in her back tense. 'You never put it on for me, did ya?' He thought she sounded angry and he couldn't for the life of him think why.

'Jean?' he called, craning his neck to try and see her face.

'But this?' Jean turned, her eyes puffy, her cheeks streaked with mascara. In her hand, she dangled his red leather G-string distastefully, still unable to believe what she had found in the bottom of his sock drawer when she was putting away the washing after getting off work early. 'I never had you down for this sort of caper, David.' She dropped it from her fingers onto the bed before adding, acidly: 'Explains a few things at least.'

Dave inhaled deeply and wondered how he could begin to explain. Flopping down onto the bed and reaching for her, he stammered: 'No, look … I know it don't look good, but …'

She spoke to him through clenched teeth, her eyes blazing. 'You're bloody right it don't.' Catching her breath to stop herself from losing it, she snapped: 'All those nights you were late back. And stupid cow here thought you were out looking for a job.' Dave shook his head No, wishing she'd let him speak, but she was in full flow. 'Well, no wonder. No bloody wonder,' she marvelled, thinking of all the nights he'd turned away from her in bed; his silent, brooding moods; his long absences from home. 'It's so bloody obvious.'

Dave, trying to interrupt, kept shaking his head. He held out his hand, palm up, to try and soothe her, to stop the tears spilling down her cheeks. 'No – I were with Gaz, honest,' he started.

Slapping the bed in anger, she jumped to her feet and rounded on him, negotiating the bed towards him, looking more and more as if she was going to belt him one. 'Oh, right. She's one of Gaz's little tarts, is she? Well, that makes sense.'

She'd never trusted Gaz, not since school days. He'd always been up to no good, and she'd tried time and again to keep Dave away from him. Stepping round in front of where her husband was still sitting and pointing to the G-string in disgust, she sneered at it. 'She'd have to be to put up with this kind of shit.' Her emotions erupting, she slapped Dave hard in the face, her rage mounting as she began beating the palms of her hands repeatedly against his head.

Dave covered his head with his hands protectively and shouted: 'Hey, hey, hey!' but Jean simply increased the intensity of her attack. Standing up, he grabbed her firmly by the shoulders and shouted in her face: 'Just listen, will ya?!' Jean, her chest heaving up and down, struggled to break free, wanting nothing more than to run from the room and this place, never to see him again, never to feel so much pain again.

Shouting at her to get through, Dave kept hold of her as she tried to make for the door. 'It's nowt to do with any fuckin' women, all right?' he yelled, holding her rigid, his face inches from hers.

Jean faltered, stopped and stood completely still, willing it to be true, hoping beyond hope that he could give her a logical explanation as to why he had such an item in his drawer, to explain what had been wrong with him these past few months. Holding her breath, she remained silent as Dave blurted: 'I'm … I were a stripper, right?'

Of all the excuses she had expected him to come up with, all the reasons he might give her, that one wasn't even on the list. She would have laughed in his face, except that he looked so deadly serious. Moving her head even closer to his, her gaze darted from one eye to the other, waiting for more.

Dave sighed and, slipping his hands from her shoulders, he started to explain. He had hoped it would never come to this, that she'd never know how low he had stooped. 'Me and Gaz and some fellas …' he began, his words tumbling out jerkily, '… thought we could make a bob or two out of taking us clothes off.'

'Strippers?' Jean repeated, unable to take it in.

Dave raised his eyes to the heavens. 'All right, all right, I know,' he began, knowing that it was not the most appetising of concepts.

'You – and Gaz? – Strippers?' Jean looked as if she were in a trance.

Defensive now, Dave reasoned: 'We weren't *that* bad.' She was waiting for him to continue. Lowering his eyes in shame, he shook his head sadly. 'Only I couldn't, could I?'

Jean shook her head, perplexed. 'Why not?' she asked, blinking.

'Well, look at me,' Dave countered, glancing down at his stomach.

Jean looked him up and down blankly. 'So?' she asked with a sniff, peering back up into his eyes, still not getting his point.

His voice cracking, Dave let the tears spill down his cheeks as he asked her: 'Jeanie, who wants to see this dance?' The stress of the past few months overwhelmed him in a giant tidal wave as he looked into his wife's distressed face from the prison of his flesh.

This is what the last few months had been all about, his self-inflicted misery at his weight, at how fat he was. Jean peered into what she had always called the windows of his soul and realised that now. Moving her face inches from his, her eyes glistening, she whispered: 'Me, Dave ... I do.' Leaning closer towards him and placing her arms up around his strong neck, she caressed his head, as he closed his eyes and wept on her shoulder.

The working men's club was packed to the gunwales with chattering, giggling women, smoking, drinking and laughing. Worse than that for Gaz, though, there were also at least fifty men, dotted about at various tables, vying with each other for the better seats, waiting for the show to begin.

The buzz in the smoke-filled club was incredible. Football chants of 'Here we go, here we go, here we go,' broke out from various tables, as the audience crowded in, with more coming in through the door all the time. It was standing room only at the back, and interspersed among the onlookers were the members of the steelworks brass band, the entire day shift from Millthorpe police station fronted by

Inspector 'Smiler', and several old mates of Gaz's and Dave's from school.

Dressed in their security guard uniforms, the five remaining members of Hot Metal were scattered around the shabby red dressing room that led directly onto the stage, preparing themselves for their big moment. Gerald was doing up his shirt buttons, Horse was tying his shoelaces, Lomper was having his tie put on by Guy in front of the spotlit artiste's mirror, and they were all waiting for the show to begin. The only person who seemed to be enjoying the situation was Alan. He had more people in tonight than for the Chippendales, and they were still queuing round the block. He couldn't believe it. Good old Gaz.

The leader of the pack was, however, the least happy of them all. A thin film of sweat on his top lip, Gaz was pale and pasty and he kept pacing the room anxiously and sitting back down on top of a table, jiggling his legs around to try and stop himself from rushing to the lavatory again. Getting up to peer at the waiting crowd one more time, but deciding against it, he rounded on Alan angrily. 'Women only, you tosser!' he complained. 'Women only! It's on all the posters, for fuck's sake.'

Alan shook his head. 'No, nobody told me,' he lied. He wasn't going to start turning away all those blokes waving tenners at him. There must be four hundred people out there.

Hearing the start of a slow hand clap outside, Gaz turned to him again and moaned: 'All the blokes from the pub are in there. The bastards.' Losing all the remaining colour in his complexion, he'd aged ten years.

Gerald did his best to reassure him. 'Ah, you'll be all right, mate,' he said, fixing the top buttons of his shirt. 'Once you're on stage.'

Gaz nearly fainted. 'Once I'm on stage!' he looked at Gerald, aghast. 'What d'you mean once I'm on stage? I'm going nowhere near the fucking stage!' He sounded hysterical. 'It's suicide, that's what it is. Suicide.' He could just imagine the heckling and booing his mates from the

Thomas Boulsover would give him. Not to mention the Old Bill. He would be mincemeat. Gerald saw the fear in Gaz's eyes and chuckled to himself. So, Gary the Lad wasn't invincible after all.

The slow hand clap increased in intensity, as the women started to get impatient. They'd paid good money for this, and they didn't want to have to wait another minute. Gaz swigged from a half bottle of scotch and cursed himself for starting this caper in the first place. 'Shit,' he said. Then to a grinning club manager, he offered: 'I'll give the money back. Alan – announce it, please.'

Alan shook his head and flashed a gap-toothed smile at his old school mate. He'd never seen the lad so frightened before and he was thoroughly enjoying it. 'To four hundred horny punters?' he said, laughing. 'Ask me another one, kid.' Peering through the curtains himself, delighted with the swelling numbers, he spotted someone he knew. 'Eh, by heck,' he said to Gaz. 'Our old English teacher's on't front row.'

Gaz gulped hard at the thought of the hard-faced Mrs Ryan, drumming Shakespeare into him all morning – a largely useless quest – and then doubling as a dinner lady at lunch time, slopping meatballs and soggy brussels sprouts onto his plate with a look that dared him not to eat every disgusting mouthful. 'We're gonna get torn to pieces,' he remarked to no one in particular.

'Well you are if you don't get out there,' Alan commented, registering the growing agitation in the expressions of his punters. Sticking the knife in with relish, he said under his breath to Gaz: 'Eh, have you ever seen a zebra brought down by a pack of wolves?' Chuckling to himself at the lad's ashen response, he looked past him to the rest of the gang, standing watching. 'Marvellous these, er, nature films, aren't they,' he said. 'Marvellous.'

Gerald, swallowing hard, nodded a little too enthusiastically. 'Oh, brilliant, aren't they?' he said, trying to remember what it was he was meant to be thinking of instead.

Skipping to his side, Guy nudged Gerald's arm leerily with a wink and gave him the fist's up sign. 'They are though, aren't they, Gerald?' He smirked knowingly at Lomper and Horse.

Gerald smiled and rounded on the lot of them. 'Oh, pack it in,' he said, pretending to be cross. The last thing he wanted to think about now was the Serengeti.

Before they could rib him further, the dressing room door opened and – to their joint amazement – in stepped Dave, dressed in his steelworks security guard uniform and beaming at them all. Two steps behind him was Nathan, his eyes sparkling. Dave took one look at Gaz's face and asked: 'Not lost your bottle have you, Gaz?'

Gaz was genuinely pleased to see him. 'Dave!' he said, jumping to his feet and temporarily forgetting his nerves. The rest of them echoed his name.

With a cheery confidence they hadn't seen in him before, Dave bragged: 'Well, there were nowt on telly, so I thought I'd give it a go.' Pointing to Nathan, he added: 'Oh, I found this one wandering about outside.'

Nathan shrugged his shoulders at his father. 'Wouldn't let me in.'

Gaz looked angrily at his son. Mandy would kill him if she found out he was here. 'What the bloody hell are you doing here?' he asked. 'Your mum'll go mad.'

Nathan grinned cheekily at his father. 'She's out front,' he said. He would save up the best news for later – he and his mum had had a long chat and she'd decided not to pursue the sole custody matter any further. Gary was Nathan's father, after all, she had told Barry, and nothing could change that. Besides, she had come to the conclusion that the two of them needed each other.

Gaz balked at the thought of Mandy in the crowd. 'Is she?' he asked, completely taken aback. 'Barry with her?' That was an even more terrifying thought.

'She wouldn't let him come. Said it were "Women Only",' Nathan answered, knowing his dad would be pleased. Gaz nodded and half-smiled, vaguely consoled.

The club began thundering to the sound of hundreds of impatient feet stamping in unison. Alan rushed breathlessly into the dressing room from the wings, a serious expression on his face. 'Right, I can't hold 'em any longer, lads,' he said. Clapping his hands together gleefully, he winked and added: 'It's now or never.'

'Shit!' Gaz cursed, his face white.

Dave made the first move towards the stage, striding purposefully through the dressing room, the others following less confidently. 'Here we go,' he told them, still hardly able to believe that he was going through with it. 'We're bloody on.' To Gerald, standing by the curtain leading onto the stage, concentrating on the Queen's Speech, he said: 'Go get your jacket on.' He was suddenly in charge.

Lomper, butterflies dancing in his stomach, got to his feet and looked at Gaz pleadingly. 'Can't we leave us G-strings on then, Gaz?' he asked, his courage slipping from him fast.

Gaz looked into the middle distance and nodded, making no move to get up and join them. 'Perhaps you better had,' he said, his voice flat.

Horse, tugging his jacket sleeves down into place, was disgusted. 'No we better hadn't,' he told the rest of them. This was all or nothing as far as he was concerned.

Dave nodded his agreement. Turning to the troupe, he straightened his neck and said firmly: 'Listen, if we're doing this, then, just this once, we're doing it right.' Daring any of them to disagree, he turned towards the beckoning lights of the stage as he heard Alan announcing them and said: 'Now, come on.' The Gang dutifully lined up behind him.

Alan saw them waiting and flicked a whole bank of switches, plunging the club into darkness. A huge cheer went up, as Alan's magnified voice boomed through the club's loudspeakers.

'All right, come on,' he bellowed. 'Put your hands together and welcome Mr Dave Horsfall.' Another enormous cheer came from the audience as Dave stepped out alone into the beam of a single spotlight, which followed him as he marched confidently across the stage.

It had been a long time since he'd been here, like this, and never to a crowd this big or this excited. But he felt strangely at home. Peering out into the darkness, Dave caught sight of Jean with her friends Sharon, Bee and Sheryl on the very first table next to the stage. Jean had her arms in the air, screaming and clapping her whole-hearted support as her husband took the microphone from the stand and began to speak.

'Okay, ladies and gents ...' he started.

A male heckler at the back shouted, 'Get 'em off, chubby.'

Dave wasn't fazed. 'And you buggers up the back there,' he said to his and Gaz's old drinking pals.

'Get on with it!' another heckler from the pub yelled.

Dave nodded. His voice filled the hall. 'All right, yeah,' he admitted. 'We may not be young. We may not be pretty. We may not be right good.' The crowd stopped interrupting and listened for the first time as Dave continued, while the others stood trembling in the wings, waiting for their cue. 'But we're here ... we're live ... and for one night only ... we're going for the full monty.'

The crowd went berserk at his final words, and started screaming as the lights dimmed again and they waited for the men they'd paid to see naked.

Gaz watched his friends and fellow dancers standing in the wings waiting for the exact moment to make their appearance. Swigging greedily from his half-empty bottle of scotch, he looked shattered. Nathan stood at his father's side, beside himself with anger, willing him to get up and join the others. 'You can't miss it,' he argued. 'Not after everything.' He hated to see him like this.

'Come on, Gaz, hurry up,' hissed Gerald, the last in the line-up. Gaz shook his head sadly. 'I'm sorry, lads,' he said, just as their cue came and they disappeared one by one onto the stage. 'Good luck, eh?' he called, but they were gone. As the men out front began taking up their positions for the opening line-up as the cheering reached fever pitch, Nathan watched his father silently.

Outside, the lights went up and Horse was the first to leap onto the stage and take his place in the line next to Dave. The opening bars of the Tom Jones number *You Can Leave Your Hat On* filled the club's smoky atmosphere. In the audience, Lomper's pals from the brass band stood up with their instruments and belted out the tune in harmony. Lomper raised an eyebrow in a delighted salute as the rest of the troupe emerged to an immense cheer. Lomper, Guy and Gerald took their places and stood anxiously in a row watching their baying audience in amazement and delight.

Still without their leader, they launched themselves into their routine at the first erotic grunt from Tom 'The Voice' Jones as the powerful music pumped through the speakers, posing much as Gaz had first posed in front of the car headlights all those weeks before.

The crowd were ecstatic. At the sight of Dave on stage, beginning to strut his stuff, Bee and Sharon turned to Jean and screamed in delighted surprise. Jean beamed back at them proudly and gave Dave a raunchy, fists-clenched gesture with her hands.

Even the policemen began cheering, along with the lads from the pub, as it quickly became clear that the dancers knew something of what they were doing, pacing up and down in formation, and swivelling their hips sexily to the opening words.

'Go on, lads!' cheered one woman, three seats away from Mandy, who sat bemused at a middle table, craning her neck left and right as she looked in vain for Gaz. Maybe he did a turn later, she wondered. He was certainly nowhere to be seen on stage.

Behind the scenes, Gaz sat pensively in the dressing room, drinking from his bottle and shaking his head at his own stupidity, feeling unusually sorry for himself.

Exasperated, Nathan rounded on his father. 'Listen, I'm gonna get really annoyed with you in a minute,' he said, clamping the security guard hat on Gaz's head. Gaz looked at his son with surprise. 'They're cheering out there,' Nathan told him. 'You did that.' Throwing a tie at him, he added: 'Now get out there ... and do your stuff.' His eyes were defiant.

In the face of such grown-up determination, Gaz knew he had no choice. Clutching his tie to his chest, he tutted aloud and complained: 'God! Is there anyone I don't get bollocked by?' but there was gratitude in his eyes.

Nathan held up his arm, his forefinger pointing to the stage, and shouted: 'Out!' The kid wasn't joking.

Hesitating only briefly, Gaz drained his bottle and, picking up the tie, got to his feet. Kissing Nathan firmly on the cheek, he threw the tie flamboyantly around his collar, rammed his security guard hat even more firmly onto his head and disappeared out onto the stage, as the biggest cheer yet went up from the crowd.

Fired up by a heady mix of alcohol and adrenalin, Gaz stepped into the line-up, perfectly synchronising his movements with the rest of the men. It looked for all the world as if the routine was planned that way. Mandy put her hands to her face in simultaneous delight and horror at the sight of her ex-husband sliding provocatively out of his jacket as the rest of them did likewise. The police, recognising the ringleader and pleased to see that he seemed to be keeping time with the rest of the dancers, roared their approval.

Genuine triumph was written on the faces of each member of the gang as they performed the various stages of their well-rehearsed routine perfectly and, egged on by the salivating crowd, began peeling off their jackets and hurling them into the audience.

Guy and Lomper, back to back, hands interlocked as they sidled to the front of the stage, jackets off now, were in love and having fun, all their past cares and inhibitions cast to the wind. Dave, his troubles with Jean over, a new era of

220

understanding looming, gave Gaz the thumbs up sign as he stepped to the front of the stage and took Gaz's hand, pairing up with him for their own spotlit moment. Gaz, the proud father of the happy-faced boy dancing rhythmically in time to the music in the wings, knew that he was about to clear all his crippling debts and start afresh with a new measure of dignity. Gerald, free of the stifling Linda for a little while, his financial future brighter than it had been in months, was doing something risky and spontaneous for the first time in his life and loving every minute of it. Horse, a lifetime of insecurity behind him, prepared himself to bare all and no longer care about what people thought.

The ties were next. Sliding them from their collars and twirling them above their heads, playing shamelessly to the hysterical crowd, each one of them found something in themselves on that stage. It was the end of a long journey of discovery that had been painful and difficult for them all, but immensely worthwhile nonetheless.

In the audience, straining to get an eyeful, Horse's mother, aunts and niece cheered and clapped their encouragement, thrilled to have another chance to see the show that they had been granted an exclusive preview of. Waving his tie raunchily above his head, Gerald threw it into the crowd and grinned as Beryl caught it and clutched it to her bosom as if she would treasure it for ever. Gerald pulled his hat firmly down onto his head and beamed gratefully at her, fighting to keep himself under control as he wondered if she'd consider making an old man very happy.

Dressed in just their shirts and trousers now, Guy and Horse leap-frogged over each other centre-stage as the women went wild, their high-pitched screams competing with the music. Lomper watched in open appreciation as the pumped-up Guy slid on his knees to the front of the stage and leered at the lust-filled women who had rushed to the front of the hall to get a better look.

The shirts were next. As the beat gave them their rhythm, the shirt buttons were undone one by one from the top, and pulled open in one smooth, synchronised movement to expose their chests. Jean and her mates formed fists with their hands and bellowed their encouragement at Dave as his manly belly was revealed for all to see. Grinning at his wife in delight and relief, Dave launched into his next step with renewed vigour and wished he'd thought of this years ago.

As the song belted out each man revealed first one then the other shoulder provocatively, before slipping out of their shirts and whirling them above their heads like helicopter rotors. As the audience clapped in time and yelled their encouragement, the shirts were hurled into the crowd, as yet another howl went up. Throwing his shirt directly into Jean's arms, Dave flashed her a delighted smile as she clutched it to her face, inhaled deeply and made a 'Phwoar!' sound to her girlfriends.

As 'The Voice' continued to give a rip-roaring performance on vinyl, the belts were pulled off and similarly thrown. Mandy caught Gaz's belt in her hands with a smile that told him all was forgiven. Winking at the mother of his child, Gaz gyrated his pelvis in a manner that showed her how he'd like to make it all up to her. She threw her head back and laughed openly at him.

Forming a perfect Arsenal off-side trap manoeuvre, with not one man ahead of the other, the dancers lined up in front of their feverish audience and, tongues out, performed their hip-thrusting shagging motion to a volley of squeals. Checking each other quickly for timing, they slapped their hands to their thighs, bent double and stood up, whipping off their Velcro-fastened trousers in one slick movement, as the club exploded to the sound of uproarious applause.

Naked now, but for their tight red leather G-strings and hats, the men removed the latter and coyly covered their groins with them, turning and twisting all the while, dancing and swivelling, revealing thong-clad buttocks and bulging pouches alternately in time to the pulsing beat. The women went wild, knowing what was coming and yet hardly daring to look.

Truly in their element, the men – led by Gaz – lined up in front of the gold scalloped curtains once again and replaced their hats on their heads, marching forwards in unison as their fingers fumbled with the quick-release catches on the side of their G-strings, holding them in place with their hands. The cry of 'Off! Off! Off!' filled the club. Hats returned quickly to their groins with one hand, the men whipped the G-strings off from behind them with the other in a simultaneous movement which sent the noise levels from the crowd to new heights.

Strutting like peacocks, dangling the tiny red leather garments from their fingers, the dancers went into their finale, flinging the G-strings into the crowd and clamping both hands to the hats held over their groins, as the women continued to chant 'Off! Off! Off!' thumping the floor with their feet, and the men in the crowd stood in open-mouthed admiration.

Jean, her face covered by Dave's shirt ever since he took off his G-string, lowered it gradually like a veil, her pupils hugely enlarged as she excitedly watched her husband preparing to bare all.

With the crowd fired up, the floorboards pounding to their stamping, the men gathered rhythmically at the back of the stage, gyrating in front of the glittering curtains. The atmosphere was electric.

Catching each other's eyes with a knowing smile, they moved into a perfect V-formation, Gaz and Dave at the front, as they prepared themselves for their final, full-frontal show-stopper.

Swaying from side to side, baiting the crowd, they turned a perfectly synchronised 180 degrees to wiggle their naked buttocks around tantalisingly in front of the audience. No thongs this time, just bare flesh, warts, dimples and all – Guy's and Gaz's buttocks pert, the others in various stages of flabbiness. But no one in the audience seemed to notice or even care. This was what they had come to see and they were beside themselves with excitement.

Jubilant at their success, grinning openly at each other and really hamming it up, the six men turned back to face the hysterical crowd and, hardly able to hear the song for the overwhelming clamour, they stepped to the front of the stage and into their final positions. Hats still firmly in place, they heard an almighty roar go up from the crowd and the audience – to a man – jumped to their feet in eager anticipation.

On the cue of Tom Jones's barely audible, final glass-shattering note, Gaz, Dave, Gerald, Horse, Guy and Lomper – the unlikely members of Yorkshire's first-ever male strip group – took a deep breath and threw their arms upwards in unison, hurling their hats off into the crowd with a tremendous flourish, arms and legs spread-eagled like starfish, stark naked and never more proud of it.